P9-DEM-566

Also by
Susan Mallery

Fool's Gold

Marry Me at Christmas
Thrill Me
Kiss Me
Hold Me
Until We Touch
Before We Kiss
When We Met
Christmas on 4th Street
Three Little Words
Two of a Kind
Just One Kiss
A Fool's Gold Christmas
All Summer Long
Summer Nights
Summer Days
Only His
Only Yours
Only Mine
Finding Perfect
Almost Perfect
Chasing Perfect

Blackberry Island

Evening Stars
Three Sisters
Barefoot Season

Mischief Bay

The Friends We Keep
The Girls of Mischief Bay

To see the complete list of titles available from Susan Mallery, please visit SusanMallery.com.

SUSAN MALLERY

best of my love

H
HQN™

ISBN-13: 978-0-373-78919-1

Best of My Love

Recycling programs for this product may not exist in your area.

Copyright © 2016 by Susan Mallery Inc.

All rights reserved. Except for use in any review, the reproduction or utilization of this work in whole or in part in any form by any electronic, mechanical or other means, now known or hereinafter invented, including xerography, photocopying and recording, or in any information storage or retrieval system, is forbidden without the written permission of the publisher, HQN Books, 225 Duncan Mill Road, Don Mills, Ontario M3B 3K9, Canada.

This is a work of fiction. Names, characters, places and incidents are either the product of the author's imagination or are used fictitiously, and any resemblance to actual persons, living or dead, business establishments, events or locales is entirely coincidental.

This edition published by arrangement with Harlequin Books S.A.

For questions and comments about the quality of this book, please contact us at CustomerService@Harlequin.com.

® and TM are trademarks of Harlequin Enterprises Limited or its corporate affiliates. Trademarks indicated with ® are registered in the United States Patent and Trademark Office, the Canadian Intellectual Property Office and in other countries.

www.HQNBooks.com

Printed in U.S.A.

This book is dedicated to Sarah S. You are adorable and charming and I hope you love Aidan and Shelby's story as much as I do. This one's for you...

* * *

Being the "mom" of an adorable, spoiled little dog, I know the joy that pets can bring to our lives. Animal welfare is a cause I have long supported. For me that means giving to Seattle Humane. At their 2015 Tuxes and Tails fund-raiser, I offered "Your pet in a romance novel" as a prize.

In this book you will meet a bichon frise named Charlie. He has a sparkling personality and couldn't be cuter. Every time he appeared in the book, I had the biggest smile. What a sweetie! I loved everything about him—from his trying to drive to his insistence that meals be on time.

One of the things that makes writing special is interacting in different ways with people. Some I talk to for research. Some are readers who want to talk characters and story lines, and some are fabulous pet parents. Charlie's real-life family adore him and he brings hours of pleasure to them.

My thanks to Charlie's family, to Charlie himself and to the wonderful people at Seattle Humane (SeattleHumane.org). Because every pet deserves a loving family.

CHAPTER ONE

"ABOUT LAST NIGHT…"

The words were softly spoken. Almost a question. Still, they were enough to make Aidan Mitchell consider pounding his head against the table. Or the wall. He was pretty sure the table was closer. Not that he was going to pick either because he honestly didn't need any more head pain. Not with the raging hangover he'd more than earned.

"I have nothing," he admitted, squinting into the, what seemed to him, overly bright light of Brew-haha, the local coffee place. Because when a man felt as bad as he did, coffee was the only solution. "No excuse, no explanation."

He wanted to say more. That it hadn't been his fault. Only it had been.

Aidan wanted to point out that he was usually a decent guy. He loved his mom, paid his taxes and ran a successful business, yet somewhere along the way, he'd become a total jerk. But why state the obvious?

The woman standing next to his table pointed to the empty seat across from his. "May I?"

He nodded, then wished he hadn't when more pain exploded across his eyes. He reminded himself it was a small price to pay for what had happened.

He pushed aside the steady thudding in his temple and did his best to focus on his new tablemate. Shelby Gilmore was petite and blue-eyed. Delicate, he thought. Pretty enough to get a breathing man's attention. But not for him, because he had it all figured out. No local women. Tourists were easier. And look where that had gotten him.

Her gaze was steady as she sipped her coffee. She seemed to be trying to figure something out. If it was about him, he should save her the trouble.

"Yes," he said, aware his voice was gravelly. No doubt yet another manifestation of the alcohol probably still processing through his system. "I'm an ass. I'm sure there's going to be a memo about it in the paper."

Her mouth curved up. "The paper's already out and I didn't see anything. Of course, I generally avoid the whole 'ass' section. It can be depressing."

"Humor at my expense. Go ahead. I deserve it."

Her hair fell past her shoulders. It was straight and kind of a gold-blond color. Long bangs covered her eyebrows. He knew she had to be in her late twenties, but she looked younger.

"I like that you're taking responsibility for what happened," she said. "A lot of guys wouldn't."

"Most guys wouldn't have gotten in trouble in the first place." He leaned back in his chair and held in a groan. "I had it all figured out. That's what kills me. I had a plan."

"The road to hell?"

Despite how he felt, he managed a grin. "Yeah. That was me. The guy with good intentions." He stopped himself a half second before he shook his head again. "Avoid entanglements. It was working for me, too."

She held her coffee mug in both hands. "So it's true. You dated tourists." The corner of her mouth twitched. "I use the word *dated* out of general politeness. Also, it's New Year's Day, which is kind of a holiday."

"Respect. I like that." He sighed heavily. "Yes, I was the dog that picked up tourists. They were friendly and willing. Not to mention, only in town for a short time. No one's definition of dating."

"I can see the general outline of a plan here. You assumed that by keeping it simple and short-term, you wouldn't have to deal with anything messy. Like a relationship. Why is that?"

He squinted against the bright light. "No offense, but do I know you?"

She laughed. "You mean beyond saying hello?" One slim shoulder rose, then lowered. "Not really. I admit that this is a very random conversation, but I'd still like you to answer the question."

His brain was working at about two-thirds speed this morning. He felt like hell, both physically and emotionally. He was the biggest jackass around and he just wanted to crawl into a hole until he figured out how he was going to fix the problem. Which would come after he figured out what had gone wrong.

But all of that didn't explain why Shelby Gilmore was grilling him. Maybe one of her New Year's resolutions was to right wrongs. Sort of a seeker of justice for those whose hearts he'd accidentally broken.

He searched his memory for what he knew about her. She'd been in town maybe a couple of years. She worked in the bakery. Or possibly owned it—he couldn't remember, exactly. He'd seen her around. He was sure she was perfectly nice, not to mention Kipling Gilmore's sister. Kipling ran the local search-and-rescue department. Aidan knew him from that, and because it was Fool's Gold—a town where everyone knew everyone else's business. Oh, yeah. He and Kipling were part owners of a local bar. Which explained why he was having this conversation in the first place. Or did it? He looked at her.

"What was the question?" he asked.

The smile returned. "Why tourists? You're a good-looking guy with a successful business. Why aren't you married?"

"I don't want to get stuck," he blurted before he could stop himself. "Is this a job interview?"

"No. I don't mean to be intrusive."

"But you're going to keep asking questions?"

"Something like that. Stuck how?"

He finished his coffee. Before he could think about standing up to get another, Patience, the owner of Brew-haha, and about forty-seven months pregnant, waddled over with a pot.

"You look awful," she said cheerfully. "Still hungover?"

"Uh-huh."

"That's not like you. I can't remember the last time you got drunk."

Aidan didn't bother responding. There was no point. He and Patience had known each other their whole lives. One of the advantages—and disadvantages— of living in Fool's Gold. There weren't a lot of secrets. Which meant everyone from here to the Nicholson Ranch would soon know exactly what had happened last night.

Shelby frowned at her friend. "Why are you working? You're due any second."

"I know." Patience rested her left hand on her incredibly large belly. "I'm so ready for him to be born. I thought maybe standing on my feet for a few hours would hurry things along. I'm not sleeping, so why make someone else get up early on New Year's Day?"

Another nice woman, Aidan thought grimly. They were everywhere. He shouldn't even be looking at her, let alone having a conversation.

"Want some aspirin?" she asked.

"No, thanks. I'll be fine."

Patience grinned at Shelby. "I don't believe that, do you?"

"Not for a second, but it's fun to let him pretend."

They were mocking him. He was about to protest that he was sitting right there when he remembered that he deserved it. That and more.

Patience finished refilling his mug and then walked back to the counter. Before Aidan could re-focus, Shelby leaned toward him.

"How would being married make you stuck?" she repeated.

She wasn't going away. He got that. So fine. He

would tell her the truth. "If you love someone, you're stuck. You have to do things you don't want to do."

"You're not talking about going to restaurants you don't like, or taking out the trash, are you?"

"No."

"I didn't think so." She studied him. "So the tourists were a way to stay safe." The smile returned. "And get laid. A twofer."

"I really wish you wouldn't put it like that."

"Because it makes you a jerk?"

He thought about what had happened the previous night. "What did you hear? About the woman?"

"This and that. Tell me your version."

He wasn't sure if she'd been sent to make sure he got that he deserved to be punished or if this was just one of those happy accidents. Either way, he was going to spill his guts and let fate take care of the rest.

"I was hanging out at The Man Cave for their New Year's Eve party. With friends." He'd been drinking beer…at least at first. A hangover hadn't been part of his master plan.

"This woman walked up to me."

"Did you recognize her?"

"Of course." Sort of. "I knew we'd probably hung out over the summer."

"Hung out being a euphemism for *had sex*?"

He winced. "You're a lot less delicate than you look."

"Thank you. So she said hi, and…?"

Aidan sighed. "She didn't say hi. She walked up to me and said she hadn't been able to stop thinking about me. That the week we'd had together had changed her. She was hoping I felt the same way because she wanted to quit her job and move to Fool's Gold to be with me."

Shelby waited. He was pretty sure she knew the punch line to the joke that was his life, but hey, he could say it. In fact, saying it out loud was probably a good thing. Or at the very least, well deserved.

"It wasn't a *week*," he said firmly. "If it had been a week, I would have remembered."

"Her?"

He cleared his throat. "Her name. I couldn't remember her name. Or when she'd been here. She got that right away. She got mad and started yelling."

The bar had gone quiet as the scorned woman had called him everything from a rat bastard to a male whore. He'd taken it because he honest to God couldn't remember her name. He'd spent at least a couple of days with her, had talked to her, laughed with her, had sex with her and walked away without being able to remember who she was.

Which made him everything she'd called him and worse. He didn't mind that he had had a lot of women in his life, but to not remember their names—that was bad. It was the hookup equivalent of a drunk waking up in a gutter with no recollection of how he'd got there. She was his rock bottom. Not that she would appreciate the fact, unless she could also bury him under said rocks.

"What happens now?" Shelby asked.

"Hell if I know. I didn't like what I saw in her face. I'm sorry I hurt her. I'm sorry I've become that kind of guy. I want to do better. I have to change. I never meant to hurt anybody. That was the point. No one was supposed to get hurt." He shook his head, held in a groan, then drank more coffee. "What does it matter? I *am* that guy." He put down the mug. "Or I was."

"You're going to change?"

"Yeah. I have to. Not wanting to get stuck is one thing, but to be such an ass… That's not me."

Shelby's gaze was steady. She looked at him for a long time before nodding. "Okay. Thanks for talking to me."

"You gonna slap me or absolve me?"

"Neither. I was curious."

"Whatever floats your boat."

She laughed. "Keep hydrating, Aidan. And the next time someone offers you aspirin, you should probably take it."

"Thanks for the advice."

"Anytime."

She stood and carried her mug to the counter and put it in the bin for dirty dishes. Aidan watched her shrug into her coat, then walk out into the cold morning.

Pretty, he thought absently. Not that her appearance meant anything to him because he knew at least part of the solution to his problem. Swearing off women would be drastic, but it would also help make things right. Yup, that was what he had to do. Give them up completely. Forever. Starting now.

THE SIDEWALKS IN town were clear, with snow piled up by the curb. Christmas trees and holly wreaths still hung in store windows, along with banners proclaiming the New Year. Fool's Gold was a town defined by the seasons and the festivals that went with them. Shelby liked the ever-changing decorations that hung off the light posts. By Monday all the signs of Christmas and New Year's would be gone, replaced by the bright colors of Cabin Fever Days. Snowmen would appear in front yards and there would be an ice-sculpture competition in the park.

She'd already heard from several of the artists who'd sent her sketches of their designs. From those, she'd created a simple template, which was turned into a cookie cutter. During the popular festival, the bakery would sell the custom cookies in the store and in their two food carts.

This would be their second year operating the food carts and the first offering custom cookies. Both had been her idea and Shelby was excited and nervous about the cookies. Excited because she was sure they were going to be a hit. Nervous because they were her second big suggestion as a new business owner.

Last fall she'd bought into Ambrosia Bakery as a minority partner. There were days she still couldn't believe she actually owned part of a business. Her! While she'd loved culinary school, she'd quickly realized that the pastry classes were her favorite and had changed her major to baking and pastry arts. Her internship had led to a job and her life had been on track.

For all of fifteen minutes, she thought ruefully.

Then her mom had gotten sick and everything had changed.

Shelby paused at the corner. It was still early in the day. The bakery was closed for the holiday, so she could go home and enjoy a rare long weekend. Or, she could go to work and play with cookies—perfecting the decorating of the custom ice-sculpture-inspired shapes.

As *home* was a small one-bedroom apartment where no one waited for her—not even a goldfish— she turned right on Second and walked toward the familiar white storefront with the pretty silver awning. Before she got there, a car pulled up next to her and a blonde woman got out.

Shelby smiled at her friend Madeline. "Shouldn't you be off being romantic with your movie-star fiancé?"

Madeline hugged her blue coat close and grinned. "I have been, but we're taking a rest. I came home to get a few things and thought I'd say hi." She wrinkled her nose. "I just knew you'd be working today."

Shelby held up both hands. "I'm not at the bakery."

"You're three feet away."

Shelby laughed. "Okay, yes. I'm going to play with the new cookie designs. Why not? It's quiet and I like baking."

"Any leftovers for hungry friends?"

"I'm sure there are."

Shelby locked the front door behind them, then flipped on the lights. She loved being the first person in the building. Everywhere she looked, there was the promise of delicious things to come. The huge bowls, the racks brimming with supplies, the massive ovens—all ready to make magic from a few ingredients.

Shelby had always enjoyed cooking, but culinary school had given her the technical expertise that had freed her creativity. While she could appreciate the perfection of a smooth and spicy sauce or a delicious entrée, the truth was most people celebrated little moments with a cookie or a brownie or cake. No one said, "Yay, you got a raise. Let's have a sandwich."

She liked that, on a daily basis, she was a part of people's lives. That Fridays were made a little brighter because of her doughnuts or pastries. That weddings and baby showers were prettier with her cakes and that birthdays came in all colors and shapes.

She pointed to the small bistro tables by the window. The bakery had more of a walk-in clientele, but they did have a few chairs for the odd tourist who wanted to eat in.

"What would you like? I have cupcakes, but they're a day old."

"I can make that work," Madeline said with a grin. "Anything day old from you is better than fresh anywhere else."

Shelby laughed. "I don't care if you're just saying that to be a good friend. I'm going to accept the compliment and hold it close to my heart."

"As you should."

Shelby went into the back and pulled out several large plastic bins, where the pastries that hadn't sold were stored. After selecting an assortment, she piled them onto a plate before starting the small coffee-maker the employees used. She collected mugs and napkins, then took everything to the front of the bakery.

Light spilled in through the big window. Despite the chill in the air, the day promised to be sunny. The mountains to the east reminded her of Colorado— where she and her brother had grown up. Those had been fun, happy times, she reminded herself. More good than bad, at least when she'd been younger. Eventually the bad would fade and she would be left with only positive recollections.

She sat across from Madeline and studied her friend. Madeline's eyes were bright with love and contentment and her skin practically glowed.

"Being in love agrees with you," Shelby told her.

"I feel amazing. Like I've been waiting for Jonny all my life. When I'm with him, I can barely breathe and when I'm away from him, I can't wait to see him again."

"Young love," Shelby said with a sigh. "I remember it well."

Madeline laughed. "Oh, please. You're twenty-eight, which means you don't get to mock young love."

"I wasn't mocking. I was expressing gentle envy. I'm happy for you and I'd like a little of that myself." She paused, then leaned forward and lowered her voice. "Not with Jonny, of course."

"I knew that."

Shelby stood. "Let me go pour the coffee, then we'll eat sugary carbs until we can't move."

"Sounds like a plan." Madeline followed her into the back. "You doing okay?"

The question sounded casual enough, but Shelby sensed the concern. Her friend had found her crying the Sunday after Christmas. She'd been phoning and texting regularly ever since.

"I'm fine. Better. I was just missing my mom."

Shelby poured them both large mugs of coffee. Madeline added creamer to hers, then they walked back to the small table by the window.

"The holidays are hard," Shelby admitted. "I always miss her, but it's worse this time of year."

"It's your second year without her, isn't it?"

"Uh-huh."

Last year had been worse. She'd been in a new place, on her own. Kipling had still been in rehab after his skiing accident. She'd flown down to spend Christmas with him, then had returned to Fool's Gold and her job. But through the entire holiday season, she'd been acutely aware of the fact that except for her brother, she had no one in the world. Something she wanted to change.

Madeline's blue eyes turned knowing. "So last Christmas you were dealing with a fresh loss, while this year, you're more settled. But Kipling's married now, with a baby on the way, so everything is still different."

"Possibly."

"I'll take that as a yes. How can I help?"

"You already are helping by being my friend."

Madeline grinned. "But that's so easy."

"I'm glad to hear that." Shelby picked up a peanut butter cookie. Even a couple of days old, they were still soft and sweet, with the perfect hint of crispness. The bite she took practically melted on her tongue.

"So," Madeline said as she leaned forward. "Have you decided? Are you going to go for it?"

Shelby thought about the alternative. Always making a bad decision for the very best of reasons. She wanted more. Of course, feeling safe was important, but she'd meant what she said before—she wanted what her friend had. A wonderful man to love who would love her in return. But to find that, to even start looking, she had to get over her fears.

Baby steps, she reminded herself. First a man as a friend, then a man as a significant other.

Shelby drew in a breath. "I'm going to do it," she said firmly.

Madeline's brows rose. "Seriously? Good for you. Have you picked the guy?"

"Aidan Mitchell."

Her friend's brows went up another half inch as Madeline's mouth fell open. "Aidan?"

Shelby nodded. "Did you hear what happened last night?"

"With Aidan? No. What?"

Shelby filled her in on the incident at The Man Cave. She'd heard a couple of different versions before getting confirmation from Aidan himself. She spared no detail of the poor woman's distress and Aidan's hungover self-loathing.

"So why is what happened a good thing?" Madeline asked, sounding doubtful.

"Because he feels awful about the whole situation. He's disappointed in himself and he says he wants to change."

For her plan to work, she was going to need cooperation. "When you think about it, he's kind of in the same position I am. We both want to be better people than we are now."

"No," Madeline said, interrupting. "You want to deal with something bad that happened in your past. He wants to stop being icky when it comes to women. There's a difference."

"Agreed, but we're both still heading in the same direction. What do you think?"

She wanted Madeline's opinion for a lot of reasons. Not only because she trusted her friend, but Madeline had grown up in Fool's Gold. She'd known Aidan all her life. If he had a dark or violent past, Madeline would tell her everything.

Her friend reached for a cookie and took a bite before answering.

"If he's serious about changing his ways, then he's a good choice. He was always nice. You know, in a guy way." Madeline's mouth turned up. "What about sex?"

Shelby rolled her eyes. "I'm not interested in sex. That part of me isn't broken."

"What if he needs the incentive?"

"I don't think he will. Not after what happened last night. This isn't about romance. It's about something more important. Both of us healing. For me, it's my heart. Or maybe my trust. I'm not sure how to explain it exactly. I just know that being friends, not lovers, is the answer."

"Good luck getting him to go for that."

"He says he wants to be a better man," Shelby said, not sure if she was convincing the other woman or herself. "If he is, then this is one way for that to happen." She bit her lower lip. She was taking a big step, but there didn't seem to be another way. "So you think he's an okay guy?"

"I do."

"Then I'm going to ask him if he's interested."

"Oh, what I wouldn't give to be a fly on the wall. You'll tell me what happens?"

"Absolutely. I think he's going to be fine with it. We'll help each other and then move on with our lives."

"The road to hell," Madeline murmured.

Aidan had used the same expression that morning, Shelby remembered. Intentions were practically resolutions. She had hers for the New Year. A plan to finally put her past behind her and move forward with her life. Now all she needed was a willing partner and in a matter of months everything would be exactly how she'd always dreamed.

CHAPTER TWO

AIDAN DRAINED HIS bottle of water. He was dripping sweat and exhausted, but in a good way. It was the second day of the New Year and he was feeling better. His hangover was gone. He'd slept the night before, had eaten a healthy breakfast and just completed a grueling two-hour workout. He was on his way to being a new man.

He was going to make this New Year's thing work for himself. He would drink more water and eat right and get lots of exercise. See his mother more often and if an old lady needed help crossing the street, he would be there. Maybe he would even get a dog. You know, to show some sense of responsibility. It would be good for him to have something other than himself to worry about.

He grabbed his gym bag and shrugged into his jacket. He would shower and change at home, then go into his office and complete some paperwork he'd been putting off. Yup, virtuous. That was his new middle name. Aidan Virtuous Mitchell.

Once outside, the cold air sucked the heat from his body. He took a couple of deep breaths as he walked to his truck. After he finished the paperwork he would—

Someone stood by his truck. A female someone.

The cold on the outside had nothing on the sudden knot of ice that formed in his gut. His throat tightened with dread as he wondered how else his past would come back to kick him in the ass. Or maybe it was the same woman, here for her pound of flesh. He wondered if he should simply let her beat him up. Maybe if he lay down, she could get in a couple of kicks. After all, he'd earned them.

He continued walking and quickly recognized the petite blonde. Shelby Gilmore was leaning against his door, but straightened when she saw him. She squared her shoulders, as if she was determined.

Her thick wool jacket dwarfed her. She had on a ridiculous red knit hat with a pom-pom on the top. She looked young and fresh and just a little bit sexy.

Aidan slowed his steps as he reminded himself that there was no sexy in his life. Not now and not in the foreseeable future. A—no women. B—no local women. C—see A.

"Hi, Aidan," Shelby said, her voice cheerful. "Have a good workout?"

"Uh-huh." He tightened his grip on his gym bag. He wanted to ask why she was waiting for him but couldn't think of a way to phrase the question without sounding abrupt. And these days he was all about the good manners.

"I brought you some cookies."

She held out a small silver-and-white-striped bag. Even from several feet away, he could smell chocolate and maybe peanut butter.

"I just ran six miles and lifted weights." He had

resolutions, he reminded himself. A need to be virtuous.

"Then you must be hungry."

Her smile was soft and welcoming. Friendly. Which was close to sexy.

Aidan put the brakes on that train of thought. No sex for him, he reminded himself. Remember A and C. And B.

"You can't show anyone the sugar cookies."

He sucked in cold air. "Excuse me?"

She offered the bag again. "Some of them are iced sugar cookies. You can't show them to anyone." The smile returned. "Because of Cabin Fever Days. Several of the artists sent me drawings of their designs so I could turn them into cookies. But the designs are supposed to be a secret, so you can't show anyone the cookies."

"Because another guy doing an ice sculpture might steal the shape?"

She nodded. "Only some of the artists are women. You shouldn't assume they're men."

"Obviously not." He eyed the bag, tempted by the delicious smell. "I'm trying to eat right." The comment was aimed more at himself than her.

"What could be wrong with my cookies?" Her blue eyes brightened with humor. "They're really delicious. You should trust me."

He wanted to ask why, then remembered she was also trusting him. With her cookies. Which almost sounded dirty. He sighed. The whole virtuous thing was harder than he thought.

"How do you turn ice sculptures into cookies?" he asked.

"I use the outline of the basic shape. I can add a few details, but not too many. If the details are too refined, they'll bake out. Plus they can't be too hard to decorate or I'll spend all my profits frosting them. Not the amount of frosting, but the time." She held out the bag again. "Sometimes I get a special order where I can really go to town, but the ice-sculpture cookies are an experiment. We'll be selling them at the festival. In our kiosk."

She was talking too quickly. Almost nervously. The bag shook a little and he instinctively grabbed it from her. Then wondered if he shouldn't have.

"Shelby, why are you here?"

"I want to talk to you."

"About cookies?"

"No. I brought those because I'm nice."

That made him laugh. "Good to know. What do you want to talk about?" He hesitated. "In case it matters, I've given up women."

Her mouth twitched. "Have you? That can't be very fun."

"It's only been a day. So far it's not so bad." He was lying, but what the hell. She couldn't know that.

Her smile returned. "Just so we're clear, I'm not here because I'm interested in having sex with you. And I don't want a boyfriend. Well, I do. But not you."

He had no idea what to make of her or what she was saying. "So I should be grateful for the cookies?"

She laughed. "No. I hope you'll like them, though." The humor faded. "The truth is…" She swallowed. "Wow, this is harder than I thought. I want…"

The ice in his gut returned. Whatever it was, he wasn't going to like it. He told himself, whatever it was, he would say no. He needed practice saying no and this would be how he started. *N-O.* Easy enough. According to his mother it had been one of his first words.

"I want us to be friends."

SHELBY UNLOCKED HER front door. She was cold and nervous. The first would be remedied by the furnace in her small apartment. The second was more of a problem.

Aidan hadn't laughed at her. That was something. Nor had he walked away. Instead he'd thought for a long second, before saying, "Go on." Which was when she'd suggested they talk at her place.

Now she waited while he followed her inside. Her already tiny apartment seemed to shrink. She pulled off her hat and fluffed her bangs, then hung both coats on the rack by the front door.

She turned and looked around her place, wondering what he saw. Or thought.

The apartment was newish, with big windows. From where she was standing, she could see the living room, the dining alcove and most of the kitchen. All in all, the place was pretty ordinary and she hadn't done that much decorating.

She'd left the walls white and added a few posters. Most of them were of wildflowers or sunsets, but the one over the sofa was of Kipling screaming down a mountain. He was in perfect focus, with the background behind him a blur. Both skis were several inches above the ground. His expression was intense, his mouth straight.

He'd won that race and she'd been there to see it happen. The picture was one of her favorites.

The rest of the room was less exciting. She had a navy plaid sofa with a single chair by the window. She's found the simple maple dining table and chairs at a thrift store. Back the other way was the short hallway that led to her bedroom. There was also a decent-sized bathroom.

Nothing fancy, but the place worked. The rent was reasonable, the neighbors quiet. She worked a lot of hours and didn't need any more. One day, she thought wistfully. One day she would have a house and husband and kids and maybe a dog. Until then, this was fine.

She pointed to the dining table. "I have cupcakes," she said. "I'll make coffee to go with them. Unless you want milk."

"You gave me cookies. I have them in my truck."

"They're for later. The cupcakes are for our conversation."

He looked from the platter in the center of the table back to her. "How can you eat like you do and still look like that?"

She felt some of her tension ease. "I taste rather than have a whole serving. Plus I work in a bakery. After a while, the good things start to be less tempting."

"I wish that were true for me."

He took the seat she offered. Shelby went into the kitchen and started her coffeemaker. She'd prepped it before she'd left, hoping things would work out. In a way, she was surprised they'd gotten this far. Her plan had potential, but it required cooperation. And Aidan not thinking she was insane.

Now that he was here, she didn't know what to say. How to start. She'd been practicing opening lines for a couple of weeks now. Ever since she'd figured out what she was going to do. She'd known the what, but not the who. Not until she'd heard about what had happened on New Year's Eve and had seen Aidan the next day.

He could have been blasé about what had happened, but he hadn't been. He'd been angry at himself and ashamed. He'd wanted to change. All of which was in her favor.

"Cream and sugar?" she asked.

"Just black."

She took her coffee the same way. Every calorie saved, she'd always thought. Now she carried two mugs to the table and took the seat across from him.

Aidan was tall, with broad shoulders. He still wore his workout clothes—a T-shirt over sweats. Both were loose, but she caught sight of the muscles lurking underneath. Given what he did for a living, it made sense that he was in good shape.

His face was nice, she thought. He was good-looking without being too pretty. She liked his dark brown eyes, the way they met hers steadily.

Silence stretched between them.

"This would be your meeting," he said as he reached for one of her cupcakes. She'd picked chocolate with a nice coconut frosting. Simple, but delicious. The best desserts usually were.

She drew in a breath and said the first thing that came to her mind. "I want to buy a house."

His eyebrows drew together. "I don't sell real estate."

"I know." She swallowed against the sudden tightness in her throat. This was going to be harder than she'd thought.

"Yesterday, you said you were sorry about what happened with that woman." She sipped her coffee. "Are you still?"

He nodded, then took a bite of his cupcake. "These are good," he said when he'd chewed and swallowed.

"Thanks. I like that you want to change. It's not easy. Old habits and all that."

"Yeah. I haven't figured out what I'm going to do yet. I'm giving up women. That's for sure."

"And how long do you think your antiwoman pledge will last?"

"I don't know. A few weeks. A couple of months."

"A long time."

His mouth turned down at the corners. "Tell me about it. But I don't know what else to do. I won't be that guy again."

"Do you want to fall in love?" She held up her hands. "Not with me. That's not where this is going. But ever?"

"I don't know."

An unexpectedly honest answer. "Because you'd be stuck?"

"I shouldn't have told you that."

"You were hungover. You couldn't help yourself. I won't tell anyone."

Emotions flashed across his face. She tried to read them and couldn't.

"I want to not treat women badly," he said at last. "No, that's not right. I was honest about what I wanted and if the lady agreed, then we had a good time. It was supposed to be okay for both of us. I don't know what went wrong."

"One of your temporaries wanted more."

"And I couldn't remember her name."

He spoke with what felt like sincere regret.

"Now you want to be different."

He looked at her. "If you think you can change me," he began.

"I don't." She shrugged. "I don't believe people can change each other. We have to make the choice to be different ourselves and then make it happen. You want to act differently around women, but you don't know how. Has it occurred to you that maybe the problem isn't that you couldn't remember her name, but that you never saw her as a person in the first place? That you don't see any of them as people?"

He glanced longingly toward the door. "Okay then. While this has been great, I need to go."

"Five minutes," she said quietly. "Give me five minutes. I'm really going somewhere with this and I think you'll be interested. Plus, it's not scary. I promise."

He deliberately glanced at his watch. "Five minutes."

"Thank you." She paused while she figured out the best and quickest way to say what she was thinking, in a way that would get him to see her plan had real merit.

"You do what you do to avoid getting stuck. Which is the same as being in love, right? You don't want the serious relationship."

He gave her a brief nod.

"Logically you go the other way. A series of short-term, meaningless flings. And while there is some pleasure in that, it's not exactly who you want to be."

Another nod, this one slightly less cautious.

"Now you want to change, but don't know how. I'm suggesting that part of the problem is you see women as either wives or playthings. You don't have any women friends in your life." She waved her hand. "I'm not counting family. Your mom, cousins and the like. I'm talking about the everyday garden-variety woman you interact with."

He leaned back in the chair. "Go on."

She told herself it was great that he hadn't bolted. Now came the tough part. Telling him about her.

"My mom was my dad's second wife. Kipling and I are half brother and sister. My mom was great. Sweet and loving. She adored my father." Shelby drew in a breath. She told herself to stick to the facts. To stay in her head and everything would be okay. It was only if she lost herself in the memories that she got into trouble.

"My dad was a difficult man," she began, then

made herself stop. Martina, her therapist, was always reminding her to talk about the past with authenticity, no euphemisms. "No. That's not true. He wasn't difficult. He was violent. He beat my mother and when I got older, he beat me."

The stark words hung in the air between them. Aidan's expression tightened but he didn't say anything.

"One of my earliest memories was of my mom screaming as my dad hit her. I remember being so scared. But when I was little, he never hit me, so in a strange way, I was safe. He didn't hit Kipling—not like he hit my mom. Maybe it was because Kipling was his son. I don't know."

She reached for her coffee, then realized her hands were trembling and put down the mug. "Kip left when I was about ten. He was a great skier and went off to train. He swore he would always be there for me if things got bad." She felt her mouth twist. "That's how we described what happened. In terms of how bad it was."

Had he put her mom in the hospital this time? Were there broken bones? Because like so many families dealing with something awful, they spoke around the truth.

"I remember asking my mom why she stayed and she said it was because she loved him so much. It didn't make sense to me, but I knew in my heart she would never go. And he didn't hit me, so we just lived like that. With the unspoken rules. Don't make Dad mad. Don't try to protect my mom. Don't get in the way."

There had been so many awful times. Nights when she'd cleaned split skin and held ice against bruises. Times when she'd tried to figure out if a bone was broken and whether or not she should call 911.

"And then I turned thirteen."

Shelby still didn't know what had set off her father. Whether it was her birthday or the onset of puberty or what. But the day after she turned thirteen, he hit her for the first time.

"It hurts," she said quietly. "I'd heard her scream a million times, but until he decked me with his fist, I had no idea how much pain there could be. The shock of it stunned me. The sense of betrayal, of helplessness. My mom tried to stop him, but he pushed her into the wall and kept coming after me."

She'd been knocked unconscious. There had been dozens of bruises but no broken bones. To this day, she didn't know if she'd had a concussion because going to the doctor was out of the question.

"I called Kip the next morning. He was home in twelve hours and he got me out of there. He was already on the ski circuit, with endorsements and stuff. So he could afford to put me in a boarding school. I stayed there through high school. My mom would visit. Only my mom. I didn't see my dad again for years."

Funny how she could get through all this without tears. Maybe she'd cried herself out years ago. She wasn't sure.

"I would plead with her to leave him," she continued. "Kip would get us an apartment. Dad never had to know. But she wouldn't do it. She kept talking about how much she loved him and how he loved her."

She looked at Aidan and was grateful for the lack of emotion on his face. His dark eyes gave nothing away and that was how she preferred it.

"She was always bruised. She did her best to cover it up, but I knew what to look for. She would stay with me for a few days, then go back to him."

She shifted in her seat and put her hands on her lap. "We lived like that for years. Then she got cancer. It was bad. By the time she told me about it, she only had a few weeks to live. I went back to be with her. Which meant being with him."

She squared her shoulders. "It all started again. I knew more and tried to protect myself, but he would come after me while I was sleeping. I would wake up with him beating me. It was horrible. More horrible than you can imagine. Kip was just starting back with his training after winning at the Olympics. I didn't want to bother him, but I didn't think I could take it anymore. Then he was injured and in the hospital in New Zealand. The doctors weren't even sure he would walk again. I knew I had to get through my mom's last weeks on my own. For her. I had to do my best not to let him surprise me. But it's hard not to sleep. A couple of times I got a hotel room for the night, but that wasn't a long-term solution. I was genuinely scared for my life when these two men showed up."

Her tension eased as she remembered the shock of opening her mom's front door and finding Angel and Ford on the steps. "They were from CDS. Mayor Marsha had sent them to protect me."

Aidan's brows rose. "How did she know what was happening?"

For the first time in several minutes, Shelby smiled. "You're asking the wrong person. All I knew was that it was a miracle. My dad was arrested on multiple charges. Apparently he wasn't only a bad guy at home. I stayed with my mom until she died and then I moved here."

Aidan leaned toward her. "I'm sorry."

"Thank you. I didn't want to dump all that on you, but I didn't know how else to explain what I want to do." Now came the hard part. "There have been men in my life. Boyfriends. Sort of. I want what most people have. Love and a family. But I'm not good at picking the right guy." She rested her hands on the table. "Because of what happened with my dad, and my mom dying, I started seeing a counselor. She helped me realize that I always pick a guy who can't commit. The delightful charmer who will never stay or be faithful, or the guy who isn't over his last relationship. On the surface, I look like I'm so together, but on the inside, I keep myself from getting involved with someone who can love me back because I'm afraid. Except for Kip, I don't actually trust men. Because of that, I pick ones that are so flawed, the relationship can never work. That way I'm never truly at risk."

AN INTERESTING SET of facts, Aidan told himself, but it had nothing to do with the building rage inside of him. He didn't know where Shelby's father was right now, but he wanted to go find him and give him a taste of what he'd been doing to his family. He wanted to reduce the man to a bloody, broken mass of pain and suffering. Then he wanted to wait a few days and do it all again and again.

He could understand being annoyed or pissed or even furious. But there was no excuse to take out any of that on someone else. He'd grown up with four brothers, so he'd been in plenty of fights as a kid. But there were rules and one of them was you stick to your own size and gender. And after about age fifteen, you give it up. Aidan believed his own father was an asshole, but even he'd never hit a woman.

"Aidan?"

He looked at Shelby. "What?"

"You're not listening to me."

"Sorry. It's your dad. Where is he now?"

"In prison. He's serving consecutive sentences. Even with good behavior, he won't be out for about fifty years."

"I want to go find him and punish him."

She reached across the table and lightly touched his hand. "Thank you. I appreciate the thought, but it's not necessary."

"I need to hurt him."

"It won't change him."

Probably not, but that wasn't what had him telling himself to let it go. Beating up her father wouldn't help Shelby. That was the real point of it.

"I wish I'd known you then," he told her. "I would have helped."

Her breath caught and she cleared her throat. "Thank you for saying that. I believe you. Which is part of the reason I wanted to talk to you. About my problem. And yours."

"That you pick the wrong guy because you're not willing to trust a man not to physically hurt you and that I pick the wrong woman because I don't want to get stuck?"

She nodded.

He tried to remember the last time he'd had a conversation this honest and couldn't. Shelby had laid it all on the line. He figured he had to do the same.

"I'm not looking for home and hearth," he admitted. "I just want to stop being a jackass."

She laughed. "A worthy goal." Her humor faded. "I thought I was doing better. I thought I was healed. Then I went out with a guy I knew was a total flake. He swore he was seeing only me, but he wasn't. It was then I realized I wasn't as far along as I thought."

She pointed to the cupcakes between them. "Everything else is great. I went to culinary school and discovered I'm more of a dessert-pastry chef. I moved here and bought into the business. I have friends, I'm going to be an aunt in a couple of months. It's all good."

"Except for Mr. Right."

She nodded.

He was no longer as concerned about what she wanted from him. Shelby had been through a lot and if he could help, he wanted to. If she was looking for the perfect guy, by now she knew he wasn't even close. Anything else was doable.

"Where do I fit in?"

"I need to learn that I can trust a man who isn't my brother," she told him. "I was hoping we could be friends. Real friends who do things together. I thought if we could do that, we could get over what's holding us back. You obviously need to start seeing women as something other than short-term sexual partners. I thought we could work on this together. Hang out. Get to know each other. Develop a relationship based on trust and respect." She wrinkled her nose. "Without the complication of the whole boy-girl thing."

Honest to God, Aidan didn't know what to say. Friends? Her points were valid and he could see how her plan might work, but damn.

"Would there be a time limit?" he asked.

"Sure. I don't know. How long until we're both better? Six months?"

So until June.

"Just friends." Because he wasn't sure he'd ever been friends with a woman before. Not since maybe high school. "Nothing else."

"Nothing," she said firmly. "We'll do stuff and talk and you'll see that women are more than a booty call and I won't be scared anymore. In six months we'll both be better people and we'll go back to our regular lives."

He wanted to protest the booty-call comment but knew he'd earned it. Friends. Just friends. Was it possible? Did he want to bother?

The thing was, if he didn't, wouldn't he stay exactly where he was? And he knew he didn't want that.

"Maybe," he said slowly.

She brightened. "So you'll think about it?"

There were a lot of ways to answer the question, but he figured they both deserved the truth. "Shelby, I'm pretty sure I won't be thinking about anything else."

CHAPTER THREE

AMBER DUTTON CLOSED her eyes and made a low moaning sound at the back of her throat. "You're killing me."

Shelby did her best not to preen. Impressing her customers was one thing, but impressing Amber was harder. Amber had owned Ambrosia Bakery for over ten years. She knew the business inside and out and she'd tasted more than her share of chocolate mousse.

Amber broke off a piece of the dark chocolate shell that held the mousse and put it in her mouth. She let it melt on her tongue before swallowing. "Amazing. You made these, too?"

Shelby nodded. "It's not that difficult. I've been working on the recipe for a while. I thought we could try adding more upscale desserts to the inventory. Maybe start on certain days to see if there's any interest. With the city's online connection, we could send out an email to men, suggesting the high-end desserts as a special surprise to take home to the women in their lives."

"We just have to give out a few samples and we'll be flooded with interest." Amber took another bite of the mousse. "This is going straight to my hips and I genuinely don't care." She pointed with her spoon.

"I thought that bread you did last week was the best new thing, but this is better."

"I have a lot of ideas."

"Hiring you that first day was the smartest thing I've ever done."

Amber dug her spoon into the mousse. Shelby smiled as she basked in pride and happiness. She loved the creative side of her job. Back at her small apartment, she had an idea file overflowing with different items she wanted to try. Cupcakes and brownies, mousses and breads. On her days off she often played around with recipes. Finding the exact combination of ingredients, the right presentation and flavors took time. But the work was so fun and fulfilling.

Culinary school had been a revelation for her. She'd discovered that there were other crazy people who dreamed up recipes. She'd loved the technical classes as much as the practical information. She'd wanted to know more and more. Getting her first job had made her giddy. Then her mom had gotten sick and everything had changed.

Being trapped in that house, knowing her father was going to find that vulnerable moment and hurt her, had left her feeling shattered. While the bruises and welts would heal, every day that she was with him had drained her spirit, and she'd worried about that a lot more than the damage he would do to her body. Having Angel and Ford show up when they did had saved her. The invitation to go to Fool's Gold had come with an introduction to Amber. Working in the bakery had been exactly what she'd needed.

Now she was a part owner and there were so many possibilities. Next on her bucket list was having Aidan agree to her wild plan so she could complete her healing and move on with her life.

Amber finished the mousse and dark chocolate shell, then licked her fingers. "I'm going to have to walk an extra hour on the treadmill to burn off those calories and it was so worth it."

"You don't have to do anything to burn off the calories," Shelby told her. "You always look great."

Her business partner—a tall, curvy, dark-skinned woman with beautiful eyes and long braids—laughed. "If only that were true. I passed forty nearly two years ago. I'm fighting gravity and a slowing metabolism, but I'm determined to win." She walked around to the front of the display case. "The blue-and-white cookies are adorable."

"I thought they'd be a quirky addition for the week."

Patience had finally given birth to her son two days before. Shelby had decided to make some baby-inspired cookies. There were little ducks and small rattles and a square frosted cookie like a baby block. The latter had taken a lot of time, so it wasn't a practical addition to their everyday menu, but she'd had fun with it.

"Maybe we could talk to Dellina," Shelby said. "Show her some samples and see if she wanted to offer the custom cookies to her clients."

Dellina Ridge was an events planner. She handled everything from weddings to corporate functions. Shelby had been trying to start a business relationship with her since she'd been hired at the bakery. Although Amber wasn't opposed to the idea, she also wasn't that enthused. Shelby told herself she could see the other woman's point. The bakery did really well already. Amber had an established business in the town where she'd grown up. Why do more?

But Shelby couldn't help wanting to expand things. There were so many possibilities.

"You exhaust me with your enthusiasm," Amber told her with a laugh. "Even so, I'm starting to see your point about working with Dellina. We could do custom work for her. It would be more time, but we could charge more. My biggest concern is the labor. We'd need extra help and I'm not sure where we'd get it. We don't need anyone on a daily basis, so this would be by the job. That's hard to find."

"You're right. Let me think about it. There has to be a solution."

Amber sighed. "To be that young and enthusiastic," she said with a sigh. "I'm envious. You work on the problem and I'll go pay our vendors. We'll meet in a couple of weeks and discuss it all. How does that sound?"

"Perfect."

Amber took a step toward the back office, then paused. She put her hand on her stomach. "I'm having the weirdest sensations lately. I just don't feel right."

Shelby didn't like that sound of that. "What do you mean?"

"Things are off in my tummy. I keep thinking it's going to be my time of the month, but it's not.

My hormones are a mess." She grimaced. "I can't be going through the change, can I? I'm way too young. At least that's what I keep telling myself." She smiled. "Don't worry. I'll be fine. And if I'm not, I'll eat more of your mousse."

"It's in the refrigerator in the back."

Amber groaned. "I so didn't need to know that. Now I'm going to be thinking about it all day."

Shelby watched her go and hoped everything was all right. Probably just a stomach bug, she told herself.

Before she could get serious about worrying more, the door opened and a very pregnant Isabel Hendrix waddled in. Shelby looked at her and did her best not to wince. It wasn't that Isabel was so very far along as the fact that she was carrying triplets.

Her friend groaned. "Yes, I know. I'm a whale. And one of the really big ones. Which, in case you were wondering, is a blue whale. They can grow to over ninety feet. Unlike the smaller killer whales that tend to top out at thirty feet."

Shelby stared at her. "How do you know that?"

Isabel grinned. "Very random, huh? And impressive. I mentioned being a whale to Felicia and she gave me a brief lecture on the species."

Not a surprise, Shelby thought. Felicia was some kind of genius who knew just about everything. She organized all the festivals in town with a precision that left most of the citizens both dizzy and appreciative.

Isabel rested her right hand on her large belly. "You know why I'm here."

"I do and I have two loaves put aside for you."

"Thank goodness. I swear I would have started sobbing if you hadn't." She shook her head. "There is so something wrong with me."

"No, there isn't. You're pregnant and dealing. Give yourself a break."

Shelby had never been pregnant, but if Isabel was anything to go by, the cravings were powerful. Her friend had developed a love for pretzel bread that bordered on fanatical. Two months before, the bakery had run out and Isabel had cried piteously. Shelby had felt so badly about the upset that she'd stayed late, baking a batch. When she'd delivered it, Isabel had cried again, this time out of joy.

Talk about powerful weapons, she thought now. If someone learned to control hormones they could rule the world.

"I have the bread on the baking schedule," she told her friend. "We'll always have it for you. And if we happen to run out, I have a half-dozen loaves of dough in the freezer."

Isabel rubbed her belly. "I'm sorry to be such a freak. I can't seem to help it. You're very good to me and I owe you. Seriously, if there's anything you ever need, tell me and I'm there. If I'm busy changing the three or four thousand diapers I'm going to have to deal with every week, I'll send Ford."

An impressive offer, Shelby thought, considering Ford was a successful businessman and former navy SEAL. She doubted there was anything he couldn't accomplish.

"You're on," she said. "I will call you first in a

crisis." For a second she thought about asking Isabel if she knew Aidan very well. They'd grown up in the same town and were about the same age. But asking the question probably meant explaining why and she wasn't ready to share her slightly offbeat plan with anyone else. Not until Aidan had said if he was game or not.

She mentally crossed her fingers that he would see that she was right about both of them. Six months of being friends wasn't a huge hardship and at the end of the time, they could both be healed. A worthy goal. But would he see it that way?

She had no way of knowing, so rather than dwell on the what-ifs, she got Isabel her bread and told herself she would hear when she would hear. If he told her no, there were other men she could approach. None immediately came to mind, but now that she knew the best way to move on with her life, she wasn't going to let anything stop her.

AIDAN DID A second check of the equipment, making sure bindings were secure and edges clean and smooth after the last trek. Taking novices out on their first snowshoeing adventure was both fun and stressful—the former for them, the latter for him. He had a perfect safety record and there was no way he wanted to risk that.

The weather was on his side. The reports were for the temperatures staying well below freezing. The trails he used for beginners had a nice base of snow without a lot of ice. More snow was predicted. After the mostly dry winter last year, extra snowpack was welcome news.

Aidan put the snowshoes back on the rack, then made sure the door leading outside was locked before he returned to the office.

Aidan's mother had started Mitchell Adventure Tours when her children had been little—mostly to provide some steady income for the family. His father's volatile personality combined with heavy drinking had meant dangerous outbursts. Not in the way Shelby had endured, he thought. Ceallach didn't hit his children. Instead he turned his temper toward his other creations. Because he was an artist who worked with glass, a couple of hours of throwing and breaking could destroy months' worth of commissions. Despite his fame and the amount people paid for his pieces, there were times when money was tight. His mother had filled in the gaps.

At first she'd offered a few walking tours of the city. Other local businesses had pitched in by recommending her to tourists. Eventually she'd started driving small groups around in the family minivan. As Del, his oldest brother, and Aidan had become teens, they'd pitched in.

Although Del was expected to take over the family business, Aidan had been the one to step up. He'd quickly grown the company, broadening the offerings and taking groups camping and fishing in the summer. Winter sports had followed. He'd bought out his mom nearly eight years ago and had added "Adventure" to the name.

Four years ago he'd moved the company to its

current location. The new building had a big reception area with lots of wall space for maps, pictures of their excursions and a list of the tours the company offered. He had a private office in back, and there was a large room for the staff. In the back was the equipment storage, along with his repair shop. The equipment he bought was expensive and he believed in keeping it in good shape.

He walked into the office, where Fay Riley was handing over tickets to a group of twentysomethings. College kids, he thought. Here for a day of snowshoeing.

They looked to be in shape, which helped, but they were also going to be a handful. They always were. Unlike his older customers, the college crowd rarely listened. He made a mental note to make sure he brought enough GPS trackers for everyone. No one was getting lost on his watch.

Fay was in her late thirties and a relatively new transplant to Fool's Gold. She and her husband had ended up settling in the area after their daughter, Kalinda, had been badly burned and started treatment with a burn specialist at the local hospital. Rather than return to their hometown, they'd decided to stay close to her doctor. Fay had started working for Aidan part-time and was now the office manager. She was the perfect combination of organized and mothering. Not only did she manage the schedule, she was great with the summer help he hired every year.

"They'll be fun," she said, motioning to the college students studying the pictures on the wall. "You head out first thing in the morning. It's a six-hour tour. They wanted longer, but I told them to start slow."

"I'm surprised they listened."

"I can be persuasive."

Aidan grinned. "You mean bossy."

"That, too."

Fay had told him once that her daughter's horrible accident had changed her in ways she couldn't explain. She'd had to learn to be strong. To make demands. To face the unthinkable and do it in a way that kept up Kalinda's spirits. He supposed that life's adversities offered a fork in the road, so to speak. Either you learned your lesson and were a better person for it, or you got crushed.

He'd been successful at everything else he'd put his mind to—his current situation wasn't going to be any different. He didn't like who he'd become, so he was going to change. Find a better way.

"The blonde is pretty," Fay added playfully in a low voice. "Last I saw, you were on a blonde kick. Of course, redheads and brunettes are nice, too."

He didn't bother glancing at the group. "No, thanks."

She raised her eyebrows. "Aren't you feeling well?"

"I'm fine. I'm not going to do that anymore."

Her expression turned quizzical. "I don't understand."

The college students left. Aidan leaned against the counter. "I'm not going to date tourists anymore."

"You don't date them. You do them. Or whatever it's called. Hook up. It's not a relationship."

A blunt assessment made all the more uncomfortable by the honesty behind it. "I'm giving up women."

Fay laughed. The sound was light and happy. She touched his arm. "Oh, honey, I don't think so. You, give up women? That's not possible."

He resisted the need to step back. "I can do it. I want to. I'm changing."

She laughed again. "Uh-huh. I'd pay money to see that. I give you a week. Maybe two. Then you'll be seducing the next pretty tourist so fast, you'll break the sound barrier." She was still chuckling when she walked into the storeroom.

Aidan knew that Fay liked him a lot. She did a good job of running things, but more than that, she cared about him and trusted him. Last year, he'd been the one to teach Kalinda to ski the few weeks they'd had snow. Because of her burns, she had lots of scar tissue that limited her movements. But she'd managed to figure it out and he'd been right beside her when she'd taken her first run down the mountain.

So he knew that Fay's teasing came from a place of affection. But it still bothered him that she didn't think he could manage a little self-control. He wasn't that much of a dog, was he?

He dismissed the question as soon as he thought it. He could do anything he put his mind to. He was a decent guy who'd lost his way. He could change and he was going to. He knew why he'd gotten where he was, which meant changing it couldn't be that hard.

Shelby's offer loomed large, as it had since she'd made it. He had to admit there was a certain logic to her plan. He liked the idea of being friends with a woman. He wasn't sure how to go about it, but maybe they could figure it out together. Plus he would be helping her and that made him feel good. Maybe if he was a part of her healing, he would make up for past behavior. Like karmic justice.

With Shelby, he could learn to see women as people. Not just objects of desire. He would grow and change. That would be good.

"I'm going out for a while," he yelled toward the back of the building. "I have my cell."

"I'll call if I need you," Fay told him.

She said something else, but he didn't hear her. Nor did he bother asking her to repeat it. No doubt she'd made some crack about his inability to change. Well, he was going to prove her wrong. He was going to prove everyone wrong.

He left his truck in its parking spot and walked across town. Midweek in the winter meant fewer tourists. Aidan had to admit he enjoyed the quiet times. Yes, there was less business, but sometimes it was nice when it was just the residents. That would change soon enough. The festivals came regularly, even in winter. And with them came the crowds.

He crossed the street and headed for the bakery. He was going to tell Shelby yes. He would be friends with her for six months and use that time to break his pattern with women. Then he would start over— a different kind of guy. Better. As if he'd grown up with sisters or something.

He walked into the bakery. Shelby stood at the counter. As soon as he saw her, he was struck by how delicate she looked. A headband held her hair off her face while the back was caught up in some kind of nearly invisible hairnet. She wore a silver-and-white-striped apron over jeans and a long-sleeved shirt. She was helping Eddie Carberry pick out cookies.

"Do those have a lot of butter?" the eightysomething woman asked, pointing at a sugar cookie that had been dipped in chocolate. "My doctor told me to watch my cholesterol. I told him I'm too old and he can watch it for me. Now I'm feeling defiant, so I want cookies with butter and later I'll have a steak."

Shelby's mouth twitched, as if she was holding in a smile. "That's one way to handle it," she murmured.

"No one can live on salads and nonfat dairy," Eddie informed her. "Because that's not living at all. It's surviving. Life's too short. Now give me a couple of brownies to go with the cookies." The old lady, dressed in a bright violet tracksuit with a matching down coat, looked him up and down. "You're working out more these days."

He was, but how did she know?

"Gladys and I see you on the treadmill when we're at the gym for our water aerobics class. You should wear tighter clothes."

"Ma'am?"

Eddie rolled her eyes. "You know what I'm saying, Aidan. You've got the goods. Let's see them. Share the bounty. Take off your shirt once in a while. Put on tighter shorts." She sighed heavily. "Young people today. You're not as bright as my generation. That's for sure."

Eddie paid for her treats and left. Aidan stared after her.

"I honest to God don't know what to say," he admitted.

Shelby laughed. "I so want to be her when I grow up. Speaking my mind and ogling younger men. It's fantastic."

"Not if you're the younger man."

"Afraid?"

He grinned. "Terrified."

She held up a chocolate-dipped cookie. "How's your cholesterol?"

"Excellent."

She passed over the cookie.

"Thanks." He took a bite. "I'm starting to wonder if you're in league with Eddie. Feeding me all this stuff so I have to work out more."

"While it's a great plan, I never would have thought of it."

"Eddie would."

She laughed again. "Yes, she would, but I promise I have no ulterior motive for offering you a cookie." She raised one shoulder. "Okay, maybe I have one reason, but it has nothing to do with Eddie. Did you think about what we talked about?"

He nodded as he finished the cookie.

"A lot?"

He nodded again.

"And?"

She was pretty. He liked how she met his gaze

steadily. He didn't have a type so much as he enjoyed all women, and while under other circumstances he would be tempted, he knew his relationship with Shelby wouldn't be about sex. It would be about something far more important.

He thought about what she'd told him about her past. How her father had hurt her. He felt the anger rise up inside of him again, along with the need to protect. Not that he could do anything, but he told himself it was good that he still had that much empathy. He wasn't a total jackass.

He wanted to be different and as far as he could tell, Shelby's plan offered a way to make that happen.

"I'm in," he said.

"Yeah?"

"Yeah."

She clapped her hands together. "That's great. I'm very excited. I was hoping you'd agree. I've been thinking about the plan and we need to make sure we agree on terms."

"Friends for six months."

She nodded. Her eyes were wide and blue and right now filled with earnest determination.

"We'll hang out and do things together," she said. "Get to know each other. Develop trust. I'll see you as a man who doesn't threaten me and you'll see me as a person, not a bed partner."

"Agree. No sex. Nothing romantic. We'll hang out and do stuff."

She squared her shoulders. "Then in six months, we'll both be better people. Healed. We'll finish our experiment and go our separate ways."

"That's easy for you to say, but I'm not sure you can keep your end of the bargain."

She frowned. "What do you mean?"

He grinned. "I'm a great friend. You might get hooked. I'm still friends with guys I knew in grade school. I can't seem to shake 'em."

She laughed. "I'm an excellent friend, as well. What if *you* don't want to stop being friends with me?"

"That could be a real possibility."

"All right," she said slowly. "What if we commit—" She shook her head. "No, you hate that word. What if we *dedicate* ourselves to our plan for the next six months? Then, if we still want to be friends, we still will be. But regular friends, without a plan for mutual personal growth."

He couldn't imagine any man on the planet coming up with something like this, he thought. Which was why women should be ruling the world.

"Sounds like a plan." He held out his hand.

She leaned across the counter and took it in hers. They shook.

"I don't work Saturday," she said. "Are you free?"

He had a couple of tours, but he could trade the afternoon one. "Sure. Say three?"

"Perfect. I'll come to your place. It's a date." She frowned. "Not a date. A…"

"A nondate?"

"An undate?"

He grinned. "A friend date."

She nodded. "Do you want another cookie?"

"No, thanks. I don't want to have to work out more and have Eddie think I'm flirting with her."

"Good point." She bit her lower lip. "Do you think this is going to work, Aidan?"

He thought about the pain in her eyes when she'd talked about her past. He remembered the accusations the other woman had hurled at him on New Year's Eve. Shelby had a good job and was part owner in a business he was pretty sure she loved. He knew he enjoyed everything about his company. Each of them had nearly all they could want and yet something was missing. Something big.

"We're going to make it work," he told her. "We know the problem and we'll find a solution. We just have to show up and put in the effort. It'll happen."

Her smile returned. "You have a little motivational speaker in you. I didn't know. I'll see you Saturday."

"I'll be there."

AIDAN PULLED INTO the driveway of the house where he'd grown up. The roof had been recently replaced and the paint was new, but otherwise it looked exactly as it always had.

The property was a few miles outside of town, with plenty of land and a workshop for Ceallach out back. A giant workshop, where the gifted artist created his masterpieces. There was even a separate driveway and parking area for his various assistants who came and went. Because glass blowing wasn't a solitary venture. Someone was needed at nearly every stage.

Aidan remembered being taken to his father's workshop as a kid. While the power and heat of the furnace had intrigued him, he'd had no real interest in creating anything. His father had despaired of ever having a son to follow in his footsteps. Then Nick was born. From about two or three, he'd been obsessed with what his father did. Even his very first crude creations had shown talent. From that day, Del and Aidan had ceased to exist. At least for their father.

Different from what Shelby had gone through, he thought idly. But still not the happy childhood from TV sitcoms. He and Del had banded together—protecting each other, talking sports instead of art. The twins—the babies of the family—had been like Nick. Talented and interested in their father's world. And so they'd grown up—five brothers divided into two camps. There had been affection between them, caring, but no real common language.

Aidan got out of his car, but before he could walk up the porch steps, the front door opened and a happy beagle dashed toward him. Sophie yipped in excitement as she raced forward, her long ears flapping as she ran. He crouched down and held open his arms. Sophie slammed into him with all the enthusiasm one delighted dog could contain.

"How's my girl?" he asked, patting and rubbing her. She squirmed to get closer, then swiped his cheek with her tongue. Her tail slapped his arm as she wiggled and whined.

His mother stepped onto the porch. "She doesn't

do anything moderately," Elaine Mitchell said with a laugh. "I've always admired that about her."

Aidan climbed the two porch steps to hug his mom. She hung on tight. Sophie circled them both and barked. Elaine stepped back.

"I wasn't expecting you," she said, holding open the door. "This is a nice surprise."

"I was in the neighborhood."

He followed her into the kitchen and took a seat at the barstool by the island. Elaine collected a filter and tin of coffee, then poured water into the carafe.

She moved with energy, which he liked to see. The previous summer she'd battled breast cancer without telling anyone in the family. After the news had come out, he'd been able to look back and see how she'd been tired, with the strain of her illness showing on her face. Now he did his best to be more observant. While his mother had promised to never keep a secret like that again, Aidan wasn't sure he believed her. Theirs was a family built on information withheld.

"How's the business?" she asked after she'd started the coffeemaker.

"Good. I have a couple of snowshoeing trips along with the usual cross-country skiing." He offered guided tours for those not familiar with the area. Most of his tour guides were college students happy to take a light load in the winter and get paid to ski. In summer he hired the students who wanted to stay in the area over the long break. Either way, it was a win-win.

Sophie crossed to her bed in the corner and

scratched the soft fabric several times before settling down. The little beagle had been there for his
mom as Elaine had gone through her surgery and
treatment. Totally faithful and supportive.

Once again he wondered if he should get a dog.
Being responsible for another living creature would
go a long way to bolstering his character. Plus a nice,
big dog would be fun. He could take him hiking and
camping. Fay liked dogs, so having one in the office wouldn't be a problem. Something to consider,
he told himself.

"Your father and I are talking about going away
again," his mother said. "Our vacation last fall was
so nice for both of us. We're looking at taking one
of those river cruises in Germany."

"That would be good," he said automatically,
thinking that being trapped with his father on a boat
was his idea of hell. But his mom would have a different view of things. "I'm glad you're getting away
more."

"Me, too. Now that your father is slowing down
with his work, we can think about other things."

Right. Because every part of their life was defined
by Ceallach's work. That came first and the rest of
it could wait its turn.

Stuck, Aidan reminded himself. Here was a prime
example of why he never wanted to be in love. His
mother was always the one who bent, who surren-
dered to whatever Ceallach wanted. He remembered
being a kid and asking her why she didn't tell his dad
to stop destroying his work. She'd told him it wasn't
that easy—that Ceallach had his demons.

At eight or ten or twelve, Aidan hadn't cared about demons. He'd cared that he could hear his mother crying because another commission had been destroyed and there wasn't any money. That she didn't know how she was going to feed her children.

Whatever the problem, Ceallach was always right, always the important one. Theirs wasn't a partnership, at least not from his perspective. He'd often wondered why she stayed. No. The real question was why she'd married the man in the first place.

She poured them each a cup of coffee. "You should think about getting away."

He took the mug and grinned. "Mom, my life *is* a vacation."

"Not the business aspect of it."

"I don't mind that."

She studied him. "I guess you never did. You were always smart that way. It's interesting how you and Del are so different from your brothers."

"You mean not like Dad?"

"I mean different." Her voice chided ever so gently. "Speaking of your brothers, have you seen Nick?"

"Sure. A few days ago. Why?"

"I worry about him. But then I worry about all my boys."

He knew that in her way, she was telling the truth. She'd always been there for her sons, loving them, taking care of them. He'd known that she would listen, would do her best to understand, even if, in the end, she would side with his father.

Like every good mother, she'd always claimed to love her five boys equally. Still, if he was asked to say who was her favorite, he would have to admit it was Ronan. The irony of that truth was the fact that Ronan wasn't even hers. As he and Del had found out the previous fall, Ronan was their half brother—the result of Ceallach's affair. Yet when his ex-mistress had abandoned her child, Elaine had taken him in and passed him off as one of her own. Mathias's twin.

More secrets, he thought, wondering briefly what else he didn't know about his family. Of course there were things they didn't know about him. Like how badly he felt about what had happened on New Year's Eve. And how he was determined to be different. But no matter how he changed, he knew one thing for sure. He would never fall in love. The pleasure was nowhere near worth the pain.

CHAPTER FOUR

SHELBY WASN'T SURE what to expect when she showed up at Aidan's house on Saturday afternoon, but the small, well-kept bungalow was something of a surprise. There was a two-car garage, a wide porch and a huge snowman in the front yard. While most of the town celebrated Cabin Fever Days with snow people of all genders and sizes, she hadn't thought that Aidan would be one to participate.

His snowman was about five feet tall, with a sturdy shape and smiling face. A ski cap topped his head and two ski poles leaned against him, as if he was about to embark on an outdoor adventure. There was a whimsical quality about the snowman—maybe in the way he seemed ready to spring to life. Aidan might not have his father's talent to work with glass, but she would guess there were a few lingering artistic genes in him.

She walked up the porch stairs and knocked on the front door. In the few seconds it took him to answer, she acknowledged the nerves bouncing around in her stomach. Part of her wanted to bolt—there was no way this was going to work. But the sensible part of her, the part that had been to therapy and read a bunch of books and really wanted to get better, knew that showing up was the first step. That if her goal of healing from the damage done to her psyche was to be reached, she had to go through the process. Running away rarely accomplished anything.

Aidan opened the door. "Right on time. Come on in."

She did as he requested, careful to stomp the snow off her boots before walking into the house.

There was a forty-second bit of busyness to distract her from her nerves—unwinding her scarf, handing over her coat before stepping out of her boots. She noticed that Aidan was also in stocking feet, but his socks were thick and dark, while hers were covered with brightly colored cats. The contrast made her smile.

They were both in jeans and sweaters. His navy, hers dark pink. She hadn't known what to do about makeup and perfume and all that stuff. Because this wasn't a date. She was hanging out with a friend. But still, she'd wondered, and in the end had done what she did for work. Mascara and lip gloss.

They stared at each other. He was tall and broad. Masculine. The foyer was small and they were standing close together. Awkwardness pressed in on her. She didn't know what to do with her hands, let alone her body.

"Should we, um…" He cleared his throat. "Go sit down?"

"Sure."

She followed him into a good-sized living room. One wall was paneled, but not like in those scary midcentury grandma homes. This was rough-hewn, obviously old and well cared for. A big wood-burning stone fireplace stood opposite, with a large mantel stretching across the wall. A huge television hung above it. The furniture was black leather, the floors hardwood. A few paintings, mostly landscapes, were scattered on the walls. A patterned rug of reds and browns and greens anchored the room. The room was eclectic, but ultimately welcoming.

"I like it," she said. "It's very masculine, but not in a no-girls-allowed way."

Aidan shoved his hands into his jeans pockets. "I picked out most of it. Nick helped with the rug. He has an eye for color."

"The artist thing."

He nodded. "That would be it." He pointed at the sofa. "Have a seat."

She sat at one end of the sofa. He took the other. They looked at each other, then away. Silence filled the room and awkwardness returned. Which made sense. She and Aidan barely knew each other. Rather than become friends in the normal way—over time, through shared interests—they were forcing it upon themselves. Where on earth were they supposed to start?

"What about—"

"Did you want to—"

They both spoke at the same time, stopped, and silence returned. Shelby decided there was no point in ignoring the obvious.

"This is really uncomfortable," she said firmly. "But I think we can get past it."

"Okay."

The slow response was more neutral than agreement.

"We have a purpose," she continued. "I want to fall in love and get married."

Aidan's expression tightened with what could only be described as panic. Some of her tension eased.

"Not to you," she pointed out. "Don't freak."

"Then don't say stuff like that."

"Why not? Why can't I be honest?"

"Because it's not what any guy wants to hear. Not right off. It means you have a picture of what's going to happen in your life and you'll use any guy to get there. It makes us feel trapped."

His words almost made sense. "Like what we want is more important than the outcome? Caring more about the bridal gown than the groom?"

"Yeah, that. Men and women want different things. You want to be committed."

"And men want to cheat."

His brows rose. "Who cheated?"

She tucked one foot under her opposite leg as she considered her words. "Wow. I honestly don't know where that came from. Miles cheated, but we were barely dating, so I'm not sure it counts. I guess what I mean is I don't trust men."

"Shouldn't you be afraid a guy would hit you rather than he would cheat?"

Talk about cutting to be heart of the matter. She held up both hands. "Yes, and maybe we could ease into the honesty just a little."

"I thought women liked a man to say what he was thinking."

She smiled. "That's a myth."

"For what it's worth, I never cheated."

"That's because you were never in a relationship long enough to get bored."

One brow rose. "So you get to be honest, but I have to be careful?"

Oops. She drew in a breath. "You're right. Sorry. I take back my request that you edit what you say. I'm tough. I can take it."

She thought he might make a crack about her being weak or broken, but he surprised her by nodding.

"You *are* tough. You're taking control of your situation and that's admirable. A lot of people are more comfortable being victims."

"Oh. Thank you."

"You're welcome."

They smiled at each other.

"So what are we going to do?" he asked.

"What do you mean?"

"With our afternoon. We have to do something."

"Why? We're talking. That's nice. We could go to Jo's Bar and get margaritas."

Aidan shifted back in his seat. If she didn't know better she would swear he was starting to sweat. "No. Guys don't go get margaritas and talk."

"You go get beers. It's the same thing."

"We get a beer and watch sports. It's not the same thing. Women want to talk everything to death. Guys don't do that. If you ignore most problems, they usually go away."

"Uh-huh. And how's that strategy working for you?"

"I'm here, aren't I?"

"Yes. Trying not to talk about what's wrong."

"We could do something," he offered. "Like watch a game. Or go skiing."

Shelby considered his options. "You realize none of those require conversation."

Aidan relaxed a little. "Isn't that great?"

"But we have to get to know each other. We have to talk about our feelings."

He winced. "Why?"

"We just do. That's what..." She felt her eyes widen. "We're totally different. The man-woman thing is real. I want to go have a conversation about my life and your life and what we can do to help each other, and you want to physically do something with only the occasional grunt for conversation. As a man, you don't want to talk about anyone's feelings, let alone your own."

"You say that like it's a bad thing. It's not. Not talking about your feelings can be very relaxing."

Which might be true but wasn't helpful. "We really didn't think this through."

Aidan leaned toward her. "No. Do not give up on me now. We have a deal. We've gotten this far, we can figure out the rest of it. You want to do girl stuff and I want to do guy stuff."

He gave her a slow, sexy smile. One that had her breath catching. But before she could do something ridiculous, like bat her eyes at him or flip her hair, she reminded herself that it wasn't a slow, sexy smile.

They weren't involved that way. It was just a smile. She would ignore any subtext her hormones might read in to the situation.

"I know," he told her. "We'll alternate. Girl date, guy date. Not date, but you know what I mean."

"That could work. We could each plan our gender event." She grimaced. Avoiding the word *date* was harder that she would have thought.

"Gender event?"

"Do you have a better phrase?"

"I'm liking gender event."

She laughed. "Okay, so you're responsible for boy things and I'm in charge of girl things. And yes on the alternating. So who goes first?"

He stretched out his arms, one hand flat, the other curled into a fist. "Rock, paper, scissors?"

She shifted until she was facing him, then together they hit their fists against their flat hands and counted to three.

"Rock," Aidan said triumphantly, then groaned when he saw her paper. "You win."

"I know," she told him. "Poor you. I grew up with a brother. Why do guys always start out with rock? It's very predictable."

"We can't help ourselves." He stood. "We're going to get margaritas and talk about our feelings, aren't we?"

"You know it."

JO'S BAR HAD been around for eight or nine years. Aidan had been there a few times, but it wasn't the kind of place he and his friends liked to hang out. For one thing, the bar catered to women.

On the surface, that might seem like a good thing—lots of beautiful women hanging out. What's not to like? Only it wasn't that kind of place. For one thing, the lighting was way too bright. There were no dark corners or ratty old booths. Instead the booths were new and scaled down in size. There were tables everywhere. The walls were painted some weird light purple color—Nick would know the name of the shade, but he didn't.

While there were plenty of TVs around, they were always turned to shopping or female-based reality shows. The menu had lots of salads on it and most of the drinks had a diet version. The only part of the bar that felt close to normal was the small room in back with a pool table, but even with that concession, Jo's generally wasn't a place men went to on purpose.

Now The Man Cave was different. More male-friendly. Not that Shelby led him there.

"Isn't this nice?" she asked as they walked inside.

"Uh-huh."

"Oh, look." She pointed to the televisions. "They're having an *America's Next Top Model* marathon. I love that show."

He'd never seen it. When he glanced at the screen, he saw women posing for pictures, which should have been appealing. Except they all looked really young and he wasn't interested in some skinny teenager, thank you very much. Not that he was interested in women at all, he reminded himself. There would be none of that for him—for at least six months.

There weren't a lot of customers on a nonfestival Saturday afternoon. A couple of groups of women seemed to be finishing up lunch. There was a young couple at a booth in the corner. He and Shelby took seats at a small booth in the back. Aidan had a clear view of a TV, which he considered appropriate punishment for all his past misdeeds.

Jo walked over and looked between them. "This is new," she said. Her gaze settled on him. "I thought you only did tourists."

"Hi, Jo." Because there didn't seem to be a better response.

"We're not dating," Shelby told the other woman. "We're friends. It's not romantic."

"If you say so. What can I get you?"

"A pitcher of margaritas and some nachos," Shelby said with a smile. "We're going to talk."

Jo's brows rose. "All righty then. I have *carnitas* nachos today. You want that?"

"Meat is good," Aidan said.

"Then meat." Shelby smiled at Jo. "Thank you."

Jo left. Aidan couldn't begin to imagine what she was thinking, or what rumors would be spreading through town over the next few days. Whatever they were, he would deal.

Shelby looked at him. "How was your week?"

"Fine."

One corner of her mouth twitched. "Could you expand on that? Maybe give me a few details?"

Because they were "talking." He drew in a breath. "Work is busy. We have a good snowpack this year, which helps with business. Lots of skiing. I'm offering a snowshoeing class for beginners. That meant buying more equipment, but I think it will pay off in the long run."

"With people coming back next year?"

"And telling their friends they had a good time."

"Is it difficult to learn how to do it?" she asked.

"No. It's like walking in sand with really big shoes. Level terrain isn't bad. Uphill is tiring and downhill is the biggest challenge."

"Gravity," she said with a smile. "It always gets you in the end. Kipling used to say that."

As an Olympic champion, he would know. "He had a bad accident a couple of years back, didn't he?"

She nodded. "In New Zealand. It ended his skiing career. For a while we were scared he wouldn't walk again, but he was determined. And lucky." Her expression turned wistful. "Now he's married to Destiny, with a baby on the way. He has it all."

Which was what Shelby wanted. A home. Family. Stability. Aidan knew her dreams would be considered normal. He should probably want them for himself. But there was no way. He just wanted to not be a jackass.

"You're going to be an aunt," he said to shift the subject to something slightly happier for her.

"My second time around. I consider Starr to be an honorary niece. She's my sister-in-law's half sister, and Destiny and Kipling have custody of her. She's almost sixteen."

He knew Destiny but wasn't sure he'd met Starr.

Jo brought a pitcher of margaritas and two glasses. "Nachos are on the way. You both walking?"

"We are," Shelby told her. "We're good."

"Just checking."

"She always does that," Shelby said in a low voice, when the other woman had left. "Makes sure we're not going to drink and drive. It's nice. People in town look out for each other."

"Or she doesn't want to get sued."

"Don't be cynical."

"It comes with the territory."

"It doesn't have to." She poured them each a margarita.

Aidan took his and braced himself for the too-sweet drink. When it was his turn, they were drinking beer. Or scotch.

"To being friends," Shelby said and touched her glass to his. "Thank you for helping me."

Her eyes were blue—sort of a medium color. Nice, he thought absently. "You're the one who's helping me," he told her.

They touched glasses again. He took a sip.

"Not bad," he said. The liquid was more tart than sweet, with a hint of salt. Not his favorite but he could get used to it.

"Wait until you try the nachos. They're amazing. So what else happened this week?"

"I'm thinking of getting a dog."

"Interesting. A big one, right?"

He nodded. "One I could take camping and fishing."

"You could teach it to snowboard. It could wear one of those cute coats and eye goggles."

"That is not happening. This is a manly dog."

"It's a dog that doesn't yet exist, at least not in your life. Maybe you'll fall for a poodle."

"Never."

"A Yorkie?" She giggled. "You could coordinate your shirt with her hair ribbon. You'd be so sweet together."

"Why are you emasculating me?"

"It's fun." She rested her elbows on the table. "But I can be serious, too. Why a dog? Are you lonely?"

He was about to say no, of course not, when it occurred to him he might be. Work kept him busy and he enjoyed his coworkers, but his relationships with them were mostly casual. Until a couple of years ago, he'd had three of his four brothers in town, but Mathias and Ronan had moved to Happily Inc. and Nick was always off doing something.

He had friends. Guy friends. But everyone was busy with their lives. As for women, as the whole world knew, he'd done his damnedest to make sure those encounters never meant anything.

"I think a dog would be good for me," he answered, aware he was avoiding the question. "I'd have to be responsible for it. Take care of it. I'd bring it to the office. Fay would like that."

"Fay is…"

"My office manager. She handles the scheduling and gets the tours ready." He hesitated. "Her daughter is Kalinda. She was—"

Shelby nodded. "I know Kalinda. She loves peanut butter cookies." She sighed. "I'm glad she's healing, but what a difficult road for her and her family."

"Fay does her best to stay strong," he said, grateful he didn't have to explain about Kalinda's burns. The teen would face more surgeries over the years. He knew for Fay there were good days and bad days, but whatever happened, she loved her daughter unconditionally.

Jo came by with a huge platter of nachos. There were plates for each of them, along with bowls of extra salsa and guacamole. Aidan inhaled the scent of the marinated pork and realized he hadn't eaten much that day. His stomach growled.

"Me, too," Shelby said with a laugh as she grabbed a chip. "I was playing around with custom cookie ideas and the day got away from me. Then I didn't have time to eat or I would be late."

"Next time, eat," he told her. "I don't expect you to be exactly on time."

"It was our first gender encounter. I wanted to make a good impression."

He liked her teasing. The fact that she could be so charming and open meant that her father hadn't broken her as much as she feared. Intense determination filled him. He was going to help Shelby get whatever she wanted, he promised himself. Not only because it would help him, but because it was the right thing to do.

They ate in silence for a few minutes, then Shelby said, "You're one of five brothers, right?"

"I'm the second oldest. There's Del, me, Nick, Mathias and Ronan. The last two are…" Twins. He always said twins. Only they weren't. They never had been. It had all been a giant lie.

"Aidan?" Shelby's voice was soft. "Are you okay?"

"You're right," he said bitterly. "Some men do cheat. My father did. I don't know how many women there were. He claims just one, but I have my doubts. There had to have been others."

"I'm sorry," she said softly. "That's so hard. Does your mom know?"

"She covered for him. For years."

Shelby frowned. "I don't understand. Why would it be an ongoing issue?"

He picked up his margarita and took a drink. "Because my youngest brother, Ronan, is his mistress's son."

Shelby's blue eyes widened and her mouth formed a perfect O. She looked shocked and strangely appealing. Sexy, maybe. He pushed that thought away and focused on what had happened with his family.

"Del, Nick and I were practically babies when my mom had Mathias. We didn't know what was going on. All I remember is that I had twin brothers. Four years ago, my dad had a heart attack. It turned out to be pretty minor, but at the time, we didn't know how bad it was. I guess he was afraid he was going to die or something and he told the twins the truth. That Ronan was the result of an affair. When Ronan's mom was going to give him up for adoption, Dad told my mom, who agreed to raise him as her own."

Shelby's eyes stayed wide. "Seriously? I can't imagine."

"It happened. Some days I think she's a saint and other days I'm convinced she's a fool. That Dad played her. He gets everything and she's stuck with some other woman's kid."

"That's harsh, but I understand your point." She reached for a chip. "What I don't get is how she did it. I mean every time she looked at him, wouldn't she see that other woman? Imagine her with her husband? It must have been incredibly painful."

Aidan hadn't planned to talk about this. He never did. He and his brothers had spoken about the situation a couple of times, but with as few words as possible. And without talking about the lingering effects on the family. But he found himself comfortable discussing it all with Shelby.

"You'd think." He took another drink of his margarita. "But it wasn't like that at all. Maybe at first—I wouldn't remember that. But by the time I was eight or nine, I knew that Ronan was her favorite."

"That's not possible," Shelby breathed.

"It wasn't anything awful. She didn't tell us that or make it obvious, but we could tell. We used to tease Ronan about being a mama's boy. She was always fussing over him. They were the closest. Even in high school, they talked all the time."

He remembered ragging on his brother. How Ronan had said it was because he was the superior brother. All good fun. Elaine had been there for all of them, so knowing Ronan was the one she loved just a little bit more hadn't meant much. He'd figured it was something every group of siblings went through.

"After Dad told the twins, they left. Packed up everything and relocated to Happily Inc."

Shelby smiled. "I've heard of that place. It's outside of Palm Desert, right? A wedding-destination town. It's supposed to be lovely, in the mountains,

with an underground spring and—" She stopped
and sighed. "Sorry, I was momentarily distracted.
I blame the margarita."

Her humor faded. "Wait a minute. I'm just now
processing. Ceallach told the twins about Ronan and
who he was and that was it? He didn't tell your mom
that he'd told the twins the truth and he didn't tell
you or your other brothers, either?"

"Not until last summer. We figured they'd gone to
Happily Inc. to get away from Dad and pursue their
art. No one thought anything of it."

"But what about them? How are they? They were
twins for what, twenty-five years, and they suddenly
find out they're not? Poor Ronan, to find out he's
not who he thought. That the woman he thought of
as his mother isn't. Has he met his biological mom?
Are he and Elaine okay? Do you guys talk about
this stuff now?"

He held up his hands in the shape of a T. "I'm willing to do the girl thing today, but you have to take it
slow, okay? Not so many questions."

To be honest, he didn't have any answers. Mostly
because he'd never really thought about the situation from Ronan's perspective. When he and Del
and Nick had found out last fall, they'd had to deal
with who Ronan was, or wasn't. Not that having a
different mother made any difference in the siblings'
relationship. They were brothers and they would always be brothers.

"Sorry. I'm just shocked. Poor Ronan. That had
to have been tough for him. And Mathias. I mean

they were a team. Special by virtue of being twins. Now that's gone forever."

"There's a cheerful thought."

"But it's true."

Not something he wanted dwell on, he thought to himself. Families were complicated—his more so than most. At least that was his impression. Maybe not. Maybe everyone else was dealing with the same level of crap.

"Do you and Nick ever talk about it?" she asked.

"No."

"Because you're men and men don't have those kinds of conversations?"

He nodded and picked up the pitcher to fill their glasses.

"Maybe it would help."

He finished pouring and put down the pitcher. "There's not a problem."

"Of course there is. Are you seriously going to tell me that your two brothers taking off like that is okay?"

She had a point, not that he wanted to admit it. "Mathias and Ronan have each other. I worry more about Nick."

The words were unexpected and made him want to swear. Where had they come from?

"Why?" she asked gently.

Hell. "Because he's not as happy as he seems. He's working as a manager at The Man Cave, but in his spare time he's hiding out in his secret art studio. I know he's doing all kinds of things up there, but he won't talk about it. He doesn't want Dad to know. God knows what the great Ceallach would say. How he would be pissed and bring Nick down. Yes, he wants his son to be an artist, but not one better than him."

Shelby put her hand on his arm. "You should talk to Nick."

"No."

"It would help."

"No."

"You're so stubborn. Guys need love, too."

"Is this really what women do when they get together?"

"Uh-huh. We talk about our problems and our feelings. It's cathartic."

"It's a nightmare."

She smiled. "You'll get used to it."

"If I do, I'll start to grow breasts."

The smile broadened. "That's very sexist of you."

"I'm okay with that."

She laughed and took another chip. Conversation shifted to the upcoming Cabin Fever Days and the ice sculptures taking shape in the park.

Later, when they'd left the bar and gone their separate ways, Aidan told himself that while he could go his whole life without having another afternoon like that, he had to admit talking about stuff was kind of good. He felt...relieved somehow. Not that he would share that piece of information with anyone. Ever.

CHAPTER FIVE

NEARLY A WEEK LATER, Shelby found herself back at Jo's Bar, but under very different circumstances. Instead of sitting across from a surprisingly chatty Aidan, she was with her girlfriends for lunch. She sat next to her very pregnant sister-in-law, who kept shifting in her chair.

"I can't get comfortable," Destiny admitted when Shelby asked if she was all right. "Some days are harder than others. I can't believe I still have a few weeks to go. I'm so huge."

From across the table, Isabel eyed her warily. "Please stop saying that. I'm going to be that big times three. All I want to hear is how wonderful you feel and how great every second is."

Destiny sipped her hot lemon water. "I've never felt better. It's nothing. You'll be fine."

Isabel sighed. "Thank you for lying."

"Anytime."

Taryn, perfectly dressed as always in a leather and wool suit and ridiculously high-heeled boots, pointed to the plate of cookies Shelby had brought to the lunch.

"Are those as good as they look?" she asked warily.

"I hope so." Shelby's voice was cheerful. "I can't believe how great the response had been. People are going crazy for the ice-sculpture cookies."

"You shouldn't be surprised," Madeline told her. "It was a great idea. We get so many tourists coming in for the festival. Who doesn't love looking at the amazing carvings, all done in ice? To be able to buy cookies that look like them is fun."

Shelby appreciated the compliment. Being a part of the bakery was still new to her. She wanted to get it right all the time. Not possible, she knew, but it was nice that her ideas had been successful so far.

"I've heard from a few more of the artists," she said. "They want cookies for next year. And a couple of people have placed orders to have cookies shipped to them at home."

Felicia, the woman in charge of the festivals, looked at her. "You could start a mail-order business at the bakery. You already have a website. It wouldn't take much to expand it."

"I've been playing around with the idea," Shelby admitted. "I need to get all my thoughts together and have more information before I talk to Amber about it."

There would be start-up costs, of course, but not that many. Still, she wasn't sure what Amber would say. Her business partner hadn't been convinced about the food-cart idea, although she'd agreed to try it. Now the Ambrosia Bakery cart was selling briskly at every festival.

"The biggest challenge is decorating them,"

Shelby said. "While the work isn't that detailed, it's time-consuming. I don't want to tie up our skilled employees with something like this, but to sell the cookies beyond Fool's Gold, we'll need a process. Plus, the sales aren't going to be regular. So hiring someone means having to fill their workday with other things when we don't have custom orders."

"You need part-time help," Madeline said. "Someone who would be willing to come in when you had orders."

"You should hire teenagers," Taryn offered. "Young ones. A group of fourteen-year-old girls would love to come in and decorate cookies for a few hours. They could do it in groups. It would give them a nice break from babysitting and offer them a chance to earn some money."

Jo arrived with their lunches. After everyone had their food, Shelby picked up her fork. "I never thought of teenagers," she admitted. "But fourteen. Isn't that too young to be working?" Training wouldn't be an issue. It was basically coloring, but on cookies.

"There are strict labor laws in the state of California," Felicia announced. "They could only work for a couple of hours a day. There are also caps on the number of hours in a week. They'd each need a work permit. If you were in the entertainment industry, it would be easier, but it's still doable."

"How can you possibly know that?" Madeline asked.

Felicia shrugged. "I can't help it. I read."

"I don't remember an article on child labor laws in my latest issue of *Vogue*, but maybe I missed it." Taryn smiled at Felicia. "You are always entertaining and I say that with love."

"Then I accept it the same way."

Shelby laughed. "Okay, now I have a starting place for my research. Thank you."

"I can be a temporary worker," Isabel offered. "When I'm on bed rest. It's not like I'll have a lot to fill my day."

"Poor you," Taryn said, hugging her friend. "I'll visit. That will be entertaining."

"Yes, but not nearly enough. I'll be going over the books for the store and ordering inventory, but I think I'll still have some extra time. Decorating cookies would be fun."

"If you didn't eat them all," Madeline teased.

Isabel wrinkled her nose. "These days I'm more into salty foods than sweet ones."

Shelby thought about Isabel's cravings for pretzel bread and figured her cookies would be safe.

"Thanks for the offer," she said. "I may take you up on it."

"Assuming you have time for your new business venture," Felicia said. "What with your love life heating up."

Everyone turned to Shelby, who was busy gaping at Felicia.

"What are you talking about?" she asked, just as Taryn murmured, "That would be my question."

"You're seeing someone?" Madeline asked, sounding hurt.

Shelby shook her head. "I'm not. There's no one."

"I heard you were out with Aidan over the weekend," Felicia said. "I'm sure my source is very reliable."

"Oh, *that*." Shelby shook her head. "No romance. Our relationship is strictly as friends." While Madeline knew the details of her past and Shelby was fairly sure there were plenty of rumors, she wasn't one to discuss her problems in a crowd.

"I don't have any guy friends," she said by way of edging around the truth. "Aidan doesn't have any female friends. We thought hanging out would be good for us."

Madeline relaxed, but everyone else stared at her as if she had grown a second and possibly third head.

"Why?" Isabel asked. "You have us."

"It's different. A male perspective is nice."

"She's right," Taryn added. "I love my boys very much. While their advice is always different than yours, sometimes it's helpful to hear it. I think all women should have male friends."

Taryn's "boys" were three retired football players who were also her business partners at Score PR, but Shelby still appreciated the support.

"See? It's not weird."

"It's kind of weird," Destiny said, "but good for you. Just don't go falling for him romantically. From all I've heard, he's not the long-term-relationship type. I'd hate to see you get hurt."

"It's not romantic," Shelby assured her, knowing in that statement she was being completely honest.

Aidan was a great guy. She'd enjoyed their afternoon together. And sure, he was good-looking and funny, but they were friends. Nothing more. She had a plan and nothing was going to stand in the way of success.

ONE OF THE advantages of being part owner of a business was having access to it during off-hours. So while The Man Cave was technically closed, Aidan had a key, which explained why he and Shelby were playing pool at ten o'clock on a Saturday morning.

He didn't know how it was possible, but Shelby had admitted she'd never played pool before, so he'd explained about striped versus solid balls and the basic rules of the game. Now Shelby was practicing how to use her cue stick to hit the cue ball. It wasn't going well.

"I think it's moving," she said as her stick sailed past the cue ball and she stumbled forward.

Aidan held in a grin. "It's not moving. You have to line up your stick with the ball."

"But what about where I want it to go?"

"Let's get you to where you can hit the cue ball consistently, then we'll worry about direction."

She glanced at him over her shoulder. "You sound very patient, but I know you're laughing at me on the inside."

"Just a little."

She wore jeans and a blue sweatshirt. Her hair was pulled back in a ponytail and she wasn't wearing much makeup. But when she smiled at him, her whole face lit up.

"Okay," she said with a sigh. "Tell me again what I'm doing wrong."

Aidan moved toward her. "Better yet, I'll show you."

He positioned the cue ball about a foot from the center pocket, then gently pushed her forward. "Stand with your feet a little bit more than shoulder-width apart. Place your left hand on the table. Bend your fingers like I taught you and rest the cue on your fingers."

She did as he instructed, then moved her right arm back and forth. The cue stick moved with her.

"Now move with a little more force."

He watched as she drew back the stick, then thrust it forward. It barely grazed the cue ball. The white ball jumped a little to the left and came to a stop. Shelby groaned, but Aidan saw what she'd been doing wrong.

"You're moving smoothly in practice, but as soon as you try to put some force behind the movement, you pull up the end."

"And that's supposed to make sense to me?"

He chuckled. "I'll show you."

He moved behind her so he could hold the cue stick with her. He rested his left hand by her left hand and put his right on top of hers.

"This is your practice movement." He slowly moved the stick back and forth, keeping it even. "This is what you do when you're trying to shoot."

He raised the back of the stick as he brought it forward. "You need to be consistent. There's no pressure."

"That's so geeky," she muttered. "Okay, let's try this again."

She completed the smooth practice shot, then went for the ball. This time she managed to keep the stick level and the white cue ball rolled across the table.

"I did it!"

Aidan straightened. "You did. Now try it again."

Shelby hurried around to the other side of the table. She got in position. "Is this right?"

He nodded because speaking suddenly seemed difficult. Something was wrong with him. He couldn't put his finger on it, but there was a tension inside him. Almost a tightness.

He shook off the feeling and circled around the table to watch Shelby get into position. He checked out her arm extension and how she held the cue, then found his gaze dropping to her butt as she bent over the table.

Her jeans pulled tight over perfect curves. Funny how he'd never noticed her ass before now and—

Shit! He took a couple of steps back and nearly collided with another table. He was attracted to her. How had that happened? They weren't dating. They weren't involved. They were friends. Non-sexual, genderless friends.

He told himself not to panic. That this was a natural reaction to close proximity to an attractive woman. It didn't have to mean anything. He wasn't going to follow up on what was little more than a biological stimulus response. Like sneezing around pollen. That was all this was. He had allergies and

Shelby was pollen. Plus he hadn't had sex in a while. Circumstances, he told himself. Not intent.

"Like this, Aidan?" she asked as she hit the cue ball.

It rolled forcefully across the table.

"You got it. Now let's try aiming at another ball."

He would focus on the game and nothing else, he told himself. He was stronger than biology. Or at least more determined. He had to be. He would not screw up his one chance to improve himself simply because he was a horny guy. He would not be defeated by his dick. Not this time.

"ARE YOU SCARED?" Shelby asked, doing her best to keep the tremor from her voice.

"No."

She and Aidan stood in front of city hall. They'd been summoned by the mayor, something that had never happened to her before. She told herself that Mayor Marsha was a very nice, elderly woman and that there was nothing to be afraid of. But she couldn't shake the sense of being called to face some kind of higher power.

"You sure?" she asked.

Beside her, Aidan shook his head. "It's going to be fine."

"You really believe that?"

"No. Everyone knows it's never good to be called in to see the mayor, but saying it's going to be fine sounds better than saying we should run for it."

She laughed.

The morning was crisp and sunny. There hadn't

been snow in a few days so all the streets were clear. The town looked like a picture postcard, or something from a made-for-TV movie. Nothing bad could possibly happen here.

"We'll be fine," she whispered.

"You don't sound convinced."

"I'm going to do my best to fake it."

Aidan put his arm around her and pulled her close. "I'll be right there with you. Faking it."

They smiled at each other and started up the stairs.

Things were going well between them, she thought happily. She liked Aidan. He was easy to spend time with. She'd enjoyed learning to play pool and he'd survived his first "girl's day." Next up was a baby shower. That was going to be interesting for both of them.

They entered the building and made their way to the mayor's office on the second floor.

"I'm a good citizen," Shelby murmured more to herself than Aidan. "I follow the rules. I pay my taxes."

"Let it go," he told her. "You'll never guess what she wants and trying will only make it worse. Every scenario will be more frightening than the one before."

"Kept you up last night?"

"A little."

They reached the mayor's office. Bailey Scott, Mayor Marsha's assistant, smiled at them.

"Hey, Shelby. You're right on time." Bailey, a

beautiful, curvy redhead, stood and walked around her desk toward Aidan. "I'm not sure we've met."

"Aidan Mitchell."

"Bailey Scott."

They shook hands.

"You're married to Kenny Scott," Aidan said. "He was such a great player. It was a shame when he retired."

Bailey grinned. "I'll let him know you were a fan. Most days he's happy to be out of it, but every now and then he thinks about those glory days. He'll be pleased to know he's not the only one." Bailey looked at them both. "Mayor Marsha is waiting to see you. Let's go on in."

Shelby had thought there would be more time to gather her thoughts, but before she could catch her breath, they were going through the large double doors that led to the mayor's office.

Mayor Marsha Tilson was California's longest serving mayor. From what Shelby knew, the mayor was in her sixties, had been born and raised in Fool's Gold and ran the town like a well-oiled machine. She was both loved and respected. To date, Shelby hadn't met anyone who didn't like her.

The mayor rose and greeted them. She wore a dark red suit with a white blouse and pearls. Her hair was twisted up in one of those old lady buns from the 1960s and while she wore pumps, they were of the sensible variety.

"Thank you both for coming," Mayor Marsha said. "I know you're busy entrepreneurs, so I'll keep this meeting as short as possible."

She motioned to the seating area opposite her desk. There was a pair of sofas and three chairs arranged around a large coffee table.

Shelby instinctively sat next to Aidan. As if he would offer protection. A silly thought, considering the mayor was unlikely to do anything scary. But still…

Mayor Marsha studied them for a few seconds. "I think what you two are doing is wonderful," she began. "Your six-month plan to be friends."

Shelby stared at her. "How did you know about that?"

The mayor smiled. "I hear things. Change is always difficult, but if you don't try, you'll never get where you want to go. I think you're both going to be very successful."

"Um, thank you," Shelby murmured, still stunned someone had talked about her and Aidan to the mayor. Why? What they were doing was important to them, but hardly interesting to anyone else. Weren't people busy with their own lives?

"I can't help but think other people would benefit from your example," the mayor continued. "While falling in love is wonderful, there is more to life than that. Other relationships that are important. Friendship, for example. Not enough men and women are friends."

Shelby glanced at Aidan, who looked as confused as she felt. Where was this conversation going?

As if reading her mind, the mayor said, "I want to try an experiment and I'd like you two to help me with it. We should have a get-together for the single people in town. A place where men and women can meet without any pressure to be romantically involved. An opportunity for them to get to know each other and be friends. Just friends."

Shelby opened her mouth, then closed it.

"You want us to plan a party?" Aidan asked, sounding as confused as she felt.

"Nothing so formal," the mayor assured him. "I was thinking of one or two events. The more casual, the better. That way everyone can relax and get to know each other." She smiled. "Bailey has a list of names and email addresses. Just get in contact with the people on the list and tell them where the first event is. Word will spread."

"I thought everyone in town was pretty friendly," Shelby said. "They have been to me."

"They are. It's part of the Fool's Gold charm. But our single people need a little help and you're the ones to offer it."

Saying no wasn't an option. Shelby knew that. Not only was she new to the town and eager to make a good impression on the mayor, Shelby owed her. When Kipling had been confined to a hospital bed in New Zealand, his body so shattered everyone feared he would never walk again, Shelby had been equally held hostage by her mother's imminent death and her father's brutal fists. Mayor Marsha had been the one go to Kipling and offer him the job in Fool's Gold. She'd been the one to send Angel and Ford to save Shelby.

"Of course I'll do it," Shelby told her. "I'll send out the emails this week."

"I'll help," Aidan added.

Shelby glanced at him in surprise. He winked at her.

"Excellent." Mayor Marsha came to her feet. "Then I'll leave you to it."

The meeting obviously over, Shelby and Aidan left. When they were back on the sidewalk, she turned to him. "Why did you agree? You could have left it to me."

"You see the movie *Titanic*?"

"Of course. What does that have to do with anything?"

Aidan grinned. "We're in this together, Shelby. You jump, I jump. She said casual. We can come up with a couple of things to do with the singles in town and then it's over. How hard could it be?"

"You say that now, but just wait. This idea has regret written all over it."

He chuckled. "Probably, but we're going to see it through anyway."

Because that was who Aidan was, she thought as they headed back to their respective offices. The kind of man who did the right thing. He was nice, she admitted as she waved goodbye at the corner and walked toward the bakery. Steady. Someone she could depend on. Good qualities in a friend.

He was also easy on the eyes and every now and then she found herself wondering what it would be like to kiss him. Not that she would. They were friends. Nothing more. Any tingles or urges were simply left over from years of dating. They didn't mean anything. They couldn't. Being friends with Aidan was important. Her future happiness was at stake. No kiss was worth that.

CHAPTER SIX

"WHAT HAPPENS AT a baby shower?" Aidan asked, not sure why he bothered. There was a part of him that didn't want to hear the answer.

"It's a party. A celebration with gifts and food and games."

"But no actual babies?"

Shelby laughed. "No babies. Well, sometimes there are. There are family showers and couples showers. This isn't either of those."

"So Destiny will be there, and her friends."

"Yes."

"Kipling?"

"No."

Their alternating gender events continued. This time it was a girl thing, which meant he was going to his first ever baby shower. The concept was a little daunting.

"Will I be the only guy there?"

They were outside Jack McGarry's house. The two-story home sat on the golf course, where there were wide lawns, plenty of space between the houses and three-car garages. Of course, Jack was a former Super Bowl–winning quarterback, so he could pretty much afford anything he wanted. Aidan thought it was pretty funny that three former Super Bowl–winning football stars had settled in their sleepy town. Not that he was complaining. Every now and then the guys hung out in The Man Cave during a game. Getting their insight into the action made the experience pretty awesome.

"You are going to be the only guy," Shelby admitted. "And I kind of had to get permission to bring you, so, um, you know…"

He laughed. "Act right?"

"You always act completely fine. Just remember, this is a girl thing."

She was cute when she was worried. He leaned in. "Do you think that by the time all this is over, I'll start to grow breasts?"

"You worry about growing breasts a lot and I don't know why." She laughed and the concern faded from her eyes. "I promise, that's not going to happen. But I think you'll be more in touch with your feminine side."

He would rather be more in touch with an actual woman, but that wasn't going to happen for a while. He told himself he would get used to the low-grade desire that seemed to fill him whenever he was around Shelby. He found himself noticing things like the shape of her jaw and the way her laugh seemed to kick him in the gut.

Five more months, he told himself, plus a handful of days. Then he would be healed. And getting some.

"So, gifts," he said, then swore. "I didn't bring a gift."

"Don't worry. I put your name on mine. You can thank me later."

"And pay you back."

She laughed. "I won't say no to that. I went a little wild with the theme."

"There's a theme?"

"Butterflies."

"Your baby shower theme is bugs?"

"Butterflies aren't bugs." Shelby wrinkled her nose. "Fine. Technically, but they're pretty and it's what Destiny wanted. We'll play some games, eat, she'll open her presents and it will all be done before you know it."

"If only that were true."

She slugged him in the arm. "Be nice."

"I'm always nice."

She looked at him. Their eyes met in one of those I-can't-look-away moments that only seem to happen in movies rather than real life. Only Aidan found he really *couldn't* look away. Nor did he want to.

"You are," she said at last. "Nice, I mean."

"So are you."

A car pulled into the already crowded driveway. The sound of the engine broke the spell and they turned toward the house.

"Butterflies," he said. "Weird."

"Get over it."

SHELBY HADN'T BEEN kidding, Aidan thought a half hour later. He wasn't just the only man at the party, but the butterfly theme was everywhere. From the pink paper plates, to the balloons, to the centerpieces, to the butterfly-shaped cake he would guess Shelby had made herself.

"Butterflies remind me of my Grandma Nell," Destiny had told him. "They're so happy and beautiful."

And bugs, but he hadn't said that. Instead he'd congratulated her on the upcoming birth of her daughter and had thanked her for inviting him to the party.

"What you and Shelby are doing is strange, but also kind of special," she'd said. "Thank you for helping her."

He'd wanted to point out that he was being helped just as much, then decided to accept the compliment. There hadn't been very many from the women in life. He should treasure the ones he got now.

Aside from the butterfly overload, the rest of the party wasn't too bad. The food was good. Plenty of sugar, he thought, taking in the pink, white and yellow cake, the jelly beans filling small baby bottles, the little cookies and sandwiches. For all that women claimed to eat salad, he didn't see a green anywhere.

Taryn, the only female partner at Score, the local PR firm owned by her and two former football players, because the third had gone on to coach football at Cal State Fool's Gold, came up to him. She held out a glass of champagne. Pink champagne.

"Don't worry," she told him with a laugh. "It comes by the color naturally. Something about leaving the skin on the grapes." She frowned. "Or maybe it's the type of grapes. All I know is that it's delicious."

So far he'd avoided the fizzy pink drink, but there seemed no way to do that now. "Thank you." He took a sip and found it wasn't that bad.

"What are they drinking?" he asked, nodding at Destiny and Isabel, both pregnant.

"Some ginger-ale-and-cranberry-juice concoction. Jo came up with it years ago. It's a way for those going through pregnancy to not feel left out of celebrations." She tilted her head. "I understand you recently hung out at Jo's."

"With Shelby. Yes."

"How was that?"

"Like the champagne. Better than I thought it would be."

"The experiment is interesting. Do you think it's going to help?"

"I hope so."

Taryn's eyes were nearly violet in color. Her hair was long and dark. She was a few years older than Shelby and had an air of wisdom about her. As if she'd seen and done a lot in her life.

"Should I worry about either of you?" she asked.

The question was unexpected. He wouldn't be surprised by her worrying about Shelby, but him? "Thanks, but I can take care of myself."

"I work with two big, tough guys. Three before Jack went off to be a coach. All of them would tell you that they can take care of themselves. You'd be amazed how often they're wrong." She sipped her champagne. "You could be, too."

"It's worth the risk."

"Then good luck."

She walked away. Aidan waited a few seconds, then went looking for Shelby. In this estrogen overload, she was his safe haven.

As he crossed the living room he heard Larissa say the word *baby*. He paused long enough to pluck what turned out to be the last clothespin from her sweater.

The fit blonde laughed at him. "You're good at this."

"You're bad at not saying the B word."

When they'd first arrived, Larissa had given each guest five clothespins and explained the rules of the game. No one was allowed to say the word *baby*. If someone was overheard using the word, that person got to take one of their clothespins. Whoever had the most clothespins at the end won. So far Aidan was cleaning up.

Shelby stood by several women. When she saw him, she stepped away from the group.

"How are you holding up?" she asked.

"Good. I like the champagne."

"We have to do our pages in the alphabet book."

"The what?"

She grabbed him by the arm and led him through the dining room to the kitchen. At the large kitchen table were squares of fabric and dozens of pens.

He sat next to Shelby and looked at several of the completed squares. They showed a different letter of the alphabet along with a drawing of an object that started with that letter. An apple for *A*, a flower for *F*.

"Here's the master list," Shelby said, pulling it

out from the stack of fabric squares. "What letters do you want?"

He took *O* and *U*, drawing an oar for the first one and an umbrella for the second. Shelby chose *G* and *Y*.

"What are you going to do for *Y*?" he asked.

"A yak. I do pretty decent animals. I took a class on how make desserts for kids' parties and part of it was learning how make animals with frosting. Pens are much easier."

Which put his oar and umbrella in perspective, he thought humorously.

"What happens with all the squares?" he asked.

"Larissa will get them bound and covered. Then Destiny will have the book for her daughter. When she reads it to her, she'll remember all of us and today."

Connections, he thought as he picked up a pen. Women did like their connections. Although in this case, he had to admit he got it. While the party was nothing any of his friends would want, there was something about it. A rite of passage maybe. Or perhaps the value was all in the caring. While he was sure there were women who needed the gifts from the shower for the baby, that wasn't the case for Destiny. She could afford to buy whatever her daughter would need.

Still, the presents were creative. Clever. A tricycle made of baby diapers. Pink elephants made out of washcloths. Gifts that were more special, not just because they were practical, but because of the time invested. Like the alphabet book.

He remembered an old movie, *Witness*, where an Amish community had gotten together to build a barn. The structure had been needed, but more than that, it stood as a testament to tradition, to acceptance and caring from the community. The shower was like that.

Later, he and Shelby walked home together. He carried the large centerpiece he'd won from the clothespin game.

"You survived," she told him. "Congratulations."

"It was fun. Different. There's no competition with your girlfriends."

"Is there competition with men?"

"Mostly. We want to know our place in the hierarchy. Sometimes we have to jockey for position. Or walk away when there's a game we can't win."

"Like you and Del with your dad."

"Just like that."

"What about the rest of the party?" she asked.

"I liked it. The food was good. A little pink, but good."

They reached her place. He walked her up to her porch and handed her the centerpiece.

She grinned. "You don't want to take it home?"

"No. I can handle our gender events, but I have to draw the line at flowers."

Her blue eyes were bright with humor. "A man with standards. I'm so impressed."

"You should be."

She giggled. "Speaking of gender events, what's next?"

"You know how to play Texas hold 'em?"

"That's a card game, right?"

"I take that as a no."

She took the flowers. "Yes, that's a no. Texas hold 'em, it is. Should I practice?"

"At least read up on the basic rules."

"Yes, sir. I guess there's not going to be any talking."

"Very little."

"And nothing pink."

"We'll be playing at The Man Cave. There's a bar. You can order a cosmo if you want."

She laughed again. "I'll be the only one drinking that."

"Yes, you will."

Without thinking, he leaned forward. To kiss her. Because he wanted to. Because he liked her. Because when he was around her, he felt need and belonging. Because…

But at the last second, he remembered she was his friend and they couldn't kiss, so he shifted and lightly touched his lips to her cheek. Then he felt like a fool and didn't know what to say.

"I'll, ah, text you the date and time," he muttered before stepping off her porch and turning away.

"Okay. Bye, Aidan."

He waved without turning around. He was an idiot. Worse, he was a horny idiot with nothing but a long line of cold showers between now and June.

SHELBY KNEW SHE was the second player to the left of the button, which meant she would be betting second. At least she was pretty sure. Despite having spent a couple of hours online learning the rules to Texas hold 'em, she was still figuring it out as she went.

The "no talking" rule of the game helped her to concentrate, and she found the relative silence kind of soothing. There was the piped-in music from the premium sound system at The Man Cave and the sound of conversation in the bar beyond the open door. But here, in the back, there was only the thud of glasses and beer bottles settling back on the table and the occasional male grunts.

She knew all the players, at least to say hi to. She was friends with most of their wives and significant others and had been to most of their houses. But this was new territory, at least from her perspective.

She wanted to ask how often the guys got together to play cards, but kept her lips carefully pressed together. Aidan had been clear. Just like she'd had to get permission to bring him to Destiny's baby shower, he'd had to ask if she could join the game. The guys had agreed, as long as she followed the rules. Apparently rule number one was no conversation.

So here she was, at a big table with eight burly guys, each one better looking than the last. Under other circumstances, she might be intimidated. But they were all in committed relationships and none of them especially appealed to her. Except for Aidan, of course. He appealed to her a lot. But in a friendship kind of way.

She thought briefly of the almost kiss they'd shared. For one heart-pounding second, she'd been so sure he was going to do it. Kiss her. Lips on lips.

Anticipation quivered ever so slightly at the memory. But of course he hadn't. Because they weren't involved. It was for the best. But still...a kiss would have been pretty darned nice.

She returned her attention to the game, placed her bet and resisted the urge to check her hole cards. She knew what they were and looking at them over and over again didn't change that. She had two kings. And the object was to get the best five cards possible using any combination of hole and community cards. If one of the community cards was a king, she would have a great shot at the pot. She mentally crossed her fingers.

"How's Isabel?" Justice asked.

Ford Hendrix, Isabel's husband, grimaced. "She's okay. It's still relatively early in her pregnancy and she's bigger every day. I don't know how her body's going to stand it. I know my mom went through the same thing and was okay, but shit. It's tough to watch."

Shelby wasn't sure what shocked her most. That there was conversation, or the fear and concern in Ford's voice. She'd seen him with his wife and knew they had a loving marriage. In her head she got that of course he would worry about her. But hearing it articulated was very different.

"Have you talked to your mom?" Jack McGarry asked. "She might have some insight."

"It's not a conversation I want to have with her," Ford admitted.

"What about talking to Dr. Galloway?" Josh Golden, a former world champion cyclist and current real estate tycoon in town, asked. "I know her from Charity's pregnancies. She's down-to-earth. I doubt anything would shock her. Make an appointment and go in to see her. She'll be straight with you."

"Trust me," Kipling said with a grimace. "She won't hold back."

Ford picked up his bottle of beer. "Yeah, I should do that. I don't want Isabel to know I'm worried. She's got enough on her plate right now with the business and all."

Shelby glanced at Aidan, who winked at her. She smiled back. Their brief interaction caused a little warm glow in her belly. He was so nice, she thought happily. A really great guy. She hoped he was getting as much out of their relationship as she was. Not only was he fun to be around, she was learning a lot. About how men and women were different. She trusted him more each time she was with him, which was her goal. To know there were good guys out there.

"Aidan, you hear from Del much?" Josh asked.

"He emails every now and then. He and Maya are still in China. They've posted some raw footage on their Facebook page. It's good."

"Funny how that all worked out," Ford said. "Del running off and you taking over the business."

"It turned out in the end," Aidan admitted. "Of course when Del first left, I wanted to hunt him down."

Josh glanced toward the open door, then lowered his voice. "Nick still doing his artwork in secret up in the mountains?"

Aidan's look of surprise told Shelby that that wasn't supposed to be public information.

"How'd you know?" he asked.

Ford placed the fifth card faceup. Shelby saw it was the king of hearts. It was all she could do not to cheer. She had three of a kind. With the two threes showing, she had a king-high full house. At least she was pretty sure that was what it was called.

"Everybody knows," Ford said as he looked at his hole cards. "Worst-kept secret in town. I'm in two. Shelby?"

She wanted to push in her entire pile of chips, but knew that would be a mistake. She added her two chips to the pile. The betting went around the table. When it was done, everyone flipped over their hole cards.

Shelby scanned them and saw that no one had more than two pairs. She wasn't very good with straights or flushes, so held in her whoop of victory until Ford said, "Damn. Beaten by a girl."

She glanced at Aidan, who grinned and nodded. "Take it. You won it."

"I like this game," she murmured, drawing in the pot.

"It seems to like you back," Josh grumbled good-naturedly.

They played two more hands or rounds or whatever they were called. Shelby didn't win again, but at least she was able to keep track of what was going on. When they finished for the night, she excused herself to go use the restroom.

When she returned, the card room was empty. She

picked up her glass of club soda and walked toward the bar. There were only a few people still there, a couple playing pool and a handful of guys sitting around one of the tables. Aidan was by the bar, talking to Nick. Shelby went to join them.

"What do you mean it came up over cards?" Nick asked, his voice tense. "What did you tell them?"

"Nothing." Aidan's tone was hard. "I didn't have to. They knew, Nick. Everyone knows. I don't know what's going on between you and Dad, but it's not good for you. Hiding your art like that. Is this really what you want to do with your talent? Work in a bar and hide out in the woods?"

Nick glared at his brother. "Get off me."

"You're letting Ceallach run things and he doesn't even know he's doing it."

"You don't know what you're talking about." Nick's voice rose to a near shout.

"Dammit, Nick. You're wasting everything you could be. And for what? He's just a mean old man."

Shelby's chest tightened. She couldn't seem to catch her breath. As the brothers continued to yell at each other, the edges of the room folded in. She knew what was going to happen. She knew the sound of fists on flesh. She knew how fast it happened and how much it hurt. She knew there was no escape. It was going to get bad and then she would be trapped.

Terror pulled at her, chilling her and making her want to run. Only she couldn't seem to see an escape. She glanced around, but couldn't focus enough to move. Panic and fear immobilized her as a scream built up inside her chest.

She had to get out of here. She had do *something*. Then she felt herself whimper as she couldn't breathe anymore. Her vision got blurry. She couldn't pass out. She couldn't! She would be too vulnerable. But there was no way out, and then he would hit her.

CHAPTER SEVEN

AIDAN SAW MOVEMENT out of the corner of his eye. He turned to find Shelby standing a few feet away. She'd gone completely white. Her pupils were dilated, with what he could only assume was terror, and her breathing was rapid.

"Get me a glass of water," he told Nick. His brother started to protest, then looked at Shelby and swore.

"Just do it," Aidan said, his tone as gentle as he could make it.

He moved toward her, walking slowly. He had no idea what to say or do, but he knew she needed him. And she needed not to be afraid.

"Shelby, honey, it's okay. Nick and I go at it from time to time but it doesn't mean anything. He's pigheaded but he's still my brother and I love him. We're not going to fight. No one's going to get hurt. I'll protect you. I promise. Shelby, can you hear me? I'm right here. You're safe. You're okay."

He lightly touched her arm. She flinched. Pain ripped through him. Not because of what she'd done, but for what she'd been through. How many times had her own father hit her? Beaten her? Left her bloodied?

"Shelby, I want you to slow your breathing. Inhale for a count of five, then exhale for the same. Can you do that for me?"

She nodded and slowed her breathing. Nick brought over the glass of water.

"She okay?" he asked in a whisper.

"I'm fine," Shelby told him, her voice trembling. "I'm okay."

Aidan took the glass. "Can you hold this?"

She nodded and reached for the water. Her fingers shook, but she held on to it, then took a sip. The glass started to slip. Nick grabbed it before it fell. Water spilled. Tears filled her eyes.

"I'm sorry. I'm sorry."

Aidan swore silently, then reached for her. Maybe it was completely the wrong thing to do, but he couldn't help himself. He drew her against him.

"I'm here, Shelby," he whispered. "I'm here."

She was stiff for a second, then relaxed against him. Her arms came around him as she began to cry.

"I'm sorry," she said again.

"Stop it. You have nothing to be sorry about. Nick and I shouldn't have gotten into it like that."

"No, it's not you. I know families fight. I know for most people it stays with yelling. I know that. I just can't always remember."

Nick put the glass on the bar. "He's right to get on me," he admitted. "About my art and Dad and all the crap going on. I can't believe everyone knows what I'm doing up in the woods."

"I didn't know," Shelby told him. "What are you doing up there?"

"Working with wood mostly. Some carving, some with a chainsaw."

Shelby sniffed, then stepped back. She wiped her face. "Are you crazy? You work with a chainsaw? On purpose?"

Nick grinned. "It's cool. One wrong move and I could ruin the piece."

"Or cut off your arm."

He laughed again. "Never gonna happen."

Aidan listened to the conversation without joining in. He watched Shelby carefully, noting the color returning to her face. Her breathing was more regular and she seemed relaxed.

"Do you sell your pieces?" she asked.

"Some. Out of state, through a couple of galleries."

"If you're that good, why do you work here?"

Nick's humor faded. "That would be the question of the hour." He glanced toward the bar. "I've got customers. I'll see you later." He walked back behind the bar.

Shelby sighed. "I got too personal."

"You did fine. He needs to figure out what he wants with his life. How are you feeling?"

She sucked in a breath, then exhaled. "I'm okay. I'm—"

He held up a hand. "Don't apologize. You didn't do anything wrong."

"I freaked out."

"You reacted to a threatening situation."

"It was only threatening to me."

"That doesn't make it any less real. Shelby, you lived through hell. Give yourself a break."

Tears filled her eyes again. "Thank you," she whispered. "For being so nice."

"I'm not nice. If I hadn't fought with Nick, this wouldn't have happened in the first place."

"I'm glad it did happen. I needed it to happen."

"What are you talking about?"

"I needed to go through this. I'll need to go through it again. I have to keep seeing that people can argue without getting physical. I have to learn what's normal."

She was probably right but he could go his entire life without wanting to see the fear in Shelby's eyes again.

She moved close, raised herself on tiptoes and pressed her lips to his.

"Thank you," she told him. "Thank you for everything."

And then she was gone. Which was probably for the best because all he could think was that he wanted another kiss, and another. He wanted her mouth everywhere and his mouth doing the same and them getting naked and—

No. That wasn't what this was about. They were friends on a mission. Because of their deal, he was becoming a better man. A desperately aroused man with no relief in sight. Talk about a hell of a way to build character.

SHELBY WOULD HAVE thought the fight between Aidan and his brother would have made her edgy for days.

But the truth was, she'd never felt better. Relaxed, calm, capable. There was a sense of freedom that she couldn't completely explain. She supposed it came from knowing she'd taken a big step in her healing.

While the argument between the brothers had terrified her, what had come from it had been wonderful. There had been anger but no violence. And Aidan had been totally there for her. He'd seen her terror and he'd reacted in a caring, gentle way.

She'd thought a lot about what had happened and had come to realize it wasn't so much that he'd understood she was afraid, it was that even though he'd been angry, he'd been *reachable*. He hadn't gone to such a place of darkness that he couldn't be brought back.

Her therapist had talked about that. How most people who weren't her father could get angry, but even flooded with that emotion, they could be reasoned with. That her job was to find men like that, men who could be trusted no matter how enraged they might be. She hadn't thought such a man existed—except for her brother—but she'd been happily wrong.

She smoothed the icing on the cake she was making for Aidan. It was one of her favorites, with three different fillings, including one flavored with Kahlúa. She had a feeling he was going to like it. She hoped so.

"That looks beautiful," Amber said as she walked into the back of the bakery. "I know a boyfriend cake when I see one."

Shelby laughed. "No boyfriend, I promise. This is for a friend who happens to be a guy."

"Yeah, I'm not a big believer in that. Twenty-one years ago I took one look at Tom and thought that I had to get me some of that." She smiled. "I still feel that way. The man moves me." She nodded at the cake. "That's an I-got-to-get-me-some-of-that cake, Shelby. You can pretend all you want, but the message is in that icing there."

Shelby just smiled at her partner. She'd already explained about her experiment with Aidan. Some people got it and some didn't. Regardless, she knew they were creating something great together and it wasn't the least bit romantic.

Not that she couldn't appreciate the allure. He was a big, strong, handsome guy. Equally necessary for her, he was someone she could trust. Gentle, smart, funny and, okay, sexy. Sometimes she thought about what it would be like if they were more than friends. She would bet he kissed like a dream. If nothing else, he had lots of experience.

That made her smile, which caused Amber to raise her eyebrows. "See. There's something going on."

"I can look without touching."

"Where's the fun in that?" Amber wrinkled her nose and placed her hand on her stomach. "I have an appointment with Dr. Galloway."

"Still not feeling right?"

"No." Her business partner sighed. "I'm probably going through early menopause. A horrifying thought."

"You're too young for that."

"I think so, but tell that to my girl parts." Amber smiled. "I'm sure it's nothing."

"You'll tell me if it isn't?" Shelby asked.

"Of course."

Shelby wanted to believe her, but wasn't sure. She and Amber worked well together, but their partnership was still very new and establishing meaningful trust took time. If Amber was sick, then Shelby would do whatever she could to help. She could keep the business going for as long as necessary. All things she would say if and when the time came.

"YOU SURE ABOUT THIS?" Shelby asked.

Aidan stared at the low, one-story building and the handful of cars in the parking lot. Sure he had doubts, but he wanted to go forward anyway. "It's the next logical step," he said firmly.

"You could start with a plant."

He glanced at her. "Very funny. I can keep a dog alive. I'll be a good pet owner."

"I believe the phrase you're looking for is *pet dad*." She smiled. "If you get into trouble, I'm close by."

"Because you know about dogs?"

"I read things on the internet."

"Well then. No worries."

They were in the front seat of his truck, with her leaning toward him. Early February was just as cold as January had been, so there was plenty of snow.

Shelby was bundled up in a thick sweater and a jacket over that. She had a ridiculous purple knit cap pulled down to her eyebrows. Despite it all, she was still sexy as hell.

Aidan breathed through the now familiar waves of need that rippled through him. June would get here eventually and then he could finally get some. He had made the right decision—not only to try being friends with Shelby, but to walk away from the short-term hookups that had dominated his life.

Despite the fact that this was the longest he'd ever gone without sex—at least since high school, when he didn't know any better—he was pleased with how things were going. He knew he was changing. He liked hanging out with Shelby. He enjoyed her company. The fact that they were never going to be lovers was okay with him. That didn't mean he didn't *think* about ways to please them both pretty much every time they were together, but he figured the pain and frustration would build character.

What was really strange was how he wasn't tempted by any of the tourists passing through town. Several attractive women had been in the office to arrange tours. He'd taken a group of single women on an overnight cross-country-skiing weekend and none of them had tantalized him in the least. A couple had flirted, but he'd been immune.

Change was possible, he thought with satisfaction, and getting a dog was the next step for him.

"You ready?" she asked.

He nodded. "The lady I talked to said not to focus on finding a dog my very first visit. She said that it's better to wait and get it right than to rush into a decision."

"So we're window-shopping?"

"Something like that. When I see the right dog, I'll know it."

Her lips twitched. "Like your souls will touch?"

"Very funny. I was thinking more of a disturbance in the Force."

She laughed. The soft, sweet sound filled the cab of the truck. He wanted to pull her close and kiss her. Not even to start on a path to something more, but because kissing Shelby felt like the right thing to do. But he knew better so he pocketed his truck key and opened the driver's side door.

"Come on," he said. "Let's go find my soul mate."

They walked into the animal shelter. A middle-aged lady named Carol took the paperwork he'd downloaded and filled out at home. She started a file, then talked to him about the shelter policies.

"We give you a two-week trial," she said. "You can take one of our pets home for a few days and see how it goes. If it turns out you're not a good match, you can return the pet and get your adoption fees back."

Aidan was less concerned about the money he would be paying than finding the right companion.

Carol, petite, with short dark hair, set the paperwork on the counter. "Do you know what you're looking for?"

"A dog," he said. "Something big."

Carol didn't look surprised. "A larger dog needs

plenty of exercise. Do you have a yard and are you prepared to walk him at least twice a day?"

Aidan nodded. "The yard has a six-foot fence. I can walk the dog and I'll be taking him to work with me. I own a tour company."

Carol glanced back at the paperwork. "Mitchell Adventure Tours. Of course. I worked for your mom when I was in high school." She smiled. "So someone you can take hiking and camping, right?"

"Uh-huh. Maybe a couple of years old. I don't think I could handle a puppy."

Responsibility was one thing, but potty training was asking too much.

"He'd prefer a boy dog," Shelby added with a wicked smile. "You know, so they could bond over manly things."

Aidan narrowed his gaze. "I think a male dog would be easier for me. But I'm open to a girl."

Shelby linked arms with him. "You're lying, but it's nice of you to pretend."

Carol laughed. "Let's go meet some dogs. We have several larger dogs in right now. Some are more active than others. There's a border collie mix who might be perfect."

Five minutes later, Aidan and Shelby were in a large, well-lit room furnished like a typical living room. There was a sofa, an area rug and a box of dog toys. Carol walked in with a black-and-white dog on a leash.

"This is Jasper," she said. "He's two years old. He's very active. Border collies need to be doing something. They're working dogs and if you don't keep them busy, they can get into mischief."

Aidan stayed seated, as Carol had instructed, and let her bring the dog to him. Jasper sniffed his hand before turning to Shelby.

"He's beautiful," she said. "Can I pet him?"

"Sure."

Shelby gently stroked his side. "Hi, big guy. How are you?"

Jasper's tail wagged. Then he walked over to the toy box and chose a bone. He settled on the rug and began to chew.

Aidan got up and approached. Jasper put both paws on the plastic bone, stared Aidan in the eye and growled. The message of "back off" couldn't have been more clear.

Carol picked up the leash and drew Jasper away from the bone. They approached Aidan again. Jasper's gaze was sharp and just a little threatening. Aidan didn't know a whole lot about dogs, but he was pretty sure this one didn't like him.

"He's not the one," Shelby said. "There's no chemistry."

"I agree." Carol walked toward the door. "Let me bring in someone else."

A Lab mix, a midsized pit bull and a Great Dane later, Aidan was thinking he wasn't cut out to be a dog owner. The pit bull had been too hyper, the Lab barely moved and the Great Dane was still a puppy and more interested in chasing its tail than paying attention to him.

"I didn't think it would be this hard," Shelby admitted when Carol had taken the Great Dane away. "There's more involved than I'd realized. You have to know you're getting the right dog. You could have him for years."

"I guess I'll come back in a few weeks," Aidan said as he stood. "Carol said they get new dogs in all the time."

The door opened and the volunteer walked in with a small white dog.

"I know, I know," she said with a slight shrug. "He's nothing like you described. But I couldn't help thinking maybe he was the one. This is Charlie."

"He's adorable!" Shelby dropped to her knees. "Hi, Charlie."

The little dog, stocky, with kind of short legs and a white curly coat, trotted over to her. He sniffed her fingers, then licked them before heading to Aidan.

"He's really small," Aidan said doubtfully. "I don't want a puppy."

"Charlie's nearly five," Carol said. "He's full-grown. He's a bichon frise. They're friendly, happy dogs. Their history is as entertainers. A lot of bichons worked in circuses."

Shelby giggled and Aidan winced. "I don't really want that kind of pet."

Carol pulled a small dog treat out of her pocket and handed it to Aidan. "Give him this. Have him sit first."

Aidan took the piece of dried meat and held it in his hand. Charlie immediately sat.

"Good boy," Aidan said. "Can he do any other tricks?"

Charlie raised both paws and waved them. When Aidan didn't give him the treat, he waved them faster as if asking, "What else do you want from me?"

Aidan grinned and handed over the bit of food. Charlie took it politely and swallowed it, then jumped on the sofa, next to Aidan.

Man and dog looked at each other. Aidan let him sniff his fingers before petting him. Charlie's coat was soft and his body was solid. His eyes were dark brown and he had a happy, doggy grin.

Shelby hugged him and got a quick kiss in return. "He's really friendly. That's good for when you take him into your office. I'd be worried that a dog like Jasper would scare customers, but Charlie would totally charm them."

Aidan had to admit the little dog was cute enough and seemed pleasant to be around, but he was so small…and kind of girly.

"I don't know," he admitted. "I was thinking of something more…"

"Macho?" Shelby asked, raising her eyebrows. "You are such a guy." She turned to Carol. "Can we take him for a walk?"

"Sure. Let me get his coat."

Aidan held in a groan. "He wears a *coat*?"

"He's small and short. The snow would cover him. It's fifteen degrees outside. Of course he needs a coat."

Carol returned with a blue cape thing with Velcro straps. She showed them both how to put it on Charlie. The dog stood perfectly still, except for his wagging tail. When he was covered, he jumped down and led the way to the door.

Once they were outside, Charlie took charge and followed what must be a familiar path. He sniffed a lot, stopped to pee a couple of times, then marched on purposefully.

"I couldn't take him skiing," Aidan said.

"You couldn't take any dog skiing."

"Okay, but what about snowshoeing? He'd disappear in the first snowdrift."

"Put him on a sled and pull him."

Aidan frowned at the mental image that suggestion planted in his brain. "I thought dogs were supposed to pull people—not the other way around."

"When life gives you lemons, or in this case, small dogs, compromises must be made. He'd be fun camping. He wouldn't take up much room. He could sleep in your sleeping bag or next to it in summer." Her expression brightened. "Cleanup would be easier. Small dog, small poop."

"There's a selling point."

Charlie barked at a couple of birds. They walked on for a few more minutes, then Aidan called to him. Charlie immediately stopped and turned. Aidan picked him up. The little dog's paws were damp and nearly frozen and Charlie was shivering.

"Hey, why didn't you say something?" he asked. "You're freezing."

He unzipped his jacket and tucked Charlie inside against his chest. Shelby helped him zip the jacket closed around the dog. Aidan supported his butt with one hand. Charlie shivered for a couple more minutes, then snuggled close and closed his eyes.

"He would have just kept going," Aidan admitted. "I can't decide if that's crazy or brave."

"Maybe it's that he would be up for an adventure."

"Carol said he comes from a line of circus dogs."

"No one has to know."

"Now you're making fun of me."

"Not only now," she teased. Her smile faded. "What do you think?"

Aidan wasn't sure. Charlie wasn't anything he'd been looking for. He'd thought he would end up with a Lab or maybe a German shepherd.

"He's kind of ridiculous," he said. "But I think I like him."

They got back to the shelter. After Aidan took off the dog's coat, Charlie dropped to the ground and rolled on his back, as if scratching an itch. The pure joy of the moment—all four paws waving in the air, his stocky little body writhing in pleasure—pretty much sealed the deal.

Carol said they could take as much time as they wanted with Charlie. Aidan led him back into the faux living room. Charlie ran around and sniffed the toys, then drank some water. When Aidan and Shelby returned to the sofa, Charlie jumped up next to them before settling on the back of the sofa. He gazed at Aidan as if he knew what was being decided.

"Well, hell," Aidan muttered. He stroked the side of Charlie's face. The dog licked his hand, then put his head on his paws and closed his eyes.

He was a good little guy, he thought. Friendly, eager and easygoing.

"I suppose a trial run wouldn't hurt."

Shelby smiled. "Silly man. There is no trial. If you take him home there's no way you're bringing him back."

Aidan looked at the little dog and had a bad feeling she was right.

AIDAN'S FIRST STOP after taking Shelby home was the pet store at the edge of town. He had a starter kit of food, along with a ball and a new collar and leash from the shelter, but that wasn't nearly enough. He knew pets needed things like beds and bowls, not to mention more than the couple of cans of food along with a two-pound bag of kibble he'd been sent home with.

"You're going to have to help out," he told the dog as he opened the passenger side door and reached for Charlie's leash, which he'd left on the floor of the truck. He snapped it into place, then lifted the dog to the ground. "I don't know what you like. Guidance would be appreciated."

Charlie stared at him, his brown eyes thoughtful, as if he was processing the request. Aidan waited, but there was no other response. Not that he'd been expecting words or a note, but still, something would have been good.

"Okay then," he said. "You ready?"

He pointed toward the store. Charlie started walking in that direction, his little tail straight up and wagging slightly.

Aidan got a big cart, then worried it would frighten the dog, but Charlie took it in stride. He sniffed the floor and looked around eagerly, as if happy to explore this new world.

Aidan started with the easy stuff. Food and bowls. He bought several cans of what the shelter had been using, along with a bag of kibble. He figured he would do some research online to find out the best kind for a dog like Charlie and transition him gradually. He picked out four different kinds of treats, including one that was supposed to keep Charlie's teeth clean and his gums healthy. He got a half-dozen bowls, then headed for the toy aisle.

Charlie showed interest in squeaky toys and a good tuggy rope. Aidan picked out a couple of nubby bones that were supposed to give the dog something to chew on. Next up, beds.

Charlie tested out every one Aidan put down on the floor. It was hard to tell which one he liked best. Aidan settled on a plush, high-sided brown bed with orthopedic foam under the cushion.

Last they cruised by the collar aisle. Charlie stood patiently while Aidan tested a couple of different collars, along with a harness. He bought one of each and the matching leashes. Last, and the item he was dreading the most—a coat.

There were several styles, along with sweaters and, dear God, dog booties.

"We're not doing that," he told Charlie.

The dog wagged his tail.

Aidan thought about how Charlie had walked through all that icy snow and never complained. How his little paws had been frozen and he'd been shivering. Then he looked back at the booties.

Everything inside of him protested. Bad enough to have a small, white fluffy dog, but one in booties?

"It's happening," Aidan told Charlie. "You're my witness. I'm turning into a woman."

Bowing to the inevitable, he reached for the booties and tossed them into the cart.

CHAPTER EIGHT

THE FIRST MEETING of the mayor-requested singles group took place on the Saturday before Valentine's Day at the outdoor skating rink at Pyrite Park. Shelby was to meet Aidan there fifteen minutes before the event.

They'd put the word out on the town's electronic community board and Bailey, the mayor's assistant, had sent an email blast to everyone who'd signed up to receive them. Even so, Shelby had no idea what to expect. They could have two participants or two hundred.

When she got to the skating rink, she found Aidan already there, sitting on a bench by the ice-skate rental shack. Charlie sat next to him, fashionably dressed in a black-and-white plaid jacket and—she squinted just to make sure she was really seeing what she thought she was seeing—black dog booties.

"Don't," Aidan said as he got to his feet. "Don't say it. I know what you're thinking and it's not my fault."

"He's very fashion forward this morning."

"Sure, make fun of the guy trying to be a good puppy parent. He gets cold. I don't want him to be uncomfortable." He reached down and petted the little dog. "He's a good boy with a lot of personality."

"You could get matching jackets."

"Very funny."

She grinned, then dropped to a crouch in front of the bench. "Hi, Charlie. How are you, big guy?" As she spoke, she let the bichon sniff her fingers. His tail wagged and he gave her a quick kiss.

She picked him up and held him close. "So you two are getting to know each other?"

"We are. He likes to drive."

"Excuse me?"

Aidan laughed. "He's been riding around with me. The other day he climbed onto my lap in the truck. I thought he wanted to snuggle, but nope, he wanted to try to drive. I told him he had to wait until he was older."

"I'm sure he understands."

Aidan reached out and rubbed the side of the dog's face. "I bought one of those books on the breed."

"Any useful information?"

He grimaced. "Sure. That bichons do well in apartments and with the elderly. I have the old-lady, Park Avenue dog."

Her lips twitched. "You're still in the trial period. Want to take him back?"

Aidan frowned. "No. Of course not. He's my dog."

She'd known that would be the answer, but hearing it still caused her heart to melt just a little. Poor Aidan—he'd had such plans for his big, macho dog. Instead he'd ended up with Charlie. He'd led with his heart and now he was committed.

She handed over Charlie. For a second their hands tangled. She ignored the odd tingles and raised herself on tiptoe to whisper into his ear.

"Look at you, making a commitment. First a dog. Next up, you'll find yourself with a girlfriend."

"One step at a time," he told her.

She was about to step away when their eyes locked and she found she couldn't move. Or she didn't want to, which was practically the same thing. She liked looking at Aidan—who wouldn't? The man was attractive. But this was more than that. This was about wanting to connect. Or something.

She told herself it was nothing but her warm fuzzies about the dog. They were friends. Only friends. Yes, she occasionally wondered what it would be like to be one of his weekend conquests. She had no doubt the man had game. But weekend encounters weren't her style. She wanted more.

Which was generally when she reminded herself that Aidan was helping her with that and repaying him by fantasizing about making love with him wasn't very nice of her.

"What's the plan?"

The question came from behind her. Shelby turned and saw Eddie and Gladys.

"We heard there were going to be lots of single guys here," Eddie said. "We're into that. Maybe someone will want to have sex with us."

Gladys grinned. "Not at the same time. We aren't comfortable with the idea of a threesome."

An unexpected conversation, especially when the

two women in question were in their eighties. Aidan took a step back.

"It's not a singles group," he began, then paused. "I mean it's for single people but not so they can get together."

Eddie and Gladys looked at each other. "What are you talking about? What else are they going to do?"

"Be friends," Shelby told them. "Mayor Marsha thought it would be good for single men and women to have a chance to be friends without the pressure of dating. Like Aidan and I are doing. We hang out and enjoy each other's company, but as friends. Nothing more."

"That's stupid." Eddie put her hands on her hips. "Are you telling me that this is platonic?" She practically spit the last word. "No one's getting any?"

"That's not exactly how I would put it," Shelby began.

"Yes or no?" Gladys asked. "Sex or no sex?"

"No sex," Shelby said.

"Ridiculous," Eddie grumbled. "Young people today. I'll never understand them."

"Let's get out of here. Maybe somebody good is working out at the gym."

The two old ladies walked away. Aidan looked from them to the crowd gathering near the rental shack. There were about fifteen people.

"You think they're going to take the news any better?" he asked.

"I'm not sure." She was genuinely confused. "Why do people act like we're doing something unnatural? This is a good thing."

"Let's go see if we can convince our new friends over there."

Shelby and Aidan walked over to the group waiting. She took Charlie while he introduced himself and her, then explained Mayor Marsha's vision for the event. Shelby put down Charlie and let him greet everyone. He was friendly and gentle and soon had all the women fussing over him.

"I don't get it," one of the guys, a twentysomething with blond hair and glasses, said. "I thought this was a place to get to know girls."

"It is," Shelby told him. "As friends."

"I don't want any more girls who are just friends. What's the point?"

Shelby looked at Aidan, who shrugged.

"It's nice," she said. "When there's no pressure. Aidan and I are friends and we've learned a lot from each other."

A tall redhead in her late thirties frowned. "I'm with him. I thought I could meet some single guys. I work a lot and it's hard to get out. I already have plenty of friends. I'm looking for something a little more interesting."

Shelby saw one of the guys shift closer to her. She looked at Aidan. "Help."

"Just give it a try," he told the group.

The twentysomething in glasses looked doubtful. "Are you being straight with us, bro? I saw how you looked at her before. That wasn't about being friends."

Shelby blinked. "What are you talking about? We're really friends. Just friends."

Aidan nodded. "She's right."

"Uh-huh," the guy said. "Whatever it takes to get through the night. I'm not going to judge."

Aidan drew in a breath. "Let's just give it a try, okay? Get your skates and get on the ice. Try to talk to everyone if you can. As friends."

There was some grumbling but the group started to get ready to go out on the ice. A few had brought their own skates, the rest got in line to rent a pair.

Shelby sighed. "I'm not sure this is going to work. But we're making the effort, so we can report back to Mayor Marsha with a clear conscience." She looked at Aidan. "What did that guy mean about how you looked at me?"

Aidan bent down to check on Charlie's coat. "I don't know. I don't think he's going to come back for our second event."

"I don't think any of them are."

Aidan straightened. "Ready to skate?"

"Uh-huh. What are you going to do with Charlie?"

"Maggie who runs the shack is going to keep him with her." Aidan grinned. "Charlie's very good with the ladies. At work, he has Fay trained. Right at ten and two, he's up and looking for a doggy treat. He sits up and waves his paws at her. If she's too slow, he waves faster, then starts to bark at her, and off she goes to get his treat."

"I knew you were smart," she told the dog.

Aidan led Charlie toward the shack. Shelby watched him go. Charlie might not be the dog he'd had in mind, but they looked good together. Watching Aidan tend to the smaller dog was just so sweet.

And kind of sexy. The tender side of him was un-expected.

For a second she allowed herself to imagine how tender he would be with her. Gentle, but strong. He would take his time and make her feel safe and cared for. Then she shook off the images. They were friends. Only friends. Despite what anyone else thought…or said.

"I WANTED TO let you know I'm fine," Amber said.

Shelby looked up from the supplies she was orga-nizing. Taking Taryn's advice, she'd put a notice up at the high school. Two-hour shifts were available at the bakery for cookie decorating. Their Valentine's Day orders had tripled from the previous year. It seemed that the entire town, not to mention several dozen out-of-state customers, wanted frosted cookies for the holiday. There was no way Shelby and their permanent staff could get everything done in time, so reinforcements were being called in.

She had eight fifteen-year-old girls due to arrive at three thirty. Which meant eight stations to be set up with frosting, cookies and little sprinkles. Not to mention hairnets, aprons and gloves.

She looked at her business partner and did her best to put Amber's statement in context. Before she could, the other woman laughed.

"Sorry. I guess I assumed it was all about me. I saw Dr. Galloway last week. Remember, I'd been complaining about not feeling well? I wanted to let you know I'm fine."

"Oh!" Shelby laughed. "Of course. I'm sorry. I should have remembered."

"You're busy."

"Still, not an excuse. So everything is good? That's so great. Does she have you on special vitamins or something?"

Amber shifted her gaze to the table. "Um, yes. I am on vitamins and some other things. I'm not sick."

There was something in her friend's voice. A particular tone Shelby couldn't put her finger on. Still, if everything was all right, she was busy enough to let the rest of it go.

"I'm glad. I know you weren't yourself."

"I wasn't, but now I'm, you know, okay." Amber pointed to the cookie stations. "I'm very curious about how this is going to go."

"Me, too. I figure we're either going to have a fantastic workforce we can call in for special orders, or it will be a total disaster."

"No middle ground?"

"I think not."

"Good luck with it all."

"Thanks."

Shelby finished setting up the stations and returned to check on the front of the store just as Madeline walked.

"Hey, you." Her friend smiled. "How's it going? I feel like I haven't seen you in forever."

"I've been busy and so have you."

Madeline laughed. "Tell me about it. A lot of young women are expecting a Valentine's Day proposal, so they've been coming in to try on dresses.

Which means lots of looking and no buying. I tell myself they'll be back. In the meantime, our samples are getting a workout."

"Speaking of samples," Shelby teased as she held out a plate with pieces of cookie on it. "We're doing some special Valentine's cookies. If you want some for your movie-star fiancé, you need to order soon."

Madeline took a piece and popped it in her mouth. "I already have. They're so delicious." She took a second piece. "Jonny's been going back and forth to LA for the past couple of weeks. It's all in preparation for his next movie. When I get his schedule nailed down, I was thinking of having a few people over for dinner. You know, couples. Can I invite you and Aidan?"

"We're not a couple."

"You keep saying that and no one believes you." Madeline smiled. "Say yes. It will be fun."

But we're not a couple. Still, Shelby didn't say the words. She was starting to understand that no one could grasp what they were doing. She didn't know why it was so hard to understand, but it was. So she should probably accept it.

"I'll check with Aidan and get back to you. I'm sure he'll say yes."

"Great." Madeline grinned. "Want to come by the store and try on some samples?"

"No. It's not like that."

"Keeping telling yourself that and maybe one day it will be true."

With that, her friend waved and left.

Shelby put the sample plate back on the counter

and sighed. Aidan wasn't going to propose. Not on Valentine's Day or ever. But thinking about him asking her to marry him made her feel all funny inside. Not in a bad way. More…unsettled. As if the possibility wasn't exactly awful.

AIDAN WATCHED SHELBY move unsteadily across the snow. They were cross-country skiing—a first for her. Her movements were jerky and uncoordinated. He had to admit that whenever they tried a new sport, he was always surprised by how badly she did. Oh, she tried and put her whole heart into it. But she lacked that innate athletic skill he would have assumed she had. After all, her brother was a former Olympic athlete. Of course, his father was a world-famous artist and he'd never gotten beyond stick figures. Genetics was a funny thing.

She continued to slide her legs back and forth while using her poles, the way he'd taught her.

"This is a great workout," she said, her voice breathless. "I get that it will whip me into shape. The fun part is less clear."

"It gets more fun as you get better at it."

"Where have I heard that before?"

But she didn't give up. She kept moving and after a few minutes, her stride evened out.

Despite the straps around his shoulders and chest to pull the small sled, he easily kept pace with her. Every few minutes he looked back to check on Charlie. The little dog was in a box on the sled, settled in a nest of old down coats Aidan had borrowed from the lost-and-found box at the office. Charlie had on his doggy coat and booties and seemed happy to watch the world go by.

Shelby moved a little faster. "Okay, I'm getting it."

She barely finished speaking when she let out a little yelp and fell over sideways. Aidan helped her to her feet.

"Always graceful," he teased as he wiped the snow from her side.

She laughed. "I know. Do me a favor, please. Tell everyone I was brilliant. It will make me feel better."

She swayed as she spoke, as if she was about to fall again. He reached out to grab hold of her. She put her hands on his chest.

The pose was an odd combination of intimate and not. The layers of clothing and outerwear, not to mention the dogsled strapped to his body, kept them physically apart. Yet there was a part of him that felt he was touching her everywhere. Feeling her soft skin and kissing her as he…

He held in a groan and deliberately took a step back. He *wasn't* touching her—that was just wishful thinking on his part. Instead he was left hard and hungry for something he not only couldn't have, but something he knew he *shouldn't* even be wanting. Shelby was his friend. He wanted her in his life, and friendship was the way to make sure that happened. Besides, they had a deal and he didn't go back on his word.

He supposed he could find someone else and scratch the itch, but that didn't seem right. Not only would it be disrespectful to Shelby, it would mean moving backward for him. He was a grown-up. He could deal with a few urges.

"You ready to try again?" he asked.

"Always." She straightened her body and began to move forward. "Tell me when this gets fun."

"Promise."

She glanced at him. "People really pay for you to take them out and do this all day? Exercise in the snow? Because they could just get a gym membership."

"Where's the thrill of that? Out here, we're in nature."

"Cold nature."

"Stop," he told her.

She obliged.

He pointed up at the tall trees around them. The dusting of snow contrasted with the green needles and brown bark. The sky was so blue it almost hurt to look at it.

"You don't get this kind of view in a gym."

She nodded. "I'll give you that, but you also don't get frostbite."

"I thought girls were supposed to be the romantic ones," he complained and they started moving again.

"That's a myth started by women to make men feel strong. At the heart of it, we're actually the ruthless gender."

She spoke cheerfully. He laughed.

"No one believes you," he told her.

"It was worth a try." She paused to catch her breath. "My friend Madeline wants to invite us to dinner. She and Jonny are having a few couples over." She held up one glove-clad hand. The pole dangled from her wrist. "I know what you're thinking. We're not actually a couple. I've tried to tell her a bunch of times, but she doesn't believe me. Or she won't. I'm not sure it matters. So do you want to go?"

She was wearing sunglasses, so he couldn't see her blue eyes, but he could imagine the combination of hopefulness and worry. Hope because she would want to have fun with her friends. Worry that he wouldn't understand.

Without thinking—because if he'd been thinking, he wouldn't have done it—he bent down and kissed her. The second his mouth touched hers, he knew he'd made a terrible mistake. He started to pull back only to realize how much he liked the feel of her lips against his. The softness. The slight chill from the outdoor temperature with a hint of warmth below.

Need and desire battled with good sense and in the end, good sense won. He straightened.

"Yes," he said firmly, as if nothing had happened. "We'll go to dinner."

Shelby pulled off her glasses. Her eyes were wide and unblinking. "You just kissed me."

He swore silently. "You noticed."

"Hard not to."

"It was an accident."

"You slipped?"

"I wasn't thinking." He glanced at Charlie to make sure the dog was okay, then returned his attention to her. "It doesn't have to mean anything. Think of it as an involuntary reaction. Like a sneeze."

"I was being cute and you had to kiss me?"

"Something like that." His mouth twisted. "I mean it, Shelby. It was a mistake. We're doing something good here. I don't want to screw that up. We still have several months left in our experiment. Let the kiss go."

He knew she was thinking, but had no idea what. While he mostly regretted what had happened, part of him simply couldn't. He'd needed to kiss her for a while and now he had.

"Okay," she said at last. "It never happened."

"Thanks."

"You're welcome." She slipped on her glasses and faced front. "Let's get going. The sooner we get done spending a bunch of time in nature, the sooner I can get back to being warm."

"There's the spirit."

Before he could say anything else, her cell phone rang. Shelby reached for her pocket.

"I'll have to tell Kipling that the new towers are working great. I know they were put in for the search-and-rescue folks to have reception way out here. He'll be so proud." She glanced at the screen. "Speaking of my brother." She pushed a button. "Hey, Kipling, we were just—"

Her body stiffened. "Now? Really? Okay. We'll be right there." She looked around. "We're out cross-country skiing, but I'm sure Aidan knows a quick way back. We'll see you at the hospital as soon as we can get there. Uh-huh. It's going to be okay."

A dozen disasters crossed Aidan's mind, but he

didn't ask anything. Instead he waited until she'd hung up. She smiled at him.

"Destiny's in labor. I have to get to the hospital. Not only to be there when she's born, but because I'm taking Starr home with me. Tell me you know a shortcut."

"Always. We're about ten minutes from the car."

She groaned. "Well, crap. You've been skiing me in circles."

"In case you hurt yourself."

"Always the planner. Okay, Mr. Mountain Guide. Get me back to civilization."

SHELBY HELD THE perfect baby in her arms. The little girl was warm and tiny, with her eyes tightly closed. Everything about her was magical—the way her impossibly small starfish-like hands moved, the slight puckering of her exquisite rosebud mouth. If God was trying to send a message saying that Shelby needed to get on with her life, He was getting through loud and clear.

She wanted this. Wanted to be holding her own baby. She wanted tears filling her own eyes, the way they filled Destiny's. She wanted her own husband looking at her the way Kipling looked at his wife. They were happy. No, not happy. That word was far too small for what they were obviously feeling.

"That baby looks good on you," Aidan said with a smile.

She laughed softly. "I can't believe you said that. You're not freaked out by this whole thing?"

"Why would I be? Not my baby." He raised one

shoulder. "Although I have to admit, it's more tempting than I thought it would be."

Shelby leaned toward him. "Want to hold her?"

Aidan backed up so fast, he nearly knocked over a chair. He held up both hands, as if surrendering. "No way. I'm not that guy."

For a second, Shelby wanted to tell him he was exactly that guy. That he would be a great father. But she knew the thought of it terrified him. Talk about getting stuck. Still, a girl could dream.

She turned back to her sister-in-law. "She's amazing. You're so lucky."

Destiny wiped away tears. "I know." She smiled at Starr, her fifteen-year-old half sister. "You hanging in there?"

Starr nodded, even though she looked a little shell-shocked. It was one thing to know there was going to be a new baby in the house and another to actually see her an hour or so after she'd been born.

Shelby made a mental note to make sure she and her honorary niece talked that night. Starr would be staying with her the first couple of nights after the birth. Just to give the new parents time to settle in. Shelby wanted to use the time to make sure Starr was adjusting all right to the sudden change in circumstances. While Starr was excited to have a baby niece, a newborn would sure change things.

Kipling grinned at the teen. "You must have friends who can give advice on having a baby in the house."

Starr smiled back. "Yes. They said to be gone when it's time to change the poopy diapers."

Later, after Kipling had dropped off Shelby and Starr at her place, Shelby led the teen into the guest room.

"You doing okay?" she asked. "For real?"

Starr sat on the bed. "It's really strange. I knew Destiny was like having a baby. I mean how could you look at her and not know. But when she had Tonya, it was all so…"

"Unexpected?" Shelby offered. "Real?"

"Yeah."

Shelby sat next to her and hugged the teen. "You know that the baby is going to get a lot of attention from everyone. Not just your sister and Kipling, but the whole town."

Starr nodded. "I know. She's small and cute."

"With those big eyes. It can't be helped. Just remember that none of that means you are loved any less. You're an important part of this family. For a while it's going to seem like everything is messed up and then it will get better."

Starr leaned into her. "Thanks for looking out for me."

"You're my favorite niece."

Starr laughed. "You have to stop saying that. Now you have two."

"Oh, right. I didn't think of that. Well, I'm going to say it for a while more and then I'll just think it." She kissed Starr's forehead. "How about pizza for dinner?"

"I'd love that."

"Me, too. Let's go pick our toppings."

Starr crossed to the kitchen drawer with the take-out menus and found the one for pizza.

"Pepperoni for sure," she said.

"Of course. It wouldn't be pizza without it. What else?"

Starr tilted her head. "You're dating Aidan."

The change in subject surprised Shelby. "We're not dating. We're friends."

"But you're together all the time and you're not seeing any other guy. You like him. How is that not dating?"

"It's hard to explain, I know, but we really are just friends."

"That's not what everyone is saying."

Then everyone was wrong. But she didn't say that, because the statements were starting to get repetitive. Instead she pointed to the menu.

"Extra cheese."

Starr grinned. "Absolutely."

CHAPTER NINE

THE SWING OF the ax followed by the *thunk* of the
blade sinking into wood was satisfying. The *crack*
as the log split. Aidan bent down to grab the split
pieces, then he tossed them into the growing pile by
the side of the house.

The sun was out, the snow steadily melting as the
temperature climbed into the fifties. He'd already
hung his coat over the railing. In another half hour
or so, he would be rolling up the sleeves of his shirt.

"You could help," he called to his brother. Nick
sat on the porch in one of the big chairs. Charlie was
settled in the other man's lap. Neither of them seem
inclined to move.

Nick waved his bottle of beer. "You've got it covered, bro. I'd only be in the way."

"You like watching me work."

"I'll admit it's satisfying." He rubbed Charlie's
ears. "What were you thinking with this dog?"

"You like Charlie."

"I do." Nick took a drink. "He's not your type."

"My type is changing. Besides, he's a good guy."

Despite his small size, Charlie was turning out to
be a great little companion. He was easygoing with
just enough quirks to be interesting. When he rode

with Aidan in the truck, he not only wanted to be on Aidan's lap, he wanted to drive. Or at least give directions. At home, he had an internal clock that rivaled anything NASA had developed. If his dinner was even a minute late, he was right there to nudge Aidan into the kitchen.

He enjoyed a good game of tug or ball, an afternoon on the sofa watching sports or going to the office. He did his business outside, waited politely for table scraps and protected the house with a fierce bark.

Nick continued to rub Charlie's ears. "How many logs are you planning to split today?"

"I'm not sure. How many do you need?"

"Seeing as winter is about over, almost none. But they'll keep for next year. You go on working through whatever your issues are."

Aidan grabbed another log. "What makes you think I have issues?"

"You're here, splitting logs. It's the kind of thing a man does when he has something to think through." Nick paused. "Shelby?"

"What? No. Why would I need to think anything about her?"

"Don't get your panties in a bunch. I was just asking."

Aidan ignored the panties comment. "Shelby and I are fine. We're friends. I like it."

"And her."

Aidan drove the ax into the log and watched it crack in two. "If I didn't like her, she'd be a lousy friend."

"You know what I mean. You *like* her."

"We're not having sex," Aidan said flatly. "If that's what you're implying. We can't. If we have sex, we won't be friends."

"Interesting." Nick put his beer on the floor and leaned back in his chair. "You're saying lovers can't be friends."

"I'm saying it complicates everything. What Shelby and I are doing is different." He wasn't going to betray her trust by revealing why she wanted to see their project through, but his brother knew him well enough to guess at his issues. "It's important. I want to change."

"By not having sex? An interesting plan."

Aidan sank the ax into a nearby log, then faced his brother and pulled off his gloves. He reached for his bottle of water.

"You're missing the point. Sex is easy for me. Too easy. I want something more. Something of value."

"Love?"

He wasn't willing to go there. Love meant being stuck. But maybe something close.

"Real love," Nick added quietly. "Not what Mom and Dad have."

"Maybe." Aidan knew his voice sounded doubtful.

"There *are* good ones out there, you know. Del and Maya, for one. All the guys in town. Most of our friends are married and they seem to be doing okay."

"I don't see you running down the aisle."

Nick laughed. "I believe it's the woman who walks down the aisle, bro. We stand and wait."

"Who are you waiting for?"

Nick picked up his beer. "Not a question that has an answer."

Aidan wondered what that meant. Nick didn't know or he wasn't interested?

Nick pointed to the pile of split logs. "Are they helping?"

Aidan was tired. That was a good thing. Maybe he would sleep tonight instead of tossing restlessly. "I'll let you know."

"How long are you going to do without?"

"Shelby and I have a deal for six months."

Nick whistled. "That's a long time. Especially for you. Until now wasn't your personal best of doing without maybe fifteen minutes?"

Aidan put on his gloves. "Funny. Very funny."

"You do like the ladies."

"And they like me back. I can hold out that long. I need some things to change."

"And Shelby's not an option because you're friends?"

"Right. I don't want to screw things up." Aidan paused. "You know what I mean."

"I do." Nick looked at him. "Most married couples would say they're friends as well as husband and wife, *and* they sleep together."

"Good for them. Now leave me alone. I have logs to split."

Nick laughed. "Go for it. Charlie and I are happy to watch you work out your frustration. When you're done here, I have a house that needs painting."

"Go to hell."

Nick was still laughing when Aidan split the next log.

THE SECOND MEETING of the single friends—and just friends—group went as badly as the first, with the added thrill of exes circling each other like wary wolves guarding territory.

"Why do they have to date?" Shelby asked, watching two people who had been making out by the end of the ice-skating party now glare at each other from opposite ends of the bowling alley. "The rules were very clear. Singles being friends. Not kissing, not sleeping together, being friends. Why is that so hard?"

Aidan walked over to pick up the black bowling ball he'd chosen. He supported it with his left hand as he walked to the end of the lane.

"Biology," he offered. "Men and women are meant to procreate. They're just doing their bit to pass on their DNA."

"There's the human condition reduced to its most basic form," she teased. "Your science teacher would be proud."

He laughed, then took several steps as he swung his right arm. The ball came forward and raced down the lane before smacking into the pins. All of them fell.

"Congratulations, Aidan," a woman called.

"Looking good," another said.

They were both sitting with Charlie. The little white dog seemed perfectly at home at the bowling alley. Shelby was sure having him there was a violation of several city ordinances, but so far no one had complained. In fact nearly every woman in the place had stopped by to pet the little dog.

Shelby told herself it was great that Charlie was getting so much attention. He was a handsome, friendly little guy so it made sense that people found him appealing. On another day, she would probably tease Aidan that his dog was a chick magnet. Only right now she didn't find the situation very funny.

Maybe she was tired. There was no other reason for her to mind the way the women came over and chatted with Aidan while they petted Charlie. It was nice that people liked him and his dog. Even without the dog, he was handsome with his broad shoulders and easy smile.

He looked especially good today, she thought absently. The way his jeans fit him. He had a really good butt and bowling only emphasized that. Even his silly rented bowling shoes didn't take anything away from his appeal. She'd noticed she wasn't the only one paying attention when it was his turn.

She watched the electronic display adjust the score for Aidan's latest strike. Their team was in the lead, but somehow even that didn't make her feel better. She felt funny. No, restless maybe. Something was wrong—she simply couldn't say what.

She walked over to the padded bench, where Charlie was holding court. He wagged his tail when she approached. When she sat down, he settled next to her, resting his head on her lap and staring into her eyes.

"Hey, sweetie," she murmured, stroking him. "Having fun?"

"I hope he is, because I'm not." The speaker was a striking redhead named Amanda. "Rob and I lasted all of two weeks before breaking up. He wasn't as nice as I thought."

"Oh, I like him fine," a pretty blonde said with a smile.

"Wait until he gets you into bed," the redhead warned. "Once he's notched his headboard, he's done."

Allison, the blonde, looked slightly startled at the information. She glanced at a team of guys. "Really?"

Shelby sighed. "You know the purpose of this group was to get to know each other without getting romantically involved."

"Why on earth would we want to do that?" Allison asked. "I have plenty of girlfriends. I'm looking for a man. Aren't you?"

"Not right now," Shelby told her. "I'm taking a break."

Which was kind of true. To be honest, she was getting tired of trying to explain her relationship with Aidan. While their situation shouldn't have been complicated, a lot of people had trouble understanding it.

Allison perked up. "You mean he's single?"

Aidan walked over and sat next to Shelby. He looked at Allison. "Am I the *he* in question?"

Shelby wanted to push the blonde away, which

made no sense. Instead she said with fake cheerful-
ness, "You are. Women continue to flock to you."

"I'm not single," Aidan said firmly.

"You're not?" Allison and Shelby said together.

Aidan raised his eyebrows. "No. I'm…" He hesitated. "I'm not single."

Allison glared at Shelby. "So you *are* dating."

"We're not."

"You're the reason he won't go out with me."

Aidan leaned back against the bench. "She kind
of has you there."

"It's not funny," Allison said, coming to her feet.
"What kind of game are you two playing?"

"It's not a game." Shelby pressed her lips together,
both happy and uncomfortable. "We're just— It's
hard to explain."

"Obviously." Allison turned and walked away.

"She's not a fan," Aidan said lightly. "Nick doesn't
get it, either."

"You discussed what we're doing with your
brother?"

"I told him the basics. Not why we're trying this."

Meaning he hadn't shared anything about her father. Shelby wasn't surprised, but still the words gave
her a warm, glowy kind of feeling in her chest. Aidan
was so nice and—

Allison returned with the redhead and Rob.

"Tell them what you told me," Allison demanded.
"Because I think you're playing some kind of sick
game."

Several other members of the group gathered
around. Charlie raised his head. His ears came

forward and his posture changed from relaxed to watchful. While Shelby appreciated that he wanted to protect his new pack, she wished there was a way to explain it wasn't necessary.

She looked at Aidan, who smiled at her. "I'll take this one," he said, before turning to the group.

"Shelby and I are friends. We've agreed to hang out with each other for six months to learn how the other half thinks and behaves. Our goal is to grow as people and learn to appreciate the opposite sex so we can have better relationships in the long term."

About a dozen pairs of eyes stared in disbelief.

"You're just friends," Allison repeated, sounding skeptical. "As in just friends, but you're not seeing anyone else?"

"No dating," Shelby told her. "It would be a distraction. This is better."

"Than what?" Rob asked. "You're spending time together and not getting any? For six months? Man, that's rough."

Amanda turned on him. "I knew it. The only reason you want to go out with a woman is to get laid. You're a real jerk, you know that?"

"Hey, if you had something interesting to say, I'd want to listen."

A couple of the guys groaned. The redhead's mouth dropped open. One of the men took Rob by the arm and led him toward the door.

"You should probably get out of here while you can."

The unfolding drama was compelling, but it wasn't enough to keep Shelby's attention. Instead she found herself watching Aidan. The Aidan who used to have a different woman in his bed every weekend. The Aidan who was currently not, to quote the eloquent Rob, getting any.

Her first instinct was to offer to fix the problem. You know, with her. And with that thought came tangled images that made her insides quiver. Holding Aidan, kissing Aidan, making love with him. Even though she knew she shouldn't, she couldn't help a minidaydream on the topic.

Then she reminded herself that he was her friend and that he deserved better from her.

"What?" Aidan asked. "You're thinking something."

"You. Sex."

His eyes narrowed. "We're not having that conversation."

"But you—"

"Nope. Not going there. Everything is fine. This is working, Shelby. We're both different. You're trusting me and I'm getting to know you as a person. We're doing what we set out to do. I'm not going to mess that up."

"But you have needs."

"I'm fine and we are done talking about this."

He stared at her until she nodded slowly. Fine. They wouldn't talk about it anymore, but that didn't mean she wouldn't think about it. Her friend had a problem and somehow she was going to have to fix it.

AIDAN SPENT A week waiting for the other shoe to drop, but Shelby kept her word. There weren't any discussions of his *needs*, or anything else that made him uncomfortable. Which was exactly how he wanted it to be. Only every now and then he found himself wondering how she would suggest solving the problem. He could think of a couple of great ideas, all of which involved them naked.

Unfortunately thinking about the problem only made it worse. And bigger. So he suffered through several cold showers, a few stern talking-tos and another log-splitting session back at Nick's. If this kept up much longer, his brother was going to have firewood for six winters.

The following Friday, he followed Charlie to the front door and opened it to find Shelby on his porch. The cold weather was less intense and she'd replaced her down jacket with a lighter leather coat. She had on high-heeled boots, instead of ones designed for snow, and tight jeans. A sexy package.

He told himself none of that mattered and that he should instead focus on the basket she carried.

"Come on in," he said, taking it from her.

She relinquished the surprisingly heavy basket and stepped into the house. After hanging up her jacket, she crouched down to greet an ecstatic Charlie, then straightened.

"We're blending," she said with a laugh. "I like that."

He led the way into the kitchen. "I know how to compromise."

They were having dinner together and just talking—a girl thing. Followed by the second half of a basketball game—a guy thing.

Two months ago he would have groaned at the thought of sitting around and talking. What was the point? But now he understood the appeal. He wasn't going to call his friends and suggest they have a boys' night in. But every now and then it was good to talk things over. Not just problems, but what was happening in life. He liked Shelby's perspective on everything from the latest festival to who was pregnant or dating.

Shelby picked up Charlie and hugged him. "How's my best guy?" The little bichon licked her chin and gave a happy yip.

While they greeted each other, Aidan emptied the basket of a casserole and four tall dessert glasses filled with what looked like parfait. Because dinner with Shelby always meant amazing dessert.

"What did you bring?" he asked.

She set down Charlie and walked into the kitchen. "That's the taco casserole that won the Great Casserole Cookoff," she told him. "I got the recipe in my email this week and decided to try it."

He chuckled. "Yet another difference between men and women."

"What do you mean?"

"I got that email, too." The same online service that sent out information about their two singles events sent out recipes. "I never thought about making any of the casseroles."

"After tonight, you're going to change your mind. It wasn't hard." She motioned to the dessert. "Chocolate bread pudding parfait. The recipe said to use bread soaked in espresso and rum, but I used chocolate pound cake instead. I think the texture will be better." She smiled. "Of course I still soaked it in rum."

"That's my girl."

Since meeting Shelby, Aidan had been forced to step up his workout routine. His job kept him pretty active, but he still tried to get to the gym a couple of times a week to get in a long run and lift some weights. But with the desserts, cookies and cakes she was forever bringing around, he'd found himself having to add another day of exercise.

He had no idea how she kept her weight exactly the same, but being a guy and therefore visual, he happened to know she never gained an ounce. No harm in looking and Shelby was a beautiful woman. He knew every inch of her…at least the inches he could see. Under her clothes was another matter. Not that he hadn't imagined, but a guy never knew for sure until he—

He firmly squashed that line of thinking. They weren't going there, he told himself. Not now, not ever. Friends. Good, platonic friends.

He left out the casserole, but put the parfaits in the refrigerator. She turned on the oven and checked out the bottle of wine he'd chosen for their dinner.

"I need to learn more about wine," she said with a sigh. "I'm forever guessing at what is good. I wonder if I could take a class or something."

"Talk to someone up at Condor Valley Winery. They'd know where to start." He leaned against the counter. "I don't know that much, either. We could take a class together." He thought about the dessert they were having. "What about learning about different wines to have with different desserts? People are always pairing wine with food, but what about sweet things? It would be a fun event to have at the bakery."

She nodded quickly. "You're right. And with the winery as a cosponsor, we could get the wine at a real discount. I wonder what it would take to get a license to sell wine in the store. If Amber was interested…"

The last sentence nearly sounded like a question. "You're not sure."

"I think I have too many ideas for her. She and I are partners, but I'm only a minority shareholder and things have been done a certain way for a long time. Not that she isn't great. She is. I really like working with her. But I try to be careful—to not push things too far."

He opened the bottle of wine. "It was like that when I first went into the business with Mom. I'd always worked there part-time, but when I took things over, I had to balance what I wanted with what my mom thought was right. It was much easier when I bought her out. Everything was on me."

"Your ideas." She took the glass of wine he offered. "So you succeeded and failed on your own."

"Right. No one to blame and no one else to take the credit. It works for me."

"I'm envious," she admitted. "I know Amber understands the business better than me but I keep thinking about all these other things we could be doing. I'd love to expand. The space next door to ours is going to be available in a couple of months. We could do so much with that. I think a tea shop would be fun to open. Tourists would enjoy it and we could limit the hours so we only needed one shift of servers."

"Have you talked to Amber?"

"I mentioned it and she wasn't that interested. I'll try again in a few months. Maybe during the summer, when we're flooded with tourists."

He crossed to her and put his arm around her. "Sorry it's difficult. For what it's worth, I value your opinion and I'm about to take advantage of our friendship by asking you to share it with me."

She leaned into him. They fit well together, he thought, realizing a second too late that what he'd meant as a friendly, comforting gesture was so much more. At least to him.

He wanted to take the wineglass from her so her hands were free. He wanted to turn her so they were facing each other, then he wanted to pull her close, the way a man drew in a woman he desired. He wanted to kiss her and touch her and—

"So the mock-ups are finished?" she asked.

The question—so at odds with what he was thinking—pulled him back to the moment at hand. He carefully dropped his arm and stepped away.

"They are. I want to know what you think."

They went into the dining room. He'd put place mats, napkins and flatware at one end of the table. At the other, he had a stack of eleven-by-eighteen-inch sheets of paper. Shelby sat at the end of the table and he took the seat next to hers.

The first poster mock-up showed a photograph of a parasailer over a huge blue lake. His company logo was on top with information on the website and the Fool's Gold address on the bottom.

"It looks both thrilling and terrifying," she admitted. "People really do this?"

"They do. Del and I did it at Lake Tahoe last fall. Lake Ciara is a lot smaller, but still plenty big. You start on a platform and the boat pulls you out onto the lake. It's awesome."

"If you say so."

The oven dinged. She got up and put in the casserole, then returned to the dining room.

"Let's see what the others are like."

He spread out the different posters and they studied the options. Shelby had some good suggestions about what she thought would work and what wouldn't.

"This one draws me in more," she said. "And the one with the kids is great. You want families to be doing this. They make up a large percentage of our tourist population."

They picked the three they like best. Aidan marked up the changes he wanted while she checked on the casserole, then they headed out to take Charlie on a quick walk before dinner.

The little dog walked along, sniffing and stopping to mark his territory. Aidan had to admit that even though it had only been a few weeks, he couldn't imagine not having the bichon in his life.

"I'm glad it's warmer now," he said. "No coats for Charlie."

Shelby laughed. "You're such a guy."

"Dogs have dignity. They shouldn't have to be humiliated by clothing."

"I don't think Charlie minded."

"That's not what he tells me."

She grinned at him. "So now you two are keeping secrets from me?"

"Just man stuff. You wouldn't understand."

"Oh, you are so going to pay for that."

Most of the snow had already melted. There were still big piles in parking lots from all the plowing, but here in the neighborhoods there were signs of spring. He pointed out the first hints of crocuses and tulips.

"The Tulip Festival is one of my favorites," she said. "All the flowers are so beautiful."

"Then we should go."

"I'd like that." She glanced at him. "Aidan, I need to talk to you about something."

Her tone warned him that he wasn't going to like the topic.

"What?" he asked warily.

"I'm worried about your sex life. Or lack of sex life."

Dammit all to hell. "No."

He turned back toward the house. Charlie trotted along with him. Aidan didn't bother checking on Shelby. His luck was such that she would be right there, too.

"We have to talk about it," she said when she'd caught up with him.

"No. We don't."

"Aidan, I'm serious."

He stopped and stared at her. "So am I. I like what

we're doing here. It's helping me and I think it's helping you. Just go with it."

"But you have needs. I worry."

"There are a lot of things to worry about in this
world. Poverty. Climate change. Me having sex isn't
one of them."

Her blue eyes were so wide and earnest as she
twisted her fingers together. "We could brainstorm
some solutions."

Why him? That was the question of the day. Why
did this have to be happening to him?

"No. Listen to me, Shelby. No. We are not having
this conversation."

"We could—"

He cut her off with a quick shake of his head. "As
my friend, you need to respect my wishes on this. Let
it go. I'm fine." He suddenly figured out how to distract her. "What about you? You must have needs."

She flushed a delightful shade of pink and ducked
her head. "I wasn't getting any before. This isn't
new for me."

"But you're dealing."

"Of course."

"Then do me the courtesy of assuming I can do
the same."

They started walking back to the house. When
they got there, Charlie led the way inside. He waited
patiently while his leash was unsnapped, then did a
couple of quick laps around the living room.

Shelby stood in front of Aidan and raised her gaze
to his.

"You're right. I'm sorry. I do worry about you,

but you obviously don't want to talk about it anymore. I need to respect that. I promise, I won't mention it again."

What he said was "Thank you." What he thought was, there was no way his luck was that good.

CHAPTER TEN

AIDAN WAS CONCERNED about Shelby keeping her word, but the next couple of weeks passed without any mention of his *needs*, or lack of getting any, or however it was she was phrasing it today. Unfortunately his desire for her wasn't as easily managed. It seemed that every time they were together, he found something even more delightful and sexy about her. Whether it was the way she spoke to Charlie in a sweet aren't-you-a-cute-puppy? voice or how she carefully carried the cake she'd made for his mom.

Elaine cut into it immediately and served up generous slices of coconut mango layer cake. Aidan took a bite and held in a groan. Talk about double the goodness. Not only did he get credit for bringing his mom the cake he hadn't made, but he got to taste it, as well.

Elaine sighed as she swallowed. "Shelby, I don't know how you do it, but everything you bring over is better than the one before. I keep thinking that's not possible. You have found your calling."

"Thank you. I've been missing summer and this cake seemed the perfect way to bring those months to mind."

"They'll be here soon enough." His mother turned

to him. "It's been a long time since you've brought a girl around, Aidan. But I have to say, Shelby has been worth the wait. Remember that awful goth girl in high school? Everything about her was so *grim*. Not just the clothes and makeup, but the way she talked about death all the time. I never knew what you saw in her. Shelby, on the other hand, makes perfect sense."

Aidan decided not to mention that part of Caitlyn's appeal had been her willingness to go to third base. Nothing his mother needed to know. As for Shelby, he exchanged a look with her. She mouthed *I know*, as if she got it.

Twenty minutes later, they were in his truck.

"I've told her at least five times that we're not dating," he said as he turned onto the main road that would take them back to town. "I don't know what else to do."

"We should get one of those giant banners and hang it in the center of town," she grumbled. "I know exactly what you mean. No one believes me, either. We are not a couple. We are friends. Why is that so incredibly hard to grasp?"

He knew why his buddies were having trouble. No male still breathing could look at Shelby and not want her. They all thought he was an idiot for not at least trying to make a run at her. And while his entire body agreed, his head knew differently. He *liked* Shelby. A lot. He wanted to be with her the way they were. Talking and hanging out and having fun. If they had sex, all that would go away. Things would get complicated.

She sighed. "I can deal if you can."

"I can."

"Good. Because this is working. I'm more comfortable around men. Last week, when we played darts with your friends, I was totally fine."

"I'm getting in touch with my feminine side." He grinned. "If you tell anyone that, I'll deny it to your face."

She laughed. "I would never tell a soul. It's just so strange. You and I are great. It's everyone else. I wish there was a way to have an honest conversation with the whole town. To just tell them what's going on."

"They would never believe us. They think we're a couple."

"Practically married." She drew in a breath. "Oh, Aidan, I have a very bad idea. Tell me no. You have to tell me no."

Blood immediately heated and headed to his groin. He had to clear his throat before he could speak.

"What is it?"

She turned to him. "It's April Fool's in a couple of days. Let's take out an ad in the paper saying we're married. A full-page ad. Everyone will go crazy. Then we can print a retraction and maybe they'll get how ridiculous they've been."

Okay, not exactly the "I desperately want you in my bed" that he'd been hoping for, but a funny second choice. Nick would freak, as would his friends.

"It might get people off our backs." He grinned. "I say we go for it."

SHELBY HELD HER beautiful niece in her arms. Tonya slept in her cocoon of blankets. One tiny hand clenched and unclenched, as if she was dreaming.

The baby's room was quiet and soothing. Destiny sat in the other chair, her red hair pulled back in a ponytail, her eyes closed.

She looked exhausted, Shelby thought, not wanting to mention that. There were dark circles under her eyes and her skin was pale. She knew better than to ask about sleep. Kipling had already told her that Tonya woke up every night. On the bright side, she ate, went to the bathroom, then fell back asleep. Still, the schedule had to be grueling.

"You doing okay?" Shelby asked.

Destiny opened her eyes and smiled. "I'm so tired I can't think. My body still feels like it's owned by aliens and I can't imagine life ever returning to normal, but I'm okay. Better than okay. She's amazing. I love her."

Her smile turned rueful. "Whatever they tell you about breastfeeding is a crock, though. It's uncomfortable and weird. I know, I know, it's how mammals do it, but still. Strange. Grandma Nell would tell me to get over it, so that's what I tell myself."

"Is it helping?"

"Some." She rolled her eyes. "My manager's already asking when Starr and I can go on tour. I remind him I have a newborn, but he's a man and not the least bit impressed."

"You finished the album, right?"

"Yes. It's going to be released in a couple of months."

Destiny and Starr shared a famous country singer father. The half sisters had written several songs together and recorded an album.

"You were going to tour later in the summer?" she asked.

"That was the plan," Destiny admitted. "Kipling will be crazy busy with work, so Starr and I were going to take the baby with us, along with a nanny. It's only a few dates and we'd have a big RV we'd call home. So Tonya can have familiar surroundings. It all seemed so reasonable, but now I don't know."

"When do you have to decide?"

"Not for another month. I want to say no, but Starr would be so disappointed."

Shelby knew that was true. The teen was wildly excited about the album's debut. "Speaking of Starr, her birthday's coming up. I'm happy to help plan the party. You've got a lot going on."

Destiny rubbed her face. "Thanks. I think Kipling and I have it covered. We still have time."

Not that much, Shelby thought, but didn't push. "I'm here," she repeated. "Just let me know. And speaking of informing people, I'm giving you a heads-up about my April Fool's prank with Aidan. We took out a full-page wedding announcement in the paper."

Destiny looked confused. "You got married?"

"No. It's a joke." Shelby waited, but Destiny only stared at her. "Because people think we're a couple?"

"But you are."

"We're *not*. We're friends."

"So you took out an ad saying you're married?"

Shelby nodded. "It's funny."

"If you say so." Destiny sounded doubtful. "I guess I'm too tired to get it. I hope you have fun with it."

"We will."

AIDAN MOVED THE cursor through the spreadsheet. Creating the summer schedule was always a balancing act. There were activities that were easy sales and others that required a more specific group. Festival weekends always booked up quickly, but for the rest of the time, he had to be more flexible. Figuring out what he would be offering when meant making sure he had both equipment and personnel.

Over the last three years he'd worked with the university, offering part-time positions for students staying in town for summer school. One of the dorms remained open, giving the students a relatively inexpensive place to stay. Parents could relax, knowing their kids were safe, and the students had a fun, outdoor job.

Several of the local ski instructors also worked for him in the summer months. They knew the mountain and were interested in more extreme sports. They also appreciated knowing there was a year-round income stream. That made it easier for them to rent apartments and share houses.

Aidan had enough returning summer staff to take care of about seventy percent of his needs. Which meant training the other thirty percent of the people he would hire.

He chuckled as he imagined what Coach McGarry's

new football recruits would think about escorting twelve senior citizens on a bird-watching hike. But all new hires started with walking tours.

"It's good to see a man who loves his work," Nick said as he walked into Aidan's office. "What's so funny?"

"A bunch of Coach McGarry's freshman football recruits have applied to work here for the summer. Jack and I worked out a schedule that gives them plenty of time to work and practice."

"It also keeps them tired enough to stay out of trouble," Nick said as he crouched down to greet Charlie. The bichon wagged his tail and licked Nick's hand, then settled back on his bed in the corner of the office.

"Unless you come to me with a special set of skills, I start all new hires out on the walking tours."

Nick settled in the chair on the other side of the desk. "Football jocks escorting old ladies out to pick wildflowers."

"Something like that." Aidan saved his data, then closed the program. He turned to face his brother. "What brings you here?"

Nick hesitated just long enough to let him know something was going on.

"I haven't told the folks yet," his brother began. "But I wanted to tell you. I'm going to be leaving Fool's Gold."

Aidan leaned forward. "What? When? Seriously?"

"I don't have a date. And yeah, I'm serious. I thought a lot about what you said to me before. At the bar. About wasting time here. You were right about a lot of things. My art is what I want to be doing. At least more than I am. I'm tired of dealing with Dad and his shit. I'll always be under his thumb in one way or another while I live here. Even if it's just in my head."

Aidan understood what Nick was saying, but also knew he would miss having his brother around. First Del left, then the twins. Now Nick.

He grimaced. "Let me guess. You're going to Happily Inc."

Nick nodded. "I've talked to the twins... I mean Mathias and Ronan."

"I still think of them as the twins, too. We probably always will." They'd been twins for too long to be anything else. But that was just his point of view. What did they think of their own situation?

"I'm going to visit," Nick continued. "See what's what. If it's all they claim, I'll move. They said they have room in their studio where I could work."

"I'm glad you'll be more focused on your art," Aidan said. "But you're not like them. You don't want to live and breathe whatever it is you're creating."

Nick leaned back in his chair. "Agreed. I'll find something else. Part-time, at least." He flashed a grin. "I'm good with my hands."

"I didn't think it was that kind of town."

His brother laughed. "I meant I could pick up some carpentry work. Home repair."

"Is that what they're calling it these days?"

They both laughed. Nick pulled his phone out of

his shirt pocket and pushed a few buttons. "There's a gallery in town. I've sent a few of my pieces."

He passed over the phone. Aidan scrolled through the pictures Mathias had emailed. The gallery was in a small square in what looked like a nice downtown. There were mountains in the background. They were different from the ones around Fool's Gold. These seemed more angular. Rock aggressively thrusting to the sky. By contrast, the Sierras seemed more refined.

He handed back the phone. "I think you're making the right decision," he said. "And I'll miss you."

Nick raised a brow. "We're going to talk about our feelings?"

"I can do that now. Pick a topic and we'll explore it."

"No, thanks. Is that Shelby's influence? What's next? You going to pee sitting down?"

"I'm looking to be a better man. I'll still pee standing up." He held in a grin. "Are you threatened by the changes? Do you worry that the family structure will be compromised? Don't be concerned, Nick. Your place is secure."

Nick's wide-eyed shock was gratifying.

"What the hell are you talking about?" his brother demanded. "What has she done to you?"

Aidan maintained a serious and concerned expression. "I'll always be your brother. We should hug. That will reassure you."

Nick swore. "Who are you?"

Aidan laughed. "Just messing with you."

Nick didn't look amused. "It's not funny. Don't talk like that. It freaks me out."

"You really need to get in touch with your feminine side."

His brother scrambled to his feet. "No, I don't. And you should put yours away. I gotta go."

Aidan was still laughing when Nick bolted out the door.

APRIL FOOL'S DAY fell on a Friday, which was perfect. The bakery was extra busy on Fridays, especially in the morning, and Shelby couldn't wait to hear what everyone had to say. Just to make sure there was plenty of chance to talk about the full-page announcement she and Aidan had taken out, she left a copy of the *Fool's Gold Daily Republic* right on the counter.

But customers came and went without saying a word. No one even hinted they'd seen anything, which made no sense. The ad was in the first section, on page eleven. How could anyone have missed it?

A little after eight, Gladys walked in. The eighty-something woman walked purposefully to the counter.

"I want to talk business," she said.

"All right." Shelby smiled. "About the paper?"

"What? No. My great-niece. Nancee. She's thinking of coming to Fool's Gold for a few months, just to get her feet under her. I want her to stay, but we'll see. The point is she makes cupcakes."

Shelby couldn't figure out why no one cared about the ad. It was huge. It was very clear. She and Aidan announced their marriage. Was no one reading the paper today, or was it one of those things psychologists were always talking about? That everyone assumed the world was talking about them, when in fact the world was too busy talking about itself?

"Are you listening to me?" Gladys asked.

"Huh? No. Sorry. You were saying?"

"Nancee makes cupcakes. Really good ones. You're always trying new things in the bakery. That has to be hard on man power and equipment. You only have so much space back there, and so many employees. Having Nancee bake your cupcakes would free up space and time."

The savvy business assessment coming from an old lady in a flowered dress was a little disconcerting. If Amber ever agreed to even half of Shelby's ideas, they would be hard-pressed to make it all work in their current location. Which was only one of the reasons Shelby wanted to expand.

"It's an interesting idea," she said. "Let me know when Nancee's going to be here. We can talk. I'll have to run it all by Amber, as well."

"That's fine. I'll let you know." Gladys smiled. "You have a good day."

The older woman turned to go. Shelby picked up the paper.

"Wait! Didn't you want to say something about this?"

Gladys stared at her blankly.

Shelby sighed. "The announcement? About me and Aidan?"

"Oh, look. You got married. Congratulations. If you want a present, you need to have a reception. Or a party, although a reception's better. And no, they're not the same thing at all."

Hardly the reaction Shelby had been looking for. "You're not surprised? Shocked? Slightly stunned?"

"No. Why would anyone be surprised?"

With that, she left.

Shelby spent the rest of the morning having customers not mention a thing. It was as if no one cared at all. So much for a fun prank, she thought ruefully. A little before eleven, Madeline stomped into the store.

"I had an early wedding gown delivery," her friend said, her expression tight. "So I had to sign for it, then iron and steam it." Her mouth turned down. "How could you not tell me? I can't believe you and Aidan eloped without saying anything."

Shelby groaned. "We didn't."

"You had to. There's no way you had a wedding here in town." Tears filled Madeline's eyes. "Was it a destination wedding and you didn't invite me? I thought we were friends."

Shelby hurried around the counter and touched Madeline's arm. "There was no wedding. Aidan and I aren't married."

"But there's the announcement."

"It's April Fool's Day."

Madeline wiped away a tear. "So?"

"It's a joke. We did it to be funny."

Her friend sniffed. "So you're not married?"

"No."

"There was no elopement or destination wedding?"

Shelby hugged her. "You're my best friend. When I get engaged, you'll be the first to know. I promise. It's just Aidan and I are friends and everyone has been talking about us like we're a couple and it's frustrating so we thought this would be funny."

Madeline hugged her back, then straightened. "I feel better. I couldn't believe it when I saw that notice. I was really hurt. I should have trusted you."

"No, it's me. I should have said something. I never thought you'd believe it. You know Aidan and I aren't a couple."

Madeline looked like she was going to say something, then she shook her head. "You two are weird. You know that, right?"

"I'm beginning to think that might be the case. We're okay?"

"We are. I have to get back to work. We'll have lunch soon. Promise?"

"Absolutely."

Her friend left. Seconds later Mayor Marsha walked in. "Shelby, I wanted to stop by and offer my congratulations. I had a feeling about you two. I'm glad I was right."

CHAPTER ELEVEN

"IT WAS TOTALLY INSANE," Shelby said, still sounding grumpy. "All of it. Mayor Marsha was the worst. Do you know how hard it was to explain to her that it was a joke? She was not amused."

"I'm glad she came to see you and not me," Aidan admitted.

"That makes you a complete wiener dog," she grumbled.

He chuckled. "I can live with that."

While he'd been startled by the lack of response to their ad, Shelby had taken it much harder. She'd been expecting shrieks and protestations. What she'd gotten instead had been silence or "I told you so's."

"I feel bad about Madeline," she admitted. "I should have let her know what we were doing. But honestly, even she wasn't totally surprised. She was upset because she thought I'd had a wedding without her being there. As if."

He closed his eyes and let the words wash over him. He'd learned that when Shelby was upset about something, it was best to let her talk it out. There was no problem for him to fix, nothing for him to do. His job was to listen.

The first few times she'd gone on a tear, he'd been

unable to keep his mouth shut. But he'd quickly realized that not only didn't she appreciate his thoughtful advice, she actually found it annoying. She didn't want an action plan, she wanted someone to hear her as she worked through the problem over and over again.

Now he was able to simply sink into the words, to respond with encouragement rather than suggestions.

She passed him a towel. "It's all very strange," she continued. "But I guess I need to let it go."

"The retraction will be out Tuesday."

"I doubt anyone will even notice or care. I thought it was a great joke. I hate being wrong about stuff like that."

He lifted his left foot out of the hot water and dried it off, then did the same with his right.

The first time Shelby had suggested they give themselves pedicures, he'd about run screaming into the night. He'd explained that he was a man and real men didn't do that kind of thing. She'd listened patiently, then had reminded him of their deal. Girl thing, boy thing. Pedicures were a girl thing.

So he'd suffered through the experience. After they'd soaked their feet, she'd given him a little kit with all kinds of strange, slightly frightening instruments. She'd taught him how to use them.

He'd had to admit—although only to himself, never to anyone else, even under threat of torture—the experience hadn't been horrible. It was now something they did together every three weeks. Although he did draw the line at buffing his nails. No way that was manly.

When they'd each completed the trimming and filing, he pulled on socks while she grabbed her fuchsia toe separators. He looked over the polish choices she'd put out and held up a bottle of bright red polish.

"You don't think it's too much?" she asked.

"After what happened, you need something cheerful."

"Good point."

Aidan shifted so he could rest her right foot on his thigh, then carefully applied a base coat. He ignored the light pressure on his leg, the fact that she was in shorts and a T-shirt and that they were alone. Nope, he was not going there. He wasn't going to notice how the T-shirt was cut low enough for her him to see the tops of her breasts. He wasn't going to stare at her mouth as she concentrated on filing her fingernails. He was going to pay attention to the job he was doing. Later, he would take cold shower number 967 and count down the days left until their deal was over and he could finally get laid.

SHELBY INSPECTED THE trays of frosted cookies. They'd had a flood of orders, so she'd called in her teen assistants. The girls had done a great job with the flowers and hearts. Nothing said spring so much as a bridal shower.

She counted a second time to make sure they had plenty for the special orders, plus enough for the walk-in sales for the weekend, then noted her inventory sheets. She walked back to her office only to find Amber sitting in the visitor's chair.

Her business partner looked up from her tablet. "There you are. I was hoping to catch you before you started making bread. I figured you'd have to come back here first. Which is why I waited."

Amber was talking too quickly and her gaze seemed to skitter all over the room. Shelby got an uneasy feeling in her stomach. Something was wrong.

She crossed to her desk and sat down. In those three seconds, a million thoughts occurred to her before she realized that she'd created the problem herself. Of course. The newspaper ad. Amber was probably wondering why Shelby hadn't mentioned the wedding to her.

"We have to talk," Amber told her.

"I know. I should have said something."

Her business partner frowned. "Why would you have said anything? It's really up to me. And how did you know?"

Okay, they were obviously not talking about the same thing. Shelby rested her hands on the table.

"You go ahead. What did you want to tell me?"

Amber ducked her head, then looked at Shelby. Her eyes were bright with an excitement Shelby couldn't define.

"I'm pregnant."

Shelby felt her mouth drop open. "I wasn't expecting that," she admitted, then laughed. "Seriously? That's wonderful."

Amber smiled. "I know. It's totally insane. I've wanted to tell you for a few weeks, but I waited. We wanted to be sure that I would get through the first trimester. I'm in my forties. Tom and I never thought this would happen, but it did. I'm thrilled and scared." She leaned forward. "I'm also four months along."

Shelby did the math. "So when you were feeling strange, it was because you were pregnant?"

"Uh-huh. I went to the doctor and that's when we figured it out. Like I said, I waited to tell you because I was so afraid I'd miscarry. But everything is going well. Tom is over the moon with happiness. I am, too."

She practically glowed with joy. Shelby got up, circled the desk, then hugged her.

"I'm thrilled for you. This is fantastic." She sat on the edge of the desk. "Wow."

"I know." Amber sighed. "It's terrifying and wonderful. I'm considered high risk, because of my age. So I'm going to do everything I can to make things go smoothly."

Shelby held up her hand. "You don't even have to ask. I'll work more hours and take on anything you want me to. Pretend you don't even own a bakery."

"Thanks. I was hoping you'd be okay with me taking it easy. There's a lot to worry about and at the same time, I'm not supposed to worry." She touched her tummy. "I'm so happy."

"I'm happy for you."

Amber stood. "We'll talk soon, okay? Oh, and if you could not say anything for a few days. I'm telling close friends and family first. My dad is beyond excited, of course. Threatening to buy one of every children's book ever published."

Shelby smiled, imagining Morgan's happiness at

finally being a grandfather. "I won't mention it until I hear it from another source."

Amber grinned. "Of course you can tell Aidan." She covered her mouth. "Oh, no. I can't believe it. I'm sorry. Here I was going on and on about the baby, when you have other things on your mind. Congratulations on the marriage. That's so great."

Shelby thought about pounding her head against the desk. "We're not married."

"What? You're divorced already?"

"No. We were never married. The ad was a joke because we…" She waved her hand. "It's not important. Pretend you never saw that announcement."

"Okay. Well, for what it's worth, I think you two make a cute couple."

"Thanks."

THE RETRACTION IN the paper got about as much reaction as the ad. Aidan watched Shelby pace the length of his office before she turned around and went the other way.

"It's just so strange," she said as she walked back and forth. "Everything is changing. With Amber pregnant, I'll have more responsibility at the bakery, which I like. But she won't be around as much, which will make it harder to change things." She looked at him. "I'm not comfortable just doing what I want without talking to her first and if she's not there, she won't be available to discuss anything."

"Right. She also might feel so stressed about the baby that she doesn't want to take on one more thing."

"I know." Shelby turned and walked back the other way. "I'm happy for her. Really happy, but the timing. I wish we'd been able to do more. Plus, after the baby's born she's going to be busy, so talking to her then will be hard."

"Are you that unhappy with how things are?"

"No. It's good. I love my work. But we could be bigger. The building next to us won't be available forever." She grimaced. "Not that it matters. Amber would never agree to the expansion now. She's got the baby to deal with. There would be expenses and construction and stress. It's just that I had all these plans."

He stood and moved toward her. "It's okay."

She came to a stop in front of him. "It's kind of not."

"Okay—then how about me saying you'll get through this. We'll talk about it and you'll come up with some solutions."

She looked at him. Her bangs were too long. They were practically in her eyes. The look was adorable.

One corner of her mouth turned up. "What you really want is to tell me exactly what to do. I appreciate that you're not."

"I'm here to listen."

She leaned against him. Her forehead rested on his chest and her hands settled at his waist. "Why does life always have to have a sense of humor?" she asked, her voice muffled against her chest. "I'm such a bad person."

"You're not. You're happy for your friend, but

frustrated because of what her news means for the business. Neither emotion is wrong."

She raised her head. "You swear?"

She was close. So close he could feel the heat from her body. It would only take the lightest of touches to pull her up against him. Then they would be touching everywhere. While it wasn't all that he wanted, it got him a good part of the way there.

"Aidan?"

He was sure it was his imagination, but it seemed to him that the word came out as a plea. A request. One he couldn't resist. He lowered his head those last few inches and pressed his mouth against hers.

He was pretty sure he'd caught her off guard, so he half expected her to pull back. Only she didn't. She stayed exactly where she was, her lips against his.

Her skin was warm and soft. Her hands moved from his waist to his shoulders. His slid around her body. He took a step forward—or she did?—then they were pressed against each other and it didn't matter who had moved first.

Wanting struck him like lightning, burning hot and bright. His breath caught in his throat as the need grew. She fit him perfectly. Her breasts nestled against his chest. Her belly rubbed against his growing erection. And then there was the kiss.

Her mouth was everything he'd hoped for. Hot and sweet and willing. She parted her lips before he asked and he eagerly swept inside. Heat grew until it consumed him and all he could think was how much he wanted her.

His hands were in her hair, stroking her neck, her back. Everywhere he touched was perfection. This was Shelby, he thought hazily, deepening the kiss until they were both straining toward each other. The woman he liked as much as he desired. The woman whose laugh made him happy. His friend and his—

Friend. The word was like a bucket of ice water. He drew back slightly, breaking the kiss and resting his forehead on hers. Their breath came in gasps. The rhythm matched the aching pulse in his groin. He was harder than he'd ever been, so ready to make love with her. He wanted her naked and writhing. He wanted to please her, then fill her until his release threw him to the other side of the universe.

The primal side of him told him she wanted it, too. That she was still touching him, still leaning into him. She had to feel his dick against her belly and she was okay with it. He nearly drowned in the images of them together. It was going to be so good.

But the rest of him—that damned sensible, civilized part of his brain, nearly starved for blood— reminded him that there was so much more on the line than what he wanted. Even if he was willing to ignore his own goals, what about hers? She needed to be healed so she could move on with her life. Sleeping with her now could totally screw up everything.

No pun intended.

"Dammit all to hell," he muttered, his voice hoarse with passion. "I respect you. I like you. I want you to have everything you're looking for. And it's not this."

Even though it was the most difficult thing he'd ever done, he took a step back.

Shelby stared at him. Her eyes were wide, her pupils dilated. She looked aroused and beautiful and it was all he could do to keep from reaching for her again.

"You should go," he told her. "Just go."

She started to speak, then shook her head before turning and walking away.

AIDAN HAD KNOWN for a while that his brother had a secret studio in the woods. He'd even visited Nick there on occasion. But he'd never explored it. Beyond looking at whatever piece Nick was working on, he hadn't thought about what else might be stored there. Now he stood beside his brother and stared at the rows and rows of incredible creations.

There were wood carvings. Dozens of them. Some finished, others in various stages of completion. He could see the traditional bears and deer, a few raccoons. But there were also life-sized human figures. A dancer with one leg in the air. A woman holding a baby. They were so real, he half expected them to move.

Nick's glasswork was just as extraordinary. Swirling shapes as big as a man. There was a glass tree, huge bowls, a slithering snake nearly six feet long.

"What's that line from that old movie, *Jaws*?" Aidan asked. "We're going to need a bigger boat."

"I've always been an overachiever."

That was one way of putting it. Aidan didn't know where to begin. When Nick had asked for help, he'd jumped at the chance to get out of his head for a few hours. He hadn't seen Shelby in a couple of days, but that didn't mean she wasn't with him. He couldn't stop thinking about their kiss. Hard labor moving heavy pieces of wood and glass would go a long way to distracting him. Or so he hoped.

"What are you going to do with it all?" he asked.

"Sell some. Put some in storage. The rest of it can be kindling. Or melted down."

Charlie walked along the rows, sniffing as he went. Aidan knew the little guy would stick close. Over the past couple of months, he and Charlie had become a team. Or was it a pack? Charlie went pretty much everywhere with him. Aidan was still playing with different designs for a sturdy wagon/dog carrier so the bichon could go hiking with him. He figured Charlie would keep up as best he could, but expecting him do five or eight miles uphill was too much.

Nick pulled a pad of stickers out of his back pocket. "Red dots are going to the gallery. Green dots are storage. Blue dots get destroyed."

Aidan winced. "How can you do that? Destroy something you created?"

"It's not hard. Some pieces aren't meant to be finished. There's a fatal flaw, either in the raw material or the design. Either way, they're never going to be anything."

A harsh assessment, but he would guess a mindset that was required for an artist. From failure came the chance to try something better next time.

He followed his brother through the huge studio. Light poured in through windows and skylights. Nick hesitated in front of a two-foot-high carving of a boy with a fishing pole.

The kid sat cross-legged. His expression was intense, as if determined to wait it out, however long it took. The features were delicate, yet masculine. Looking at the perfectly carved hands reminded Aidan that his brother was an incredible artist.

Nick stuck on a blue dot.

"What?" Aidan demanded. "That's a brilliant piece. Even I can see that."

Nick turned it so Aidan could see the crack running down the back. "I doubt it's going to split further, but I can't sell it."

"I'll take it."

Nick looked at him for a second, then smiled. "Thanks."

They finished going through the pieces, then began to move them into different parts of the studio. Some of them could be simply carried into place, but others required the two of them to wrestle them or use a hand truck. A few of the bears had to wait until they had more man power.

Charlie supervised for a while before settling on the small sofa in the front part of the studio. After a couple of hours, Aidan and Nick joined him to take a break.

Aidan opened the beer his brother had handed him and took a drink. "You're really going."

"If not to Happily Inc., then somewhere."

"Have you told Mom?"

"No. I want to have a plan before I mention it."

"She's not going to appreciate having yet another of her sons leaving town."

He thought Nick might crack a joke, but instead his brother's expression turned serious. "It's all going to be on you now. The family thing. I'm sorry about that."

"I can handle it. I don't get her relationship with Dad, but there's no getting around the fact that she loves him. He's her world. The rest of us are a distant second." He took another drink. "I think that's how it's supposed to be when you're married, though. Sure the kids are important, but they grow up and move away. If you lose your partner while dealing with your children, then one day you have nothing."

Nick's brows rose. "What is Shelby doing to you?"

Aidan laughed. "Nothing bad. We talk about stuff. Sometimes it's good to talk."

"No, it's not." Nick swore. "Maybe you're the one who needs to leave."

"I belong here."

"Because of the business?"

"Some. I like it here." There had been a time when Aidan had chafed against what he'd seen as being trapped. When Del had left, the family business had fallen to him. But over time, he'd realized this was where he was meant to be.

"Are you happy?" Nick pressed.

"That's a very girly question."

"You, of all people, should be forgiving of that," Nick pointed out.

"I am." Aidan thought for a second. "Yeah, I am. What I was doing before, going from woman to woman, it was a way of hiding. I thought I was playing it safe, but acting like that came at a price. I was a jackass."

"And now?"

"Less of one, I hope." He reached over and rubbed Charlie's ears.

"This is Shelby's doing?"

"Some of it is her and some of it is me."

"You're still not..." Nick's voice trailed off.

Aidan thought about the kiss and how much he'd wanted her. How he'd resisted. How he hadn't talked to her since.

"No. It's not like that."

"But you want it to be like that." Nick raised his bottle of beer. "That wasn't a question, by the way. You want her."

"Who wouldn't?" Aidan exhaled. "But we're friends. And I like being friends with her. I like her. Sleeping together would change everything."

"Maybe not. Maybe if you did it, you could get her out of your system and go back to the way things were."

Aidan had a bad feeling that wasn't likely to happen. Shelby wasn't the do-it-once-and-forget-her kind of woman. "That's not gonna work."

"Then sleep with someone else."

"I can't."

"Why not?"

"We have a deal."

"One that's not working."

"Then we should probably talk about that."

Aidan turned and saw Shelby standing in the open door of Nick's studio.

CHAPTER TWELVE

"I AM SO out of here," Nick said.

"You don't have to go," Shelby told him, because it was the right thing to say. In truth, she needed Nick to go so she could talk to Aidan.

She'd been avoiding him for forty-eight hours. If she'd been able to avoid herself, she would have done that, too. Because she was nothing if not confused. Confused about the kiss and what it meant. Confused about what to do next. When she'd suddenly realized she had to talk to him, he hadn't been at his office. Fay had told her where to find him.

Now she waited, shifting her weight from foot to foot as Nick collected his car keys.

"Lock up when you're done," he told his brother and left.

Charlie hurried to greet her. She crouched down to pet the dog, grateful for the distraction. But eventually she had to stand back up and face Aidan.

They stared at each other from across the room. She had no way of knowing what he was thinking. For all that they were friends, there were still mysteries between them.

He motioned to the sofa. "Have a seat."

She settled at one end. Aidan took the other. Charlie curled up between them and put his head on his paws. Silence filled the open space.

Shelby tried to think what she should say first. Or maybe she was just hoping he would start talking, because that would be so much easier.

"I miss you," Aidan said.

The unexpected statement shocked her into confessing, as well. "I miss you, too. It's been hard not hanging out. Or talking on the phone or texting."

She glanced at him, then away. She drew in a breath and returned her gaze to his. "We have to talk about the kiss."

"I know."

"Really?"

"I'm not saying I *want* to talk about it, I'm saying we should. Unless you agree that it was just a kiss and we should let it go?"

He sounded so hopeful, she had to smile. "No."

"I didn't think so."

"But you made the effort. That counts."

"Not enough." He leaned toward her. "Shelby, we're not going there. It would be a mistake. I want you, that's pretty obvious. Being together would be amazing. But that's not why we're here."

He *wanted* her? Little butterflies danced through her tummy. He wanted her! Anticipation filled her as she thought about how good she'd felt in his arms. How safe and sexy and hungry.

"It's not the worst idea," she began.

He cut her off with a shake of his head. "It would be a disaster."

"Why? You have a lot of experience. You know what you're doing."

She'd been hoping he would at least crack a smile, but he continued to look serious.

"We're doing something good here," he told her. "I don't want to lose that."

"So if I threw myself at you right now, you'd refuse me?"

"Regretfully, yes."

Ouch. "But you won't sleep with anyone else until the six months are over?"

"No, I won't. We had a deal."

Talk about an honorable man, she thought glumly. One with integrity. She should be thrilled. Impressed. Instead all she felt was rejection and mild annoyance.

While she'd never considered herself a prude, she wasn't exactly anyone's ideal of a temptress. So seducing Aidan was out of the question. Besides, as much as she didn't like to admit it, she kind of respected his stand. If only it weren't so confusing.

Because he was right. They were doing something good. But after that kiss, well, everything was different now.

"I can't decide if I should applaud you or beat you with a stick," she admitted.

"How about we go back to being friends?"

Her cell phone rang before she could answer. She glanced at the screen and saw it was her sister-in-law.

"It's Destiny," she said as she pushed the green button. "Hi. Everyone okay?"

Destiny's voice cracked. "N-no. It's a mess. I'm a mess. I really need your help."

"You sure you know what you're doing?" Destiny asked, her voice doubtful.

"He's fine," Shelby assured her, before Aidan could admit that he was clueless.

He still wasn't sure how everything had changed so quickly. One minute he'd been trying to convince Shelby they couldn't be lovers—what kind of twisted world had it become that he was saying *that* to a beautiful woman he desperately wanted?—the next they were driving to Destiny's house.

The new mother looked exhausted. She was pale and there were dark circles under her eyes. Shelby had taken the baby from her and handed it over to him, then had started making tea.

Aidan held the six-week-old in his arms, careful not to wake her. He had to admit, she was a beautiful little thing, with a tiny nose and a sweet mouth. As long as she stayed asleep, he could handle this.

Destiny sat at the kitchen table. "Kipling's been gone for two days. He offered to cancel his trip, but he'd been looking forward to the conference. I said everything would be okay. And Starr's busy with her life, so it's just been me and Tonya. She's a really good baby, but half the time I don't know what I'm doing. What if I break her?"

Shelby spooned tea leaves into the mesh basket, then set it inside the pot. The kettle on the stove was already starting to make a low whistling sound. She turned off the heat and poured the water into the teapot.

"You're not going to break her," Shelby said. "Destiny, you're one of the most organized people I know, but you need to learn to ask for help. You've just had a baby. Everything is new and scary and you don't have to do this alone."

"I know." Destiny wiped away tears. "It's just I feel like such a failure. I'm tired all the time."

"Do you get any sleep?" Aidan asked.

"A couple hours every now and then."

"Not nearly enough."

Destiny sniffed. "Starr's a teenager. I don't want to ask her for too much. She needs to be having fun with her friends. But her birthday's coming up and I can't find the time to plan it like I should and I'm trying to write a couple of songs and there's all kinds of prepublicity for the tour and I'm fat!"

She started crying again, this time covering her face with her hands. Shelby pulled up a chair next to her. After wrapping her arms around her, she drew in a breath.

"Let me see if I understand the situation. You're dealing with a baby. You're breastfeeding, so you have to get up every couple of hours to do that. You're cooking for your husband and your sister, taking care of Tonya, taking care of the house, all the while you're trying to write new music, planning a national tour, doing publicity for the tour and maybe rehearsing the songs with Starr? There's also her birthday and you're trying to get back into shape after, hey, giving birth."

"Uh-huh. Oh, and they sent over DVDs with the choreography on it. I have to learn that."

Aidan felt exhausted just hearing the list. "Get a housekeeper," he said. "And a part-time nanny.

You're going to need one for the tour, so find one now so you're comfortable leaving the baby with while you're performing. Tell Kipling to get his ass back here. He's the dad. He needs to take a little more responsibility. You're right about Starr. She's a teenager. Let her live her life. Shelby and I can handle the birthday party."

Both women stared at him. Destiny's mouth dropped open.

"What?" he asked defensively. "Was I supposed to be just listening?"

Shelby smiled. "No. You were supposed to be fixing and you did a very good job."

SHELBY SKIMMED THE Pinterest board. People were so creative, she thought happily, making notes as she studied different music-themed cupcakes. The crisis with Destiny had been managed, and one of the results was that she and Aidan were planning Starr's sixteenth birthday party.

Aidan had suggested a music-themed party and Shelby agreed. They were going to have a lot of fun with that. They'd decided on the 1950s as their musical era, which opened up so many possibilities.

Amber walked into her office and took a seat. Her business partner wore a loose yellow shirt over jeans. Her hair was pulled back, her makeup light. She was barely showing, but she radiated a contentment Shelby hadn't seen before.

"You're glowing."

Amber laughed. "Thank you. I feel good. Healthy.

The morning sickness is gone, thank goodness. That was awful. How are you doing?"

"I'm great. Business is fantastic, as you know. My teens are doing wonderful work with the cookies. I want to start putting a schedule together for the summer tourist season. We have the food cart for the festivals and some of the other projects we've been talking about." She held up her hand. "Don't worry, I'll handle it all."

She expected her business partner to tease her about her plans, but instead she seemed to crumple a little.

"I've made a decision," Amber said as she squared her shoulders. "I know it's the right thing to do, but it's going to mean a lot of changes."

Shelby didn't like the sound of that. "What kind of changes?"

"This pregnancy is so unexpected. So life-altering. I want to experience it fully. I want to be there for my baby." Amber drew in a breath. "Shelby, I'm going to sell the bakery and I'd like you to consider buying it from me."

AIDAN HAD PROMISED that riding a BMX bike up the side of a mountain would clear her head. Shelby was less sure. Mostly because she wasn't able to think at all. Or breathe. But maybe that was the point. Maybe all the panting and gasping and dealing with the shooting pains in her leg were meant to distract her from the indecision she'd been wrestling with for the past couple of days. And if they were, they were working.

It was a beautiful day. Sunny and cool. Signs of spring were everywhere. Buds and new leaves covered the trees. Wildflowers carpeted the ground. She could hear birds calling to each other, and a light breeze whispered through the branches.

All of which would have been much easier to observe if she weren't so worried about falling off her bike.

"Stay in the middle of the trail," Aidan called from behind her.

She didn't know which was more annoying—the instruction or the way he was barely breathing hard.

She was in shape, she told herself. She worked out. Although apparently not enough, she thought as she bounced over a rut in the path. She rounded a corner, then came to a stop when she saw the trail went *up* the mountain. Pretty much in a straight, vertical line.

Aidan pulled up next to her. "I promise, the view is worth it."

"Couldn't we just buy a postcard?"

He laughed.

The sound made her smile. Being here like this, even on a bike, was good.

"My butt's going to hurt later, isn't it?" she asked.

"No pain, no gain."

"That's total crap, invented by a masochist. You can't convince me otherwise."

He pointed to the top of the trail. "Can you make it?"

"Let's find out."

She began to peddle. Her thighs screamed in protest and her lungs soon followed. She kept her head down, focusing only on the next couple of feet. Up and up. Eventually she would get there.

"Come on, Shelby," Aidan called. "Just a few more feet."

She made it over the crest of the trail and found herself staring down at the town in the valley below. A view that would be a lot prettier if she stayed conscious.

She lowered the bike to the ground, then pulled off her helmet and braced her hands on her trembling thighs as she gulped in air.

Aidan passed her a bottle of water. "Drink slow. A sip only."

A sip? Her throat was dry, her body hot and her heart racing. None of it in a good way. She took the bottle and straightened, then parted her lips and let mouthfuls of the cold water pour down her throat.

"Shelby, stop—"

That was all he got to say before she felt the first spasm. She dropped the bottle and clutched her stomach. Seconds later, all the water came up as she vomited.

The retching continued for several minutes. When she was done, she collapsed to her knees and braced herself with her hands on the dirt.

"I hate biking," she managed between gagging and coughing.

"It doesn't seem to be your sport," he agreed. "Can you sit?"

She rolled onto her butt and rested her head on her knees. She was hot and sweaty and humiliated. What was she supposed to say after something like that?

He kneeled next to her and used a damp cloth to wipe her face, then handed her the bottle of water.

"Sip," he said firmly. "Wait twenty seconds, then sip again."

"I'm sorry."

His mouth turned up. "Don't be. It happens a lot. Nobody listens and then they pay the price."

"I'll never doubt you again."

He laughed. "If only that were true."

She got down a few sips and began to feel better. The mountain air cooled her and her heart rate returned to normal. Even the view was more appealing than it had been.

And while she would love to sit and admire it, there were decisions to be made and things to talk about.

"Thanks for offering to help with Starr's party."

"Are you kidding? It's going to be the best. I've gone online and looked around. There are a lot of great things we can do."

"I never thought you'd enjoy planning a party for a sixteen-year-old girl."

He touched his chest. "You wound me. Why wouldn't I? I like Starr and turning sixteen is a big deal. I wonder if Kipling's teaching her to drive."

Shelby started to take a drink of her water. She put down the bottle and stared at him. "No! We are not having that conversation. Don't you think there's enough going on without us dealing with whether or not Starr learns to drive?"

"She has to learn. I just worry that Kipling doesn't

have time. Not with Destiny and the new baby. Starr shouldn't get lost in all of this."

"Now I feel guilty," she admitted. "You're being more sensitive than me."

"I'm a very sensitive man."

"Apparently."

All humor aside, he had a point. Starr needed to learn to drive. It was a rite of passage for every kid in America, plus it would be a big help at home. Destiny was already overwhelmed. Shelby could understand that. Hearing her to-do list had been shocking. Wasn't it enough to have a new baby, a new husband and a half sister in the house? But there was everything else.

"It's really hard when you're a better person than me," she grumbled. "Fine. We'll talk to Kipling about the whole driving thing."

"I am pretty amazing," Aidan said with a grin. "You're very lucky to have me."

"All I hear is buzzing," she told him.

He laughed.

The happy sound drifted across the mountains. She sipped her water and let herself enjoy the moment. A couple of problems solved, and a few more waiting in the wings. Wasn't that always the way?

"Ready to talk about it?" he asked quietly.

She knew what he meant. The "it" in question was Amber and the bakery. "Sure." Not that she knew what to say.

"You kind of have to go first," he told her. "I can guess, but I'll probably get it wrong."

She looked at him and smiled. "You're saying

the W word. Won't you be drummed out of your gender?"

"Not if you don't tell on me." He touched her face, then lowered his hand to the ground. "What are you thinking?"

She was thinking that it felt nice to be with him. That she'd puked up her guts and he was still right there. She was thinking he was a great guy and she'd done well when she'd chosen him. She was thinking she didn't want the friendship to be over in six months. Oh, sure, they'd still be friendly, but it would be different. He would be dating and she knew that would change everything. They wouldn't have organized time together, like now, and she would miss him.

There were other thoughts, too. Swirling images of their kiss and how that kiss had made her feel. She'd known he was right to pull away. That getting involved on a physical level would change everything. But... How was she supposed to forget? How was she supposed to let it go? It wasn't the wanting that haunted her, it was the rightness of it all.

Which was nothing but a distraction. A *handsome* distraction, but a distraction all the same.

"I don't know what to do about the bakery," she admitted. "I know what I want. But is that what makes sense? I'm still in shock, of course. I didn't see this coming. I knew Amber was pregnant, but it never occurred to me she would walk away from her business."

"You want to buy her out."

Not a question, she thought. A statement. But

then, guessing that was hardly a challenge. Aidan knew her.

"There's so much that could be done there. Ways to expand the business. But Amber's the one with all the experience. Maybe there's a really good reason she didn't do all this before. Maybe my ideas are stupid and if I implement them, the business will completely fail."

His dark eyes were gentle. "Do you really believe that?"

"Sometimes. I don't know what to think. I don't know what to do. I'm excited and scared and confused, all at the same time."

"Let's look at this another way," he said. "What *don't* you want?"

Talk about the right question at the right time. She drew in a breath. "I don't want to be stuck." She smiled at him. "Which I believe I get from you. I don't want to be stuck somewhere that makes me unhappy. I'm not saying I don't want to work for someone else. That might be okay, depending on who it was. I don't know. I love my job, but sometimes I feel too contained. I have all these ideas and maybe some of them are crazy, but some of them are really good. I want the chance to experiment, to try new things. I want a fleet of food carts at every festival and my cookies shipped across the country. I want to be synonymous with happy good times. Okay, not me. The business."

"Breathe," he told her. "You can't make any of it happen if you don't breathe."

She did as he suggested, then took another sip of water. "What are you thinking?"

She had to ask, because she couldn't tell just by looking at him. But she knew whatever he was thinking, it was kind and supportive. She wasn't afraid of what he would say. Even if he told her he thought buying the business was a mistake, she would know he meant well. That he only wanted the best for her.

She would have to remember this feeling. When their six months were over and she went looking for a man to fall in love with, she wanted to feel just like this when she was with him. Safe and cared for. And she wanted to make him feel the same way.

"I think you should buy the business."

That was a lot more blunt than she'd been expecting. "How can you say that? What do I know about running a business? What if I do everything wrong? What if everyone quits and no one ever buys another cookie from me again? I'll die broke and alone and humiliated."

"That's the positive spirit we all admire."

She glared at him. "Is this you being funny? This isn't funny. This is very serious."

Aidan didn't look the least bit impressed by her outburst. He stretched out his legs in front of him and smiled. "Did I mention breathing? That's rule number one. After that, everything else is easy."

"What do you know about breathing? You have a successful business. It's easy for you to say what I should and shouldn't do. You're not the one who's going to fail."

"Neither are you. You want this, Shelby. You've

wanted it for a long time. You talk about being stuck. Well, you were stuck with Amber. You wanted to fly and she never wanted to get off the ground. I'm not saying you were right and she was wrong. We won't know that for a while. But this is your chance. Run with that. Not that many people get the opportunity to go for their dream. This is your moment. Grab it with both hands."

She opened her mouth, then closed it. What was she supposed to say to that? If this was her dream, then she was a fool to let the chance get away from her.

"I'm scared," she admitted. "Really scared."

"All the more reason to go for it."

Was he right? Or maybe that wasn't the correct question. Maybe the real question was, how would she feel if she never even tried?

CHAPTER THIRTEEN

SHELBY HAD NEVER considered herself an overly emotional person. She'd been through a lot in her life and she'd had to deal with some horrible situations. Because of that, she'd spent time in therapy. She was pretty confident that she understood how her psyche worked. She watched people, tried to understand them and respond appropriately. She almost never sat in a business meeting fighting the urge to cry.

Yet here she was blinking rapidly, hoping she didn't look as upset as she felt. No, not upset. Touched. Grateful. She'd come to Fool's Gold with nothing. She'd been accepted, taken in and welcomed in every way possible. Even if she tried to forget, she was reminded over and over again.

"Business valuation is both simple and complicated," Sam Ridge was saying. "There are the tangibles. The value of the equipment, the value of the inventory. As this is the bakery, I'm assuming most of your inventory is disposable." The former NFL Super Bowl–winning kicker smiled. "I'm thinking brownies rather than cars."

"You're right," Shelby said. "We don't have very many cars to sell."

"So no real inventory other than ingredients.

There is an income stream—how much is made each week, each month. From that you subtract what you pay out. The cost of flour, sugar and butter. Employee wages. Insurance, rent. Now's where it gets tricky. Everything has to be given a value. The mailing list for out-of-town customers. The recipes, the logo, the goodwill the bakery has established. The reputation is worth something. The question is how do you put a price on that?"

Patience Garrett wrinkled her nose. "No offense, Sam, but you're scaring me and I already own Brew-haha. I can't imagine what you're doing to poor Shelby."

Sam looked surprised. "I'm giving her advice. I thought that's why we were here."

"There's a difference between advice and torture." Patience patted his arm. "You're such a guy. Luckily, Shelby and I happen to like that in a person." Patience turned to her. "Shelby, are you doing okay?"

Shelby nodded, mostly because it was too hard to speak. Her throat was tight and her eyes were burning. Now if she gave in to the tears, the symptoms would go away. But then she would embarrass the very nice people who had come to help her. And that help, that very unexpected help, was the reason for the tears.

Apparently she wasn't the only one Amber had told about selling the bakery. Word had spread everywhere. In the past couple of days Shelby had received lots of unsolicited advice on what to do. The consensus was very clear. Everyone wanted her to buy Ambrosia Bakery.

When Patience had called to ask her to stop by, Shelby hadn't known what to expect. The fact that Sam Ridge was also at the meeting had surprised her. Then Patience had poured her a cup of coffee and Sam had started talking. Unlike the other people who had come by the bakery to offer their opinions, Sam and Patience had actual, practical advice. Twenty minutes into his explanation on business valuation, her head was spinning but she was also feeling more confident. At least now she knew what to ask.

"Amber will be really fair," Patience said. "I've known her my whole life. She's very sweet."

"This is business." Sam sounded firm. "You don't mess around with business. Get everything in writing. Do you have an attorney?"

"I need a lawyer?" Shelby hadn't thought of that. There were a lot of things she hadn't thought of. Doubts crept in, but she pushed them away. Aidan was right. This was her chance to follow her dream. "I guess I'm going to need an accountant, too."

"I can recommend both," Sam told her. "You're going to need a loan to buy the business. There are several ways to structure that. The loan officer can go over those terms with you, but I can give you a basic rundown now."

He spent five minutes going over amortization and balloon payments. Shelby's head started to hurt. She was good at designing cookies and coming up with new brownie recipes. Not talking about finance. How much was the bakery going to cost? She had a small savings account, but she was beginning to see it wasn't even going to be close to enough.

Patience reached across the table and put her hands on top of Shelby's. "Don't freak out," she instructed. "I know this is overwhelming." She smiled at Sam. "No offense, but you're way too thorough."

"I'm just trying to help."

"You are," Shelby assured him. "I really appreciate this. You've given me so much to think about."

Patience's expression was sympathetic. "But?"

Shelby drew in a breath. "It's a lot," she admitted.

Patience drew back her hands and smiled. "Here's what I can tell you. I had dreamed about opening my own business for a long time. But there was no way it was ever going to happen. I didn't have the money or the experience. When I got the chance, I was so excited. And I was scared. It was a risk. I knew that. I could have just put my inheritance in the bank and gone on with my life. But I knew I would regret that always. I had to choose between playing it safe and following my dream. Now, a couple of years later, I'm so grateful for the decision I made. Only you know what's right for you, Shelby. I'm just reminding you that the chance to follow your dream doesn't happen very often."

"So I'm here to offer the scary advice while you get to be the motivational one?" Sam asked.

"Pretty much." Patience's voice was cheerful.

"I'm not even surprised." But Sam was smiling as he spoke.

"I really appreciate this," Shelby told them. "Not just your time, but your words. A lot of people have been telling me to just go for it, but you two offered me practical steps. That means a lot. There's so much to think about."

"You'll get there," Patience assured her. "Just listen to your heart. We can all give advice, but you're the one who has to decide what's right for you. No one else." She grinned. "I'm so glad Aidan called. This has been fun."

"I agree." Sam winked at her. "We could take our act on the road."

Shelby blinked. "Aidan phoned you and asked you to talk to me?"

"Uh-huh." Patience sighed. "You two are such a great couple. He's worried about you. I love that in a man. I never thought I'd see that player brought to his knees, but here he is, acting like a man in love."

Shelby didn't know what to deal with first. "We're just friends."

"Is that what we're calling it?" Sam asked, as he rose. "Let me know if you have any more questions." He handed her his card. "You can stop by the office or set up a meeting. Whatever works for you. In the meantime, I'll get you those names."

"Thank you."

He left. Shelby hugged Patience and thanked her, then walked out onto the street.

She was no longer fighting tears, but did still have a spinning head. Aidan had taken the time to get his friends to help her. Talk about supportive. And unexpected. Not that he wasn't a great guy, but still. This was above and beyond.

Patience was wrong. They weren't in love. They were friends and today that seemed so much more important.

HAVING SURVIVED DESTINY'S DELIVERY—albeit from a distance—Aidan considered himself an old hand at the giving-birth thing. So when he heard that Isabel Hendrix had gone into premature labor, he knew supplies would be required. Which was why he swung by the bakery instead of Shelby's house. She'd said that Isabel would want pretzel bread and he knew better than to ask why.

He barely had time to stop his truck before she raced out of the bakery. She had two tote bags with her. One was filled with loaves of bread, the other had boxes of cookies.

"Thanks for coming to get me," she said with a smile. "You didn't have to. I could have done this myself."

"And miss out on all the fun? No way. Plus this probably gets me out of a girl thing later."

Shelby put the bags in the backseat, then climbed up beside him and fastened her seat belt. "You can pretend all you want. I know you like the girl things."

Aidan knew what she meant. But at the mention of "girl things" all he could think about were the differences between men and women. More physical than emotional. How much he liked those differences… and missed them.

For the greater good, he reminded himself as he drove to the hospital.

"Like them or not, it's always good to have a rain check in my back pocket."

"I'll give you as many as you want," she said. She shifted in her seat until she was angled toward him. "I can't believe what you did for me. No, I take that back. I totally believe it."

Her voice was earnest, her body language intense. As if she wanted to make sure he understood what she was saying.

"What are we talking about?" he asked cautiously.

"You having Patience and Sam talk to me. It was scary and wonderful at the same time. They had so much information." She straightened in her seat. "Hey, wait a minute. You have a small business. Why didn't you tell me all this yourself? You must know everything there is about running a business."

"While I enjoy you thinking of me as a god, the truth is I know what I need to know to make *my* company work. Not what you need to know. I figured talking to someone with a financial background, like Sam, would be helpful. And I knew Patience had been through something similar. You could bond over your joint experience."

"Is that sarcasm? Women don't automatically bond over every little thing."

"You kinda do."

She sighed. "Fine. Maybe. Regardless, thank you. And I owe you. You're really a good friend."

Her compliment warmed him. Not that he needed much warming when she was around. Still, he appreciated the sentiment. "You're a good friend, too. So did they help?"

"Patience gave me a lot of moral support. Sam was more practical. I have a very long and growing to-do list. There's a bunch of people I need to talk to. A lawyer, a banker. I don't think I've ever talked to a banker. Oh, I take that back. I started to take out a loan to buy into the bakery. It was a brief conversation. And a little scary. I guess a lawyer's going to be even worse."

"They're not my favorite people, but they're very necessary. At least that's what I tell myself."

They pulled into the hospital parking lot and found a space near the door. Aidan carried the bags inside. He and Shelby got on the elevator. "I can't believe this our second pregnancy visit in such a short period of time," she said.

"We are a town of breeders."

She laughed. "That must've made you nervous, with all your lady friends."

"Not me. I'm a big believer in protection. Easier for both of us."

One corner of her mouth turned up. Her eyes began to sparkle and he knew he was in trouble.

"Whatever you're thinking," he warned her, "don't say it out loud."

The doors to the elevator opened on to the maternity floor. She smiled sweetly and said, "The condom companies must've really loved you. Did you get a Christmas card every year?"

"Funny," he grumbled. "Very funny."

Finding Isabel's room turned out not to be a problem. It was easy to spot from all the people milling about outside in the hallway. Aidan would guess that a good percentage of her family, not to mention her husband's, had already arrived.

Madeline saw them and waved them over. "She's doing great," Isabel's business partner said. "She had a C-section, of course. It was triplets. Three girls! They're all above three pounds, which is fantastic. The big issue with triplets is low weight at birth. It sets them up for all kinds of problems."

Shelby hugged her friend. "Someone's been on the internet."

Madeline laughed. "I wanted to appear knowledgeable. I figured people would be asking questions. Hey, Aidan."

"Maddie."

Madeline wrinkled her nose at the nickname. "One of the disadvantages of living somewhere your whole life is the person who can always make you feel like you're six years old."

"You loved it then and you love it now."

She grinned. "Shelby, honey, when all this settles, remind me to tell you about the time Aidan got very powerful glue on his hands and then had to pee."

He groaned. "You wouldn't."

Madeline smiled. "I would and I will. Now come see the beautiful mother."

The crowd made room for them as they walked into the hospital room. Aidan didn't know if all maternity rooms were singles, but with the number of people visiting Isabel he doubted the hospital would've had a choice either way. Her parents were there, along with her husband's impressive family. Ford was one of six children and his three sisters were also triplets. Denise, Ford's mom, had her boy-friend, Max, along. Aidan winced as he thought the B word in association with a woman well into her fifties. But Denise and Max weren't married and he didn't know what else to call the man. *Life partner* just seemed so weird.

Shelby rushed to her friend's side and they em-braced. Aidan sidled over to where the men were standing. Ford looked a little shell-shocked.

"How you holding up?" Aidan asked him.

"I'm not," Ford admitted. "I've seen combat. I've seen a lot of bad stuff. Nothing prepared me to watch a doctor slice open my wife's stomach like a water-melon and pull babies out. They should warn you."

Aidan didn't know if he should laugh, offer a hug or run for the hills. The latter seem to make the most sense but he told himself to suck it up. He only had to hear about it; Ford had had to live it.

"I mean I knew it was triplets," Ford continued, shaking his head. "I saw an ultrasound. The doctor was very clear. But jeez, when they pulled out one baby after the other and they were so damn small." He stared at Aidan. "I'm talking *small*. What are we supposed to do with them?"

Aidan was saved from answering when Shelby waved him over. She showed Isabel the pretzel bread and the new mother promptly burst into tears. The hormone bath continued as the other women rushed into see what was wrong. He busied himself setting out the boxes of cookies, then slowly, very slowly, backed into the hall. He figured Shelby would know where to find him.

What he didn't expect was to see his parents in the hallway outside the room. His mother, maybe, but his father? Ceallach wasn't really interested in anything but himself.

His mother smiled when she saw him. "We heard the good news and came to see Isabel and the babies. Have you been down to the nursery? They're so beautiful. Tiny, but beautiful. She must be so happy." His mother hugged him. When she straightened, her gaze was direct. "I want grandchildren."

Aidan took a step back and held up both hands. "Don't look at me. Del is the one who's engaged. Talk to him and Maya."

"I want grandchildren from *all* of you. You need to get started on that. Shelby is a perfectly nice girl. What are you waiting for?"

Aidan held in a groan. There was no way he was getting into the we're-just-friends conversation yet again. He turned to his father.

"Hey, Dad. How's it going?"

His father looked at him. Ceallach's gaze sharpened as if he just now realized who was in front of him. "You! This is all your fault."

"There's five of us. The grandkid thing is not just on me."

"You're the reason Nick's leaving. You're the one chasing him away." His father's voice rose with each word.

"Is that what you really think?" Aidan asked. "That I have anything to do with this? You're wrong. This is all about *you*, Dad. This is all *your* doing.

There's a reason every one of your sons have left Fool's Gold. Do you ever stop to think about that?"

Elaine put a restraining hand on his arm. "Aidan, don't. You'll upset your father."

"Yeah, we wouldn't want that, would we?"

He turned away and started for the nursery. Anything to get away.

A few minutes later, as he stared unseeingly at the tiny babies behind the glass, he felt more than heard Shelby come up beside him. She stood close.

"I heard the fight," she told him quietly.

"I don't want to talk about it."

"Okay."

"Just like that?"

"Sometimes talking isn't required. You've taught me that." But she did reach for his hand.

They laced their fingers together as they watched the sweet new babies sleep through their first day in Fool's Gold.

"YOU DON'T REALLY need my help," Shelby teased. "I've seen you make much more complicated things."

Aidan dumped the graham-cracker crumbs in the bowl. "Are you kidding? This is done in three parts. I've never made a three-part dessert before."

She wondered how many desserts he'd *ever* made before they'd met. Maybe cookies. With the help of a girlfriend. Since they'd started hanging out together, he'd learned how to cook all kinds of things. At first Shelby did most of the work, but these days she simply supervised and offered advice.

On the menu for today—key lime pie. Aidan had

already squeezed a cup of key lime juice. He'd been shocked when she'd told him it would take over a pound and a half of limes to get that much. Then he'd seen how tiny they were and how little juice came out.

They were at his place. His kitchen was a little bigger than hers. More important, he had to get used to working there. Because she wasn't always going to be around to help. A thought that made her feel strange, so she didn't linger on it. Even so, the truth was there. June was getting closer and closer. Their six months would end and they would resume their regular lives. While she was sure she and Aidan would always stay in touch, she knew that everything would be different.

He pulled the melted butter from the microwave and added it to the graham crackers. He put on disposable gloves, then mixed the two ingredients with his hands before pouring the mixture into the pie pan.

"You want to get it even," she told him from her seat at the island. "I know it's counterintuitive, but do the sides first. Try to get the thickness the same before worrying about the bottom. If there's too much crust left, we can scoop it out. If it's too thin, we can make a little more."

He worked intently, pressing the graham crackers into the side of the pie pan.

"I'm sorry about my dad."

The statement was unexpected. Since they'd run into Ceallach and Elaine at the hospital, he hadn't said anything about the incident. She wasn't sure he would ever want to talk about it.

"If you're apologizing for what he said, you don't have to. I know he's a jerk."

Aidan looked at her, his brows raised. "Are you being critical of my father?"

"Yes, and he deserves a lot harsher than what I said. He's awful. I'm sorry—I know he's family and I should keep my mouth shut, but I can't. You never say very much, but I hear things. And now I've seen him in action. What's wrong with him? Why on earth would he blame you for Nick leaving? You had nothing to do with that."

"I might have suggested it when we had our fight. That night in the bar."

The night that had changed everything, she thought. The night she'd watched Aidan and his brother argue and not hit each other. When she'd realized that even furious, Aidan was still reachable. Everything she'd read in her self-help books, everything she'd talked about in therapy, had suddenly made sense. What her father had done, *who* he'd been, wasn't normal. She didn't have to be afraid all the time.

"Are you saying Nick is so spineless that you tell him to do something and he does it?"

Aidan grinned. "Of course not."

"So how is this on you? Besides, you're not the problem. Ceallach is. He's not a nice man."

"No, he's a genius."

She snorted. "That's no excuse for bad behavior. Kipling was a world-class athlete and he manages to be a decent guy. Being gifted isn't an excuse to be a jerk."

"You're so fierce," he teased.

"You're my friend. I don't want anyone hurting you."

His humor faded. "He can't hurt me, Shelby. That power ended a long time ago."

She knew he believed what he was saying, but she was less sure. From all that she'd learned and experienced personally, parents could always hurt their children. It was just one of those things that came with being a kid. Being someone's child wasn't a connection you outgrew.

"I think the problem is no one expected anything of him," she said. "Emotionally, I mean. Because of who he was and what he could do, he wasn't required to live up to the rest of society's standards. He got a pass and somewhere along the way, bad behavior became synonymous with brilliance."

"Speaking of standards." Aidan showed her the pie pan. "Even enough?"

She inspected the crust. "Perfection. Okay, into the oven and set the timer."

He pulled off his gloves, did as she requested, then read over the next step of the recipe.

"It wasn't just society," he said as he collected eggs from the refrigerator. "Mom always told us we had to work around Dad's schedule. She enabled him from the start. He doesn't have a bigger fan than her. She would walk through fire for him."

Shelby leaned against the island counter. "Is it just women who do that?" she asked. "I hate to generalize, but how often do men act that way? Surrendering to another person because they're supposedly so gifted. I'm sure it happens, but we seem to hear about women doing it more. Do you think we're biologically more ready to serve?"

"By *we* you mean all women?"

She smiled. "Yes, Aidan. I wasn't including you in the *we* statement."

"Good. Because I'm the only other person here. I accept getting in touch with my feminine side, but I'm not ready to start a gender-changing journey."

She looked at his broad shoulders and the handsome lines of his face. "Not something you have to worry about. And you didn't answer my question."

He grimaced. "I was hoping to distract you."

"I promise you won't get in trouble for your answer."

"I'm taking you at your word." He pulled a whisk out of a drawer. "Yes, I think women are more willing to worship, for lack of a better word, when it comes to the men in their lives. I don't know if it's biological or cultural. But more women than men will live in servitude. My mom is a prime example. She would tell you it was for the greater good. That the world is a better place because of what Ceallach Mitchell has created. If there was a price paid for that, she would say it was worth it."

"Would you?"

One shoulder rose. "I don't know. We all survived. We're all doing fine. Every childhood has a few bumps and bruises."

She knew what he meant by the phrase, but found

herself thinking of her mother. Of how she'd allowed Shelby's father to beat her. When did a parent cross the line from supportive spouse to monster?

"Shelby? You okay?"

She shook off the thought. "What? I'm fine. Why?"

"You went white." Aidan circled the island and stood in front of her chair. "What happened?"

"I thought of my mom as a monster. How could I? I loved her so much."

He cupped her face in his heads. "This is so above my pay grade, but I'll make a run at it. Yes, you loved her. But she didn't protect you. I agree that a married couple has to stand together. One day the kids will be grown and they need to be there for each other. But sometimes one of them is just plain wrong. Whether or not you believe in spanking a child, there's never an excuse to beat one. Your father was wrong to ever touch you, and your mom was wrong to let it happen. Leaving or not leaving was her decision to make for herself. I don't pretend to understand the psychology of being an abused spouse. But what I do know is that she should have stood between you and your father's fists. Whether or not she left, she should have protected you. She should have kept you safe. Whether she could have done it or not, I don't know, but she should have tried."

Shelby stared at him. "He's not the reason I can't trust," she whispered in shock. "She is. I knew he was broken. I knew there was a darkness inside of him. But she was different. Normal. But she let him do those things. It's not him, it's her."

Tears filled her eyes. She willed them away, but they fell. Aidan pulled her close and wrapped his strong arms around her.

He didn't say a thing. There were no promises that everything would be okay. She liked that. She liked his strength and that he didn't seem to mind her getting his shirt wet.

She tried to process what she'd finally figured out. She felt lighter and a little sick to her stomach. Men like her dad were easy to avoid, she thought. Brutes rarely wore a disguise. But her mother was different.

"I still love her," she whispered. "How sick is that?"

He drew back and cupped her face again. "You're not sick. You're incredibly strong. Look at all you've been through, yet here you are. Happy, successful. Most people would never have figured out there was a problem, let alone done something about it. You came up with a plan to get better. You roped me into it. You're one of the most impressive people I've ever known, Shelby. I'm honored to be in your life."

His words settled over her like a blessing. She took them in and let them fill the broken bits of her. Healing would take time—it always did. But she'd made a start. A good one.

"Thank you," she murmured.

He kissed her forehead. "You're welcome. Better?"

She nodded.

"Good. Because in a couple of hours, we'll have pie."

She laughed.

He lowered his hands and took a step away. Without thinking, she grabbed the front of his shirt to hold him in place. His dark gaze settled on her face.

She read the questions there. He wanted to know if she was okay. If she needed more from him. Because he would give it.

He was a good man. Next to her brother, he was the best man she knew. She liked him. She liked being with him.

"Let's make love."

Aidan swore and retreated to the far side of the kitchen. "Dammit, Shelby."

"I mean it. I'm not playing. It will be great."

He sucked in a breath. "I can't believe I'm going to say this, but no. We're not screwing this up with sex. This is the best relationship I've ever had with a woman. I care about you. I'm not going to let some random hookup change that."

Interesting how she felt disappointment but not rejection. Maybe because she knew he wanted her. And while his determination to do the right thing was annoying, it was also pretty darned wonderful.

"It wouldn't be a random hookup."

"You know what I mean."

He looked frustrated and desperate and on the verge of bolting. The timer dinged.

The relief on his face was nearly comical. He hurried to the stove and pulled out the pie crust.

"Oh, look. It's done." He pull it on the cooling rack, then turned to her. "We can't."

"I know. I'm sorry. I won't ask again."

"Like I believe that." He swore. "You're killing me. You know that, right? Because saying no is the right thing and I want to and I won't." He groaned. "I really am a woman."

She laughed. "You're not. You're wonderful. This is the best relationship I've ever had, too. I really am sorry."

"That you asked or that we're not doing it?"

"Both."

CHAPTER FOURTEEN

SHELBY WALKED THROUGH the vacant property next door to the bakery. She knew nothing about construction, but she wasn't about to let that stop her from dreaming. Assuming it was possible to break through at least part of the wall between the two storefronts, she could have easy access front and back, with the ability to close it off. So a tea shop in front and a bigger kitchen in the back.

Adding a professional kitchen would be expensive and time-consuming. She'd been doing some research online and the prices had nearly made her faint. But if she was going to go for it, now seemed like the time. The space was there. If she didn't rent it, someone else would.

The advantage for her was that she could help design the new kitchen. She could put in extra ovens to increase her capacity on the bakery side.

She alternated between excited and terrified. Both emotions were probably normal, considering what she was doing. Talk about a huge leap into the unknown. But not doing it wasn't an option. She didn't want to spend the rest of her life wondering "what if?"

She carefully locked up behind her and put the

key in her pocket. Josh Golden had agreed to give her forty-eight hours to make up her mind. She was going to have to let him know by this time tomorrow. Not that she would need that long. She already knew what she was going to do.

She returned to the bakery. Eddie Carberry stood by the counter.

"I've been waiting for you," Eddie announced. "She wouldn't tell me where you were."

The clerk behind the counter smiled apologetically. "I offered to take a message."

"You're fine," Shelby assured her. "What can I do for you, Eddie?"

"I want custom cookies for my bowling league. Let's go in your office and talk about them."

Shelby generally had those kind of meetings up front, in the small eating area. But Eddie seemed resolved. It was kind of surprising how a woman in a lime-green tracksuit could radiate determination, but Eddie did.

Shelby led the way. When Eddie was seated on the visitor side of her desk, Shelby walked to the bookshelf by the door.

"I have lots of samples of cookie designs here," she said. "Or if you have a sketch, we can work from that."

"Shut the door."

Shelby looked from the old woman to the door, then shrugged. She doubted Eddie was going to rob her, or threaten her. She shut the door and then sat at her desk.

"I didn't want anyone overhearing us," the other woman said in a low voice. "This is private."

Shelby couldn't imagine what the "this" was. Maybe Eddie had fallen in love and wanted a surprise wedding cake? Or there was going to be a birthday for someone?

"I have money," Eddie said abruptly. "Not millions, but plenty."

Shelby tried to stay relaxed. "Okay," she said slowly. "Congratulations."

Eddie rolled her eyes. "I'm not looking for praise, you silly girl. I'm offering you a loan. So you can buy the bakery. You could pay me back over time. With interest. And if I die before it all gets returned, then I'll forgive the loan."

Eddie's eyes narrowed. "Let me be clear. That's not a license to off me. I'll have a provision in my will that if my death is suspicious, you're the first one they're to investigate." Her expression softened. "But I don't think you'd do that."

Shelby opened her mouth, then closed it. "I honestly don't know what to say. Thank you. I'm stunned, but thank you."

Eddie clutched her large purse in both hands. "You're welcome. I've been watching you ever since you moved here. You were such a frightened mouse in the beginning. You've grown since then. Blossomed. You have backbone and that can't be taught. You're smart and honest. You'd be a good bet."

The words were as lovely as they were unexpected. "Thank you," she said. "You're being so nice."

"Humph. Don't tell anyone. I have a reputation in town. Anyway, you think about it." Her expression turned stern. "You are going to buy the bakery, aren't you? Because if you don't, you're an idiot."

Shelby laughed. "Yes, I am. I'm going to tell Amber right now."

"Good. I'd hate to be offering my money to an idiot." She rose. "Let me know what you want to do."

"I will."

Shelby stood and circled the desk. Before she opened the door, she hugged the old woman. Eddie was smaller than she seemed. Like a little bird. But when she hugged back, her hold was fierce and powerful.

Shelby walked her out, then went into Amber's office.

"Do you have a second?" she asked.

Her business partner looked up. "I do. Have you made a decision?"

"I'd like to buy the business."

Amber laughed. "I'm so glad. I was hoping you'd say yes. This is fantastic. We have a lot to do. I'll get my lawyer going on the paperwork and we'll need to get the business valued. Oh, Shelby, you're going to do great. I know you are. You have so many ideas and so much energy."

"I'm excited."

"Me, too! Let's celebrate with a cookie."

Shelby laughed. Because champagne was out of the question. But there would be plenty of bubbles later. With Aidan and the rest of her friends.

THE WEARY CAMPERS stepped out of the van as Aidan unloaded their backpacks and set them on the ground. Charlie, who'd already spent five minutes greeting Aidan, sniffed everything.

"Best time ever," a teenage boy told his dad. "We have to do this again next year."

"Maybe we'll bring Mom along," his father said.

The teen laughed. "Like that'll ever happen."

The rest of the group seemed equally pleased with their long weekend. The weather had been perfect—warm during the day and cool at night. The signs of spring had been everywhere in the mountains, from the wildflowers to the newborn fawn they'd seen.

Aidan ushered everyone into the office, where they signed the forms that confirmed they were back where they'd started, then checked the van one more time for forgotten gear or cell phones.

He hadn't slept much while on the trip. He never did. Now all he wanted was a hot shower and about ten hours in his bed.

The latter thought had him picturing Shelby, but he carefully pushed that image away. Sleep. He needed sleep.

"How about a walk before we head home?" he asked the dog.

Charlie wagged his tail and followed Aidan into the office. Fay was finishing up with the last of the customers. She pointed to where Charlie's leash lay on the counter.

"Kalinda played with him most of the morning," his office manager told him. "I knew you'd want to crash and that wouldn't work if your boy was rest-less. So he should be tired, too."

"Thanks for that, and for taking care of him."

Fay petted the dog. "Are you kidding? We all love having him. You should go on more trips where you can't bring him. I won't complain."

"I'll keep that in mind." He yawned. "I'll be back to check messages, then I'm heading home."

"See you in a few."

He clipped on Charlie's leash. They opened the front door just as Aidan's mother was reaching for the handle.

"Mom. What are you doing here?"

Elaine looked at him. "I just wanted to stop by. I haven't seen you in a while." She frowned. "You look like you haven't shaved."

"I was on a backpacking trip for three days. I'm going to take Charlie for a walk, then go home and crash."

"Oh. Well, can I walk with you?"

He wanted to say no. There was nothing his mother could say that he wanted to hear. Only that wasn't how he'd been raised. So he nodded and pointed to the trail he and Charlie liked to use.

They walked in silence for a few minutes. When they were clear of the office, Aidan let Charlie go off-leash. The bichon gave a quick bark of apprecia-tion before trotting off to investigate the trail.

"Will he be all right?" Elaine asked.

"He doesn't go far and he always checks back with me," he told her.

"He's sweet, like Sophie."

Aidan thought that Sophie was a bit more of a mischief maker than Charlie, but didn't say anything.

"Your father is sorry about what happened at the hospital."

"No, he's not."

His mother sighed. "Aidan, you're too hard on him."

"Am I? I'm happy to see you, Mom, but you don't have to apologize for him. He's no different now than he's ever been."

He remembered what Shelby had realized. That her fear, her anger, was as much toward her mother as her father. Was it the same for him? Ceallach had been difficult for years, but his mother was the one who didn't demand better for herself and her children.

"He loves you," she insisted. "He'll never say it, but I know he feels it."

"If you say so."

Which was more polite than what he was thinking. As far as he was concerned, his father barely knew who he was. Without having the ability to create art, Aidan couldn't possibly matter. The statement had no moral value. It simply was. His father would never change. Neither would his mother.

Aidan had never thought about that before. That his parents simply *were*. He struggled to understand what Elaine saw in her husband, but maybe that wasn't his job. Instead of trying to make sense of it, he could accept the facts as they were.

Charlie trotted back to check on them. Aidan gave

him a quick pat, then picked up a small stick and threw it. The little dog raced after it.

"I wish you and your brothers could see things from his perspective," she said with a sigh.

"There's a scary thought."

"Why?"

"I'm not ready to peek into the mind of an artist."

"It's so interesting that three of you have his gift and you and Del don't."

Interesting wasn't exactly the word he would have used.

"Are you ever sorry?" she asked.

"I can't miss what I've never had. I don't know what it's like to create in the way Nick and the twins do." He paused as he realized what he'd said. "Sorry, Mom. I still think of them as the twins."

"I do, too," she admitted. "They'll always be that to me."

"And Ronan will always be your favorite?"

She stopped. "He was never that."

Aidan waited.

Elaine made a tsking sound. "It wasn't like that." She linked arms with him and they started walking again.

"When your father told me what he'd done, I was devastated. I had to forgive him, of course. Because if I didn't, I couldn't stay."

"You wanted to be with him always." Not a question. How could it be when he knew the answer?

"Of course. He told me about the baby and that she wanted to give it up. I knew what he was asking. What he expected. I couldn't agree, but I did say I would go see the baby. That's how I thought of him then. As the baby."

Her expression turned wistful. "I knew I'd hate him on sight. That I'd have to refuse. Then I held him and in that moment my heart told me the truth. That I could love him as if he'd been one of my own. We took him home that day."

"What happened to his birth mother?"

"She died a few years later. We were notified through a lawyer. I'd already adopted Ronan legally, so that wasn't an issue. He's your brother, Aidan. As much as if I'd given birth to him."

He couldn't imagine that level of love. To take in your partner's bastard child and raise it as your own. Joyfully. He would bet his mother never once regretted what she'd done. Never had a moment's doubt. He might not agree with her feelings about his father, but he couldn't question the size of her heart.

He put his arm around her and drew her close. "You're an extraordinary woman, Elaine Mitchell."

"Don't be silly. I'm just like everyone else."

He knew that wasn't true on so many levels. He supposed the character that kept her stuck with his father had been the reason she could love Ronan so deeply. The good with the bad.

Maybe there weren't answers, he thought as they continued walking along the trail. Maybe there was only acceptance and the knowledge that most people did the best they could with what they had.

ONE OF THE things Shelby liked best about living in Fool's Gold was the rhythm of the seasons. Festivals, banners, decorative flags and window art marked the passage of time in a charming and engaging way. There was a sense of community. Of belonging. Which meant when the call went out that help was needed to plant flower baskets, everyone volunteered.

So she wasn't surprised when she showed up at the Plants for the Planet parking lot and found over a dozen people already there. She waved at several friends, then smiled when she saw Aidan had taken charge of things. He'd divided them into groups of three. Baskets and soil were being distributed, as were flowers. Shelby walked over to join him.

"Look at you, all in charge."

He shrugged. "Felicia was here about fifteen minutes ago and passed the baton to me. It's planting flowers. How hard could it be?"

"You should take more credit."

"I will later. When I'm talking to my friends, I will have single-handedly done all this myself."

She laughed and went to join a woman working by herself. She was in her midforties and Shelby thought maybe she'd seen her at one of the single's group functions.

"Shelby, right?" the woman asked as Shelby approached. "I'm Fran. Nice to see you again."

"Hi. This should be fun. Very spring-like."

Fran handed Shelby a pair of gardening gloves. "I like to get my annual volunteer project done early. Then I don't have to feel guilty for the rest of the year."

"I hadn't thought about it that way, but you're right. Good for us."

Shelby collected a half-dozen baskets while Fran opened a bag of soil. Together they maneuvered it into place so they could fill the baskets to the designated mark.

"He's good-looking," Fran said, nodding toward Aidan. "When I first met you two, you said you were just friends. Is that true?"

"Uh-huh."

"I'm sorry to be nosy, but why? If you're both available, why wouldn't you want to take advantage of that?"

Shelby didn't know how to answer the question. Oh, she had plenty of words, but no one ever believed them. "It's an experiment," she said at last. "I needed to learn to trust men and Aidan, well, he needed some time off his regular life." Because what Aidan was dealing with was his business, she thought.

"We agreed to be friends for six months. To get to know each other and simply hang out and do things without letting sex get in the way."

"But sometimes sex is the best part," Fran pointed out. "Don't you miss it?"

"Of course. Aidan's totally hot and I'd have to be dead not to think about it. But doing without is better."

"Why?"

"We're focused on what's important. I've really grown and changed in the past few months. I'm a better person."

"Sure." Fran sounded doubtful. "I guess that's

worth something. I'm not saying sex is the only thing that matters, but honestly, I don't know how you're doing it. I would simply throw myself at him."

Shelby busied herself with smoothing the soil so that Fran couldn't see her face. She *had* thrown herself at Aidan. More than once. And he kept telling her no. She knew why. At least, she was pretty sure she did.

Unless he was just being kind.

The concept was so shocking, she nearly fell over.

"You okay?" Fran asked.

"Yes. Sorry. I lost my balance. Let me start taking the flowers out of the plastic containers. You can put them in the pots."

"That works."

Shelby concentrated on removing the little squares of soil and roots, then passing the plants over to Fran. Her fingers were moving in one direction, but her brain was somewhere else.

Was that it? What if Aidan had no interest in her? What if he really did just think of her as a friend? Maybe he was saying all that other stuff to be kind. She knew that he liked her…at least as a friend. So he wouldn't intentionally hurt her.

Was that it? She didn't want it to be, but maybe it was. Maybe he was embarrassed by her behavior. Or worse—maybe he felt sorry for her! She couldn't stand that. Just thinking about it made her face get hot. She wanted to run. She felt embarrassed and ashamed.

She watched him circulate among the groups and

knew it was just a matter of time until he joined them. What was she going to say?

Whatever was most appropriate for the situation, she told herself. She hadn't done anything wrong. Liking someone wasn't bad. Wanting to make love with Aidan didn't make her an evil person. She was attracted to him. There was no shame in that.

"You ladies doing all right?" Aidan asked.

Shelby forced herself to look up and smile. "We're great. With so many people helping, we'll be done in no time."

"We still on to visit Destiny later?"

She wanted to say no. She wanted to say there'd been a change of plans. But after she'd moved to Fool's Gold, she'd promised herself she would never react out of fear again. So she nodded. "We are."

"Good."

He walked away. Fran stared after him.

"You're a stronger woman than me," she said with an appreciative sigh. "I would so want me a piece of that."

Shelby and Fran continued to work on their baskets. About an hour later Felicia returned with several guys driving trucks. The baskets were loaded up to be distributed and displayed around town. Shelby stripped off her gloves, got a bottle of water and started to walk home. She had an hour until Aidan would be by to pick her up and she wanted to shower.

But before she got to the end of the street, she heard a woman calling her name. She turned and saw Taryn Whittaker walking toward her.

Despite Taryn's five-inch wedge heels, she moved

quickly. Her white fitted dress emphasized her lithe figure. Her dark hair was pulled back in a braid that moved in time with her steps. She looked cool and elegant, not to mention totally at odds with the town. But that was Taryn. She didn't let living in Fool's Gold keep her from her love of all things designer.

"I've been looking all over for you," Taryn said as she approached. "Were you gardening?"

Shelby glanced down at her dirty jeans and smudged T-shirt. "Does it show?"

Taryn laughed. "I garden, too. At home, where I can give Angel instructions while I watch. I do enjoy watching that man lift and tote." She sighed. "Which isn't why I wanted to talk to you. Do you have a second?"

"Sure."

Taryn pointed to a bench. They walked over to it and sat down. Shelby ignored the sense of being a peasant next to a princess. For all her extensive grooming, Taryn was a regular kind of person. At least on the inside.

"So I've heard about you buying the bakery. I think that's fantastic," Taryn began. "This town is all about female power and I don't want that to change."

"I'm not sure buying a small business qualifies as female power, but okay."

"It does. Trust me." Taryn lowered her voice. "I've been very fortunate in my career. Score is successful and with success comes financial reward. Jack helped me when I was young. He didn't have to, but he did. Ever since, I've made it a point to do the same. Help other people. Buying a business is expensive. Rumor is you want to lease the space next door and add a commercial kitchen. Also not cheap. I absolutely think you should go for it. To that end, I'd like to offer you a loan. My terms are fair, slightly better than the bank, and I require less paperwork."

Shelby sucked in a breath. "Taryn, that's so generous. And shocking."

"I've done it before," the other woman said. "To be honest, I have my finger in a few pies around town." She laughed. "Pies is a fun metaphor considering you're going to buy a bakery, but you know what I mean. It's up to you. Just think about it. I don't want to be your business partner. We'd make sure there was a buyout strategy. I'm just saying, if you want it, the money is yours."

Shelby didn't have all the numbers yet, but she'd gotten some preliminary estimates from a contractor and the remodel was going to be over seventy thousand dollars. When added to how much she would need to buy out Amber, it was a lot of money. She thought about asking Taryn if she was prepared to offer that much, then realized the question was silly. Taryn would have done her homework before seeking her out.

"You're even more well-off than I'd thought," Shelby admitted.

Taryn laughed. "Like I said. I've done well. I want to pay it forward. Or whatever that phrase is." She smiled, then rose. "Think about it."

"I will. I promise."

CHAPTER FIFTEEN

"YOU'RE GOING TO let him run the meeting?" Destiny asked, her voice teasing.

As the question wasn't directed at him, Aidan didn't bother answering. He wasn't concerned with what Destiny thought about him. Instead he found himself oddly relieved that she seemed so much better.

"Aidan is a very capable party planner," Shelby murmured in a low singsong voice. "Isn't he, my beautiful girl? Yes, he is. Yes, he is."

Had she been anyone else, he would have totally freaked at her obvious affection for Destiny's baby. Even from across the living room, he could hear the *tick-tick* of her biological clock. But it wasn't his problem, he told himself. He and Shelby weren't together that way. She wasn't going to look to him to be her baby daddy.

A good thing. He wanted to improve his character. Not settle down. At least that was what he'd always told himself.

Destiny sipped what looked like a disgusting green smoothie and eyed him. "A party planner, huh? How many parties have you planned?"

"My entire business is about getting people from

point A to point B and back safely, on skis or bikes or while parasailing. I can handle a birthday party for a sixteen-year-old."

Her eyebrows rose. "Aren't we confident?"

"Aren't we feeling better than we were last time?"

Destiny laughed. "Okay. Point taken. I'm giving you sass because I'm feeling pretty good. I'm sorry about the meltdown the other day."

"You're a new mother. You have a lot going on." Shelby touched the gurgling baby's face. "Your mommy is a famous singer. Yes, she is."

"I'm not famous."

"Not yet. You will be."

"Maybe. I'm not sure I want that," Destiny admitted. "I saw what too much fame did to my parents. But some kind of success would be nice." She sipped her drink and looked at Aidan. "Let's talk about the party."

She was completely different from the last time he'd seen her. The dark circles were gone and she seemed more relaxed. He knew that in addition to letting them take care of Starr's party, Destiny had started sharing the responsibility of Tonya a little more. She'd also told her manager to back off for the next month while she continued to recover from childbirth. An impressive turnaround.

He supposed the lesson was that everyone was capable of changing, when motivated. Look at him. He'd come a long way.

Tonya began fussing. Shelby rocked her. Destiny took one more sip of her green drink, then stood.

"Sorry, guys. She's hungry. I was hoping she'd

eat before you got here, but we're having another schedule shift. Give me ten or fifteen minutes and I'll be back."

She collected the baby and walked out of the room. Shelby watched her go.

"She has to be so happy," she said wistfully.

"Feeling the need?"

"A little. I always knew I wanted kids, but I was scared. If that makes sense."

"Sure. You wouldn't want anyone to go through what you went through. Why wouldn't you be cautious?"

"You're becoming so insightful."

He gave any exaggerated sigh. "I know. Perfection looms. Soon I'll be a demigod."

She laughed. "If only that were true. I could say I knew you when. Do you want kids?"

And they were back to that.

For a second, he felt a tightening in his chest. The precursor to panic. But there was no need for worry. Not with Shelby. He would trust her the way he wouldn't trust other women.

"Sure. Kids would be great. I like kids. I come from a big family, so more is better."

"I'd like four," she told him.

"That's a lot."

"I like the idea of happy chaos and noise. Plus they'd be there for each other the way Kipling was there for me. That was always a good feeling."

Aidan nodded. "When I was growing up, Del had my back. We both took care of the younger ones.

Especially the twins." He paused. "I'm never going to think of them as anything other than the twins."

"Does that have to change?"

"They're not twins. They never were."

"But it's how you think of them. I wonder if it's how they think of themselves."

Aidan had no idea how Mathias and Ronan had worked things out. Or even if they had. "They live in the same town, work in the same studio space. They must have come to terms in some way."

"It had to have been hard, though. One second they thought they knew who they were and the next, their whole identity had changed. Ronan lost his family and Mathias lost a part of himself."

He wanted to say she was being dramatic, but he wasn't sure. Maybe she was the one who had it right. Ronan must have felt like a fraud, or at the very least, an interloper. Mathias would have, as Shelby had pointed out, lost a piece of who he was. He knew for his two youngest brothers, their "twinness" had defined them. What had it been like to find out it had never existed?

"Look at us, all philosophical," Shelby teased. "Next thing you know, we'll be solving global problems."

"Or attempting to."

She laughed and stood, stretching her arms over head before bending down to touch her toes.

She was petite, with small bones and a slightness about her that belied her internal strength. He should have realized how tough she was when she'd first approached him about her plan. That had taken guts and determination.

"What are you thinking?" she asked when she'd put her arms at her side.

"About how you stalked me back in January."

"I didn't stalk you. I considered you a good candidate and I was right. We're good together."

"We are."

He wouldn't have guessed that they would become such good friends. When the six months were over, he knew things would change between them, but he hoped they would still spend time together. He liked being with her.

But wanting it might not be enough. She would be busy with her new business and he would be in the high summer season. Plus they would probably each be looking for a relationship. Shelby had been very clear about what she wanted. A man she could fall in love with. While he was looking for—

"Okay, that's a serious expression," she said. "What?"

"I don't know what I want."

"In life?"

"When this is over. You and me. You're going to go find Mr. Right, get married and have four kids. What am I going to do?"

"What do you want to do?" She raised a hand. "No, that's the wrong question. Does being in love still mean you're stuck?"

A question he hadn't considered in a long time. When he'd been a kid, he'd seen his mother's devotion to her husband as a bad thing. Now he was less sure. He didn't agree with her choices, but he thought maybe he understood them more.

Shelby sat next to him on the sofa. She angled toward him and took his hand in hers.

"She could have stood between you and Ceallach, but she didn't. That was her decision. That decision speaks to her and not to the entirety of being in love."

"You're saying I learned the wrong lesson?"

Her blue eyes were wide and filled with compassion. "Yes. Love simply is. Each of us reacts differently to the feeling. Your mom and my mom are a lot alike. They both fell in love with difficult men. They both chose to sacrifice their children in the name of that love. We saw what happened and made connections. You learned that love makes you stuck. I learned that love makes you weak. We've been unable to trust in love ever since. At least not romantic love."

"And now?" he asked.

She smiled. "I trust you."

"I trust you, too."

Simple words. Easy words, yet they hit him like a freight train. He was momentarily immobilized by their impact. He trusted her. Wholly and without reservation. He'd never trusted a woman before. Not that way. In fact, outside of his brothers, he wasn't sure he'd ever trusted anyone as much.

He reached for her just as she leaned into him. She went into his arms as if she'd always belonged in them. In the second before their lips touched, he felt desire mingle with certainty. This was right. Being with Shelby was right. He wasn't sure why he'd resisted for so long.

At the first brush of his mouth against hers—

"Ha! I knew it." Destiny walked into the living room with her baby on her shoulder. "All this we're-just-friends crap. You're not just friends. You were *kissing*!"

Shelby scrambled to the other side of the sofa. "We weren't."

Destiny's smug expression never changed. "Really? Did Aidan faint and you were giving him mouth-to-mouth?"

"It was an accident," Shelby amended. "We really aren't together."

"It's my fault," Aidan said. "Leave her alone."

Destiny stared at him. "Is that how it is?"

"Yes."

She studied him for a second. "All right. Let's talk about the party."

Shelby looked between them. "What just happened?"

"Aidan won't let me tease you," Destiny said. "He's being protective."

Shelby relaxed. "He does that all the time."

"Interesting," her sister-in-law said. "Now, about the party."

Shelby pulled a notepad from her bag. "We're still thinking about a 1950s-music-themed party. I saw the most creative cupcakes online. There were a couple of ideas that I really liked. My favorite was cupcakes in the shape of a guitar. They were iced to look like one, too."

Destiny grinned. "Starr would totally love that."

"We'd have music from the fifties," Aidan told her. "There are plenty of playlists we can buy. For games, we'll do old-fashioned board games like Scrabble and Candyland. Along with Twister."

"It's girls only, right?" Shelby asked.

"That's what she says she wants," Destiny told them. "Kipling and I are so grateful. I didn't want to have to sweat that much supervision."

"You could also do fun manicures." Aidan took the notepad and read from the list he and Shelby had put together. "The supplies would be easy to assemble and then the whole kit could be put in some kind of pretty bag. That could be the party favor."

Destiny's mouth dropped open. "You know about parties like this having a favor?"

"I was at your baby shower."

"I know, but…" She looked at Shelby, then back at him. "Um, sure. The manicure kits are a great idea."

They talked about the party for another few minutes. When it was time for Destiny to put Tonya down for her nap, they said their goodbyes and left.

"The party is going to be so much fun," Shelby said as they got in his truck. "Starr is going to love it."

"I hope so. Plus we'll enjoy putting it together."

"I'm very excited about the cupcakes."

He wasn't surprised. Shelby would enjoy the challenge of creating something that special.

"You could play around with different kinds of cupcake cakes," he said. "Take pictures and offer them to your customers. Especially for kids' parties.

Cupcakes are easier than having to cut up a cake. You could make some kind of template for the design. Like if somebody ordered a dinosaur cake. You make it out of cupcakes, then number the individual cupcakes on the bottom so the parents can use the template to re-create that shape and design wherever they wanted it. A park or someone's house."

She looked at him. "That's a great idea. I love the template. I've used them myself, but I've never thought of offering them to customers. They would be easy to do on the computer and then print out." She laughed. "You're so much more than a pretty face."

"Thanks."

He drove without thinking and found himself pulling into his driveway rather than the office, where he'd left Charlie and she'd left her car. She looked around.

"I thought you were taking me home. Did you want to do something instead?"

An innocent question. He knew how she meant. He also knew exactly what he wanted to do.

"I'd like you to come inside," he told her. "Then I'd like to make love with you."

She swung her head back to meet his gaze. Her eyes were wide, her expression surprised. "But you said…"

"I was wrong."

"About us being friends?"

"About me being able to resist you. I can't. But I need you to be sure. It's going to change everything."

SHELBY KNEW HE was right. That their relationship would forever shift.

She wanted him. That much was clear. And she loved knowing he wanted her, too. But what about the risks? She liked Aidan so much—she liked how they were together. She most especially liked how he always looked out for her. Even now, he wanted her to be sure. If she said no, he would back off in a second.

"Do you have condoms?" she asked.

He laughed. "Yes. A large box."

She smiled. "Is that a large box of condoms or a box of large condoms?"

"I guess you're going to have to wait and find out."

He turned off the engine and they both got out of the truck. Shelby waited for him to walk around to her side. In that heartbeat of time, she poked at her emotions to make sure she was completely comfortable with her decision. There were nerves, but they were the anticipation kind. More pole-dancing butterflies than frightened ones.

He reached her side and took her hand. Their fingers laced together with an ease that made her relax, even as his touch warmed her.

"About my reputation," he began as they walked to the front door. "You seem to have a certain expectation."

"I do," she teased. "I'm going to see stars and touch the moon and all that stuff."

"I'm not sure how I feel about that."

"Pressure?"

He opened the door and let her go first. "Some."

"So I shouldn't expect too much?"

He walked in behind her, then closed and locked the door. He turned to her and pulled her close.

"I wouldn't say that."

The confidence in his voice sent a shiver through her. The feel of his body against her caused her to start melting from the inside out. And when he lowered his mouth to hers...well, thinking became impossible.

They'd kissed before. Friendly kisses, brief kisses, even a kiss or two with passionate undertones. But they'd never kissed like this. She hadn't known what it was like to be claimed by Aidan.

He held her firmly, yet gently. His mouth moved against hers, exploring, teasing, promising. When she parted her lips, he moved his tongue inside and brushed against hers with a rhythm designed to take her from interested to aroused to begging.

He moved his hands down her back to settle on her hips. That was all—the possessive touch of his hands on her body. He didn't move them, but the weight, the pressure, the firmness of the hold mesmerized her. Maybe it was the promise of what was to come. Maybe it was slight kneading of his fingers. Maybe it was all in her head, but she didn't care.

She rested her hands on his shoulders, then moved them to his back, where she could feel his strong muscles and the warmth of his skin below his shirt. She liked the broadness of him, the scent of him, the way he tasted.

He drew back just enough to kiss each corner of her mouth, then her cheeks. He kissed his way along her jaw, then nibbled the lobe of her ear. The combination of warm mouth and sharp teeth had her catching her breath.

Heat burned hot in her chest and radiated out in all directions. Her skin grew more sensitive, as if nerve endings were pushing closer to be touched by him. She wanted to crawl inside him so she could experience all of him.

He continued to kiss his way across her neck. Her head fell back. At the same time, his hands moved up her sides, across her ribs, to her breasts. Through the layers of her T-shirt and bra, he cupped her breasts. His thumbs moved across tight nipples in a single, light touch. Pleasure shot through her and her breath caught.

He did it again, then again. It was as if he knew the exact way to touch her. As if he was part of the feedback loop in her mind.

He dropped his hands to the hem of her T-shirt and pulled it up and over her head, then he kissed her. His tongue plunged in deeply, and she met him with needy strokes of her own. At the same time, he reached behind her and unfastened her bra. The garment fell to the floor. She felt the cool air on her breasts seconds before his hands covered her.

He took her curves in his large hands, pressing in slightly. Thumbs and forefingers settled on her nipples and played with the tight tips. A direct line of need and enjoyment formed between her breasts and her groin. Heat and arousal began to move back and forth, growing with each round trip. When he lowered his head, she caught her breath in anticipation. He closed his lips around her left breast and sucked deeply.

She gasped as the sensations surged through her. Delicious wanting grew as he circled his tongue around her nipple. He flicked over the very tip and then used his teeth to gently grate against the sensitive skin.

Down low in her belly, she felt the rising tension. Her thigh muscles were stiff in an effort to support her, while her knees threatened to give way. She was swollen and wet and desperate. When he moved to the other breast and repeated his efforts, she had to hold on to him to stay standing.

He straightened. "Shoes. Take them off."

She did as he instructed. He did the same and pulled off his socks, then hers. Then he moved behind her. "Hold up your hair."

She complied.

He nibbled his way from shoulder to shoulder. The light touch made her shiver. Her breathing increased. On the return trip, he moved his hands to her breasts and used just his fingertips to trace circles on her skin.

The contrast of her paleness next to his tan was unexpectedly erotic. As was the barely there brush of his jean-clad erection against her butt. He moved his hands down to the button on her waistband and unfastened it. He pushed her jeans and her panties to the floor. She stepped out of her clothes as he eased his fingers between her thighs.

She still had her hands holding up her hair and he continued to kiss the back of her neck. One hand teased her breasts while the other found the very center of her and began to circle her swollen clit.

There was too much going on. She couldn't think, couldn't focus on any one thing. Sensations poured through her from every direction and what she knew for sure was that she didn't want any of this to stop.

"Take one step to the right," he said, his breath hot against her neck.

She did and realized that she'd just parted her thighs for him. He moved in farther, slipping a finger inside of her. Her muscles immediately clamped around him. Deep, deep inside, she felt the first whisper of her soon-to-be release.

"Aidan," she breathed.

He kissed her neck, her shoulder, then right behind her ear. At the same time the movements against her breasts and between her legs continued. He withdrew and found where she was most swollen and rubbed slowly at first. Slowly enough that she involuntarily pulsed her hips. Then faster and harder.

She groaned as her muscles tensed. The sweetness was just out of reach, just beyond grasping. She was so close that she—

He straightened and pushed against her back. "Down the hall on the left."

"Wh-what?"

He was stopping? Did the man know she was about to have an orgasm?

"My bedroom. I want to finish there."

Oh, right. In a bed. That made sense.

She took two steps, realized she was completely

naked, then didn't know what to do. Aidan gave her a gentle push. "Keep moving."

She reached the bedroom and walked over to the bed. Aidan was right behind her. He'd already pulled off his shirt and was working on his jeans. He got them undone and pushed down, along with his briefs. His massive erection sprang free. Her insides clenched in anticipation.

"You have a favorite side?" he asked, his voice hoarse.

"No. You?"

"At this point, I don't give a damn."

He sounded desperate and ready. Two excellent qualities in a lover, she thought as she pulled back the dark navy comforter. He got out a couple of condoms and tossed them on the nightstand, then slid in next to her. She was still shifting onto her side, then he pulled her close and kissed her.

At the feel of his mouth, his tongue, his body, she relaxed into the moment. This was right, she thought happily. All of it.

He moved his hand across her stomach, then lower. She parted her legs and he moved directly to her center, where he began to rub as he had before. At the same time, he kissed his way down to her breasts.

She quickly returned to the breathless, on-the-edge place where she'd been before. Her breathing increased and tension filled her muscles. She moved her legs and closed her eyes and her body spiraled higher and higher. She was so close that she—

Her orgasm caught her by surprise. One second she was reaching and then next she found herself flung into a vortex of pulsing pleasure. She might have called out his name—she wasn't sure. All she knew was that every cell in her body was happy to dance and sway in surrender to the wonder of her release.

As the contractions slowed, he kept pace, slowing as well. When she was still, she opened her eyes. He watched her intently.

"All done?" he asked.

She nodded.

He turned and ripped open the packet, then pulled on the condom. It was barely in place before he kissed her once, shifted between her legs and pushed all the way in.

They both groaned. She wasn't sure what he was thinking, but she knew that she loved the way he filled her. Deeply, completely. She shifted to draw him in deeper, then drew back her knees and wrapped her legs around his waist.

"I've been waiting for this," he told her. "You have no idea."

"I can guess," she teased as she traced her fingers down his back. "It's been a long time."

His dark gaze settled on her face. "This is about you, Shelby. Not about getting off. I want to be clear."

Because she trusted him, she believed him and smiled. "Then what are you waiting for?"

He took her at her word, drawing out and then filling her again. The delightful friction stimulated already excited nerves into a quivering state. It didn't take long for her breathing to match his. She gave herself over to the moment, to the feel of him going in and out, deeper and faster. The pressure built and she bore down to get as much of him inside as possible.

She rotated her hips and pushed from the inside every time he surged in. His body tensed and she knew he was close. The thought of his release excited her and she arched her body. That brought the head of his penis in contact with some deep place that immediately began to burn with an arousing hum of want.

She gasped and he thrust in again, just as deeply. "Oh, yes! Like that."

He thrust in just a little deeper and she felt herself going over the edge. It was different from before—it was from the inside rather than the outside. The contractions of her muscles were more in her belly. She grabbed his hips, urging him to keep the rhythm going. He kept pace with her for a few more seconds, then he shuddered his release and groaned her name.

She had no idea how many minutes they lay there, tangled, trying to catch their breath. Aidan finally moved off her and reached for a tissue. When he'd gotten rid of the condom, he rolled back on his side and looked at her.

She had no idea what he was going to say. What she didn't expect was him to start laughing. But the combination of relief and happiness was contagious and she began to giggle, then laugh. He collapsed back and she snuggled up next to him. He wrapped his arm around her and pulled her close.

"Well, damn," he murmured.

"I knew we'd be great together."

He kissed her forehead. "We are that."

"Friends with benefits," she told him.

"Wasn't that a movie? Or a book?"

"Probably. But it's still what we are. We can make it work. You'll see." She half sat up. "Unless this was a one-time thing."

He looked at her for a long time, then smiled. "Do you really see me being able to resist you again?" He pulled her on top of him and kissed her. "Now, for round two."

CHAPTER SIXTEEN

AIDAN HAD TO admit it—he felt good. Better than good. He'd awakened with that feeling of smug contentment combined with being a god. He was the man. Conqueror of worlds, or at the very least, conqueror of his world and pleasurer of Shelby.

They'd spent the rest of the night together. After their second amazing session of lovemaking, they'd surfaced long enough to dress, collect Charlie and grab some take-out for dinner, then had spent the evening snuggled together on his sofa before retreating to the bedroom to continue putting a dent in his condom supply.

He leaned over and absently rubbed Charlie's ears. "Hey, guy," he murmured. "How you feeling?"

Charlie wagged his tail.

"Yeah? Me, too."

Aidan leaned back in his chair. Part of him was still concerned that everything could fall apart now that they'd crossed the line, but he wasn't about to feel anything close to regret. Being with Shelby had been great. Right.

He turned his attention back to his computer. He had a spreadsheet that detailed the activities the company offered, separated by season. He'd already started work on the scheduling, but kept going back to the list.

There were lots of fun things for people to do. Everything from the very traditional walking tours to the more adventurous whitewater rafting and parasailing. In between were hikes and campouts that could be adjusted for the skill and fitness level of the group. But it was all so predictable.

He walked into the front office, where Fay was printing out passes for the day's tours. Charlie trailed after him. Fay looked up from her work.

"What?" she demanded. "You're thinking something."

"How do you know that I'm thinking? Is it a woman thing? Or that we've worked together for a long time?"

"Both. Now talk."

"I'm looking at the schedule. We have a lot of things for families and for guys and couples, but nothing for women. Nothing female-based."

"Like?"

"I don't know." He opened the bottom drawer of her desk and pulled out a yellow ball, then tossed it down the hall for Charlie. The little dog raced after it. "Something from the Máa-zib, maybe. This town was founded by a group of powerful women. There's the festival where the guy gets his heart cut out. What if we did a ladies' weekend around that? With a bike ride and an afternoon of shopping. Maybe some spa stuff. We could approach the businesses in town to co-op with us."

Fay nodded slowly. "That could be fun. It wouldn't

have to be around the festival, although that's great. What about bachelorette weekends?"

He grabbed a pad of paper from her desk and started making notes. "That would work. We could do packages or something. Include meal vouchers." He looked at her. "What about more couples stuff? A romantic sunset kayak for two with a picnic? Ana Raquel has her food truck all summer. She could put together the food and wine. We already have blankets and kayaks. We'd give a quick lesson for the novices, send them out with a map and GPS locator."

Fay grinned. "Unless they don't want to be found."

"They'll want to be found eventually. The food will run out." He chuckled as he wrote.

"I'm impressed," she added. "Usually when you want to make changes, you're only interested in going faster or making the ordinary more dangerous. This isn't like you."

"I want to mix it up," he said, when what he was thinking was that this was Shelby's influence. She'd forced him to do "girl things." While he'd resisted at first, he had to admit there was value in having a conversation. In learning to listen and offer encouragement without offering advice. He would always prefer doing over sitting, but there was a time and place for both.

"Women either influence or make all family vacation decisions," he continued. "I need to keep that in mind."

Fay petted Charlie. "Our little boy is all grown up. I'm just so proud."

THE HELP EMERGENCY RESPONSE OPERATIONS, or as it was known in town, the HERO office, was designed to handle a crisis. There weren't a lot of unnecessary touches. The walls were covered with maps of the surrounding forests, the desks had state-of-the-art computers and the command center looked capable of a space launch.

Shelby had always felt a little intimidated when she visited her brother at work. He rescued people and saved lives—she made cookies. Not that the comparisons were new. After all, he'd been a world-class athlete before heading up the town's search-and-rescue organization, while she'd, well, baked cookies.

Kipling smiled when he saw her and pulled her close for a hug. "How's my favorite sister?" he asked when he released her.

"Good. How's my favorite brother?"

"Tired. Happy, but tired. Tonya's sleeping longer between feedings, but we are weeks from her sleeping through the night." He waved Shelby into a chair and sat behind his desk again, swiveling so he faced her. "It's great."

"You like being a dad."

"It's the best thing ever. She's so tiny and perfect. I never thought I could love anyone this much."

Shelby thought about all the women that had paraded through her brother's life for years. As he'd gotten older, he'd started to settle down, but he'd always had a wild streak. Until he'd met Destiny.

Theirs had been an unconventional courtship—with Destiny's unplanned pregnancy first drawing them together before tearing them apart. In the end, they'd realized they were in love and wanted to be a family.

Shelby had watched it all from the sidelines. She'd hoped things would work out. Not only did she long to see her brother happy, she genuinely liked Destiny and Starr. Now there was one more Gilmore in the family.

"You're surrounded by women," she teased.

"I know. Isn't it great? How are things with you and Aidan?"

Three days ago, Shelby would have pointed out—for the nine hundred and forty-seventh time—that she and Aidan were *just friends*. Only she wasn't sure about that anymore. Making love had changed everything. She wasn't sure of the consequences, but was sure they existed. With luck, they would all be happy ones.

"Excellent," she said, thinking of the flowers delivered to the bakery that morning. And the way he texted her at least once an hour.

"Aidan's a good guy. He was a bit of a player, but he seems to have changed his ways."

"You've been checking up on him?"

"Of course."

Which was totally what Kipling would do, she thought fondly. He'd always taken care of her. No matter what, her big brother would be there for her.

"You know about the bakery," she said. "That I'm buying it."

He nodded. "It's going to be great."

"I'm excited. Well, scared, too, but mostly excited.

I'm working on my business plan. I've already met with a contractor to discuss expanding into the space next door. The landlord is holding it for me. If everything comes together, I'll have the lease by the end of next week. Once Amber and I get the paperwork signed, I'll be moving forward."

There were a thousand details to work out. For one thing, she wanted to change the name of the business to Flour Power. She wanted a new logo and fresh, new boxes and bags for her customers.

He leaned toward her. "I'm glad you're doing this," he told her. "When you first wanted to buy into Amber's business, I know I resisted. I wanted you to be sure. I was wrong about that. You've settled into living here as if you were born here. Owning your own business is the next logical step."

"I'm glad you think so." She smiled. "Because I'm here to ask you for a loan."

She had more to say. Like how she wanted a loan, not a partner. That she would be paying him back with interest. That her business plan had been reviewed by both a lawyer and an accountant. But she didn't get to go there with any of it because Kipling was standing and pulling her to her feet.

He hugged her hard, squeezing until she couldn't breathe. But that was okay, because she felt the love between them.

"Thank you," he said and kissed her forehead. "I wanted to offer but didn't know if I should."

She smiled at him. "There was a line of people trying to give me money. It was kind of cool. Even

Morgan, Amber's dad, offered me a loan. There's a surprising amount of money in this town."

She hugged her brother. "I knew you'd want to be a part of this, so I came to you first. If you only want to take on part of it or would prefer me to go to a bank, I'm—"

"I have the money. I want to give you the loan."

Kipling had made money skiing, but most of his fortune had come from endorsements. When you had multiple gold medals, the big guys came calling. In addition to the usual equipment deals, he'd had international campaigns with a fast-food restaurant and had been the face—and body—of a clothing line. While the size of her loan terrified her, she doubted it would amount to a single quarter's interest payment for him.

"Thank you," she told him. "I was hoping you'd agree. Want me to offer you free cookies for life?"

"No. I get enough of your baked goods as it is. Too many more and I won't be able to exercise off the calories." He winked. "I'm married to a country star. I've got to look good."

"I think Destiny would love you regardless."

"I hope so, but I'm not testing the theory." He hugged her again. "I'm proud of you, Shelby."

"Thank you. I'm kind of proud of me, too."

Aidan wanted to ignore his cell phone but Nick had called twice in two minutes. "It must be important," he said as he pushed the button to accept the call.

"You at Shelby's place?" Nick asked by way of greeting. "I'm coming over."

Aidan looked at the equipment spread out around them and grimaced. "It's not a good time."

"Don't give me that. I know you're not naked because you're not getting any. Whatever you're doing can wait."

Before Aidan could protest, there was a knock on the front door. He ended the call and swore.

"Nick's here."

"I got that," Shelby said with a laugh. "Should I let him in?"

Aidan swore. "You're going to have to."

He pulled his feet out of the hot water and reached for a towel just as his brother walked into Shelby's living room.

Nick came to a stop and stared. "Holy crap. What is she doing to you?"

Charlie raced over to greet him. Nick bent and petted the dog as he looked around. "You're scaring me, bro."

Aidan glanced at the soaking trays for their feet, all the files, clippers and other equipment on a towel on the coffee table. There were bottles of nail polish, toe separators, buffers and things he couldn't name but knew how to use.

"I'm the only one who gets her toes painted," Shelby offered.

Nick swung his head to look at her. "You're the devil, aren't you?"

Shelby laughed. "So speaks the man who's never had a pedicure. Sit."

Nick looked between them. "I'm not playing your sick game."

Aidan moved out of the way. "The lady said to sit."

Nick cautiously sat down. Aidan replaced the water and set the soaking tray in front of his brother.

"You're going to want to take off your shoes and socks, then roll up your pants."

Nick looked skeptical. "Then what?"

"Then you wait for things to get soft," Shelby said, her voice soothing.

Nick swung his head to look at Aidan. "It makes it go soft?"

"No, you ass. The skin on your feet." Aidan glared at him. "What's wrong with you?"

"With me? You're the one having a pedicure."

"Yeah, a beautiful woman wants to hang out with me and touch my body. It's miserable."

"Hey, she's only touching your feet."

That was what Nick thought and Aidan wasn't about to correct him. He saw Shelby hide a smile as she helped Nick roll up his pants. The other man reluctantly took off his boots and socks, then put his feet in the warm water.

"What's in this?" he asked, his voice suspicious.

"Does it matter?" Shelby winked. "You're already committed."

Nick glared at her, then relaxed back in the seat. "Is this what you two do together? Take care of your feet?"

"Among other things." She sounded serene as she spoke. "Sometimes Aidan braids my hair."

"She's kidding," he said quickly.

"I'm not so sure," his brother told him. "Man, now I really have to worry about you."

"Don't. I'm fine."

"You're not seeing the big picture."

Aidan sat next to Shelby. She shifted so she could put her feet on his thigh. She handed him the base coat.

"Why are you here?" Aidan asked as he began to paint her toes.

"I wanted to tell you about my trip to Happily Inc.," Nick told him.

Aidan glanced up. "Yeah? You saw Ronan and Mathias?"

"Uh-huh. They're doing great. It's an interesting town. East of Los Angeles, in the foothills. High desert, I guess it's called. But there's a hot spring and caves and mountains for skiing. It's more stark than here."

Aidan looked at him. "Do not, under any circumstances, start describing the colors of everything, I beg you."

Nick laughed. "Would I do that?"

Shelby sighed. "You would so do that. Did you like it there?"

"I did. I wasn't sure. It's smaller than Fool's Gold by a lot. The big industry is destination weddings. There are venues all over for them. Houses that look like castles or Southern plantations. You can have any kind of wedding you want, with Roman chariots or cowboys."

"I like cowboys," Shelby said.

Aidan turned to her. "You do?"

"Who doesn't?"

"They smell."

She laughed. "They don't smell. They're nice. Zane Nicholson is nice."

"He's married."

"I'm not interested in him in that way. I'm just saying…" She sighed. "Go ahead, Nick. Cowboy weddings."

He glanced between them, obviously confused. "You two okay?"

"We're fine," Aidan told him. "The town?"

"Right. Like I said, there are a lot of weddings. Back in the 1950s, the town was failing. Some guy who owned the bank knew that if the town went under, the bank would go with it because people couldn't repay their loans. He came up with the idea of changing the town history."

"You can't change a town's history." Aidan took Shelby's other foot and started putting base coat on the nails. "It is what it is."

"Not for this guy. He came up with this story about how, during the California gold rush, a stagecoach full of brides heading for San Francisco broke down in town. Each of the brides fell in love so by the time the stagecoach was ready to leave, none of the women wanted to go."

"Oh, that's so nice," Shelby said. "I want to go there."

"See?" Nick pointed at her. "It works. The town changed its name. Hollywood types caught on. Remember, this was the 1950s, when celebrity weddings were a huge deal. From that, Happily Inc. grew to what it is today—a destination wedding town. There's also a sleep center, where they help you sleep better. Something about a convergence of forces or mystic stuff like that. Anyway, I saw the gallery where Ronan and Mathias sell their work. The lady who runs it is really knowledgeable and she doesn't take a lot of crap." He thought for a second. "She kind of reminded me of Mayor Marsha."

"I don't know if that's good or bad."

"Me, either. The space where Mathias and Ronan work is awesome. Big and bright. There's room for me, too. I looked around and found a few short-term carpentry jobs, so I won't have a problem finding a job."

Aidan reached for the nail polish. Shelby shifted so he could start painting her other foot. "You're doing it, aren't you?" she asked. "You're moving?"

Nick nodded. "I rented an apartment. I'm going to give notice at the bar."

Aidan concentrated on the task at hand. He didn't want think about his brother leaving Fool's Gold. His gut told him this was the right thing for Nick. That his brother needed to get away from Ceallach. But his heart, well, his heart was going to miss having a brother around.

"Hey," Nick said. "I know what this means. You're the last one here."

"The last what?" Shelby asked.

"The last Mitchell brother in Fool's Gold," Aidan told her. "Del's traveling the world with Maya and the other three are going to be in Happily Inc."

She nodded slowly, then reached out her hand and

put it on top of his. The touch was brief, but he got the message. She was there for him. She understood. Whatever else had happened between them, they were still friends.

"You gotta do what's right for you," Aidan told Nick. "You can't stay here. We both know it. This is better."

"You can come see me anytime you want."

"Gee, thanks."

Nick grimaced. "You know what I mean." He brightened. "Did I mention there's an animal preserve?"

"What do you mean?" Shelby asked. "Like a zoo?"

"Naw. Way better than that. There's this open, grassy area at one end of town with all kinds of grazing animals. There are zebras and gazelles and even a giraffe named Millie."

"Okay, now you're just making stuff up," she teased.

Nick made an X on his chest. "I swear. Besides, Fool's Gold has an elephant."

"I know, but Priscilla's different. More like family."

Aidan smiled. "You'll accept an elephant as family, but not a giraffe?"

"When you put it like that, I guess we can have both." She turned to Nick. "Okay, you've soaked long enough. Use one of the towels to dry your feet and we'll move on to the next step of the pedicure."

Nick did as he was told. "You're not going to tell anyone about this, are you?" he asked his brother.

"Back at you," Aidan said.

"Deal."

CHAPTER SEVENTEEN

Jo PLACED THE pitcher of margaritas in the center of the table. "There's something not right about this," she muttered.

Felicia nodded. "It's difficult when social norms are violated. In this case, the girls-only lunch. But it's for a good reason. I doubt Aidan will be a regular fixture." She eyed him. "Your quest to be friends with Shelby is admirable, but you will need to have boundaries for that relationship to work."

Shelby felt her lips twitch as she tried not to smile. "Yeah, Aidan. We're going to need to talk boundaries. You're crowding me a little."

He held both hands, palms up. "I asked for help and this is what I get? Aren't you always telling the men in your life that it's okay to admit you don't know something? But when I do, this is the response? You're going to have to decide on your message."

Taryn picked up her margarita. "Well, damn. That's an interesting tactic. I hate to say it, Aidan, but you're right."

Larissa grinned. "Oh, no. Hell is freezing over as we speak. Run for your lives."

"It's all funny until you want to talk trash about

the guys," Jo warned. "Then he's going to be sitting here and what will you do?"

"Talk over him," Shelby said cheerfully. "He won't mind."

She half expected Aidan to protest, but he only smiled. The man had confidence, she thought happily. She would give him that. And mad skills in the bedroom. Maybe one came from the other.

When Aidan had asked her advice on his ideas for more female-focused summer tours, she'd suggested he join her and her friends for lunch. When she'd put out the word about what he wanted, several of her friends had immediately agreed to help him. From there plans had morphed into a margarita lunch, which meant no work was going to get done that afternoon.

"Enough torturing Aidan," Patience said as she picked up her glass. "A toast. To friends."

They all touched glasses. Even Aidan. Taryn leaned toward him.

"You realize this makes you an honorary woman."

One corner of his mouth turned up. "You say that like it's a bad thing."

"And here I thought you'd be flustered. All right." She sighed. "Shelby, you can keep this one. He's special."

Shelby felt an odd kind of lurching sensation in her belly. Before she could say anything, Felicia shook her head.

"It's not like that. They're friends. Shelby explained it all to me when they first started spending time together. I think it's an excellent experiment. I don't suppose you'll be writing a paper about your experiences when it's all over, will you?" Her voice was wistful.

"You're a freak," Larissa cheerfully told the other woman. "And we love you."

Conversation flowed all around them. It was the usual mishmash of getting caught up and sharing fun gossip. Who was dating, who was pregnant, who was going where on vacation. Shelby participated but her attention was on Aidan. Four months ago, he would have been squirming—both uncomfortable with the situation and anxious to get to his stuff. But now he simply sipped his margarita and ate chips. Every now and then he added a comment or two.

She liked that he liked her friends. She liked how they could hang out together. Being around him was so easy, she thought. Comfortable. They never ran out of things to say. The fact that the man could turn her on with just a glance was simply a bonus.

Jo returned with their lunches. When she left, Taryn smiled at Aidan.

"This is the quietest we're going to get, so if you want to talk about your business, now would be the time."

"Thanks." He glanced around the table. "I'm thinking about making changes in what I offer tourists. Most of my tours are adventure-based. Outdoor activities. While a lot of women enjoy that sort of thing, there's a whole indoor market I've been ignoring. Fay, my office manager, and I did some brainstorming. What if I had things like girls' weekends where we co-oped with other businesses in town to offer a night or two at the lodge, a spa experience with dinner somewhere?"

"Why wouldn't women just book it themselves?" Larissa asked. "Why go through you?"

"To make it easier."

"Not good enough," Taryn told him. "You need to be able to offer a unique element. What's your next overnight tour?"

"I'm taking a group camping next weekend," he said.

"Why can't they go camping by themselves?"

Shelby thought Aidan might get defensive, but he stayed completely relaxed.

"I provide the equipment. I'm the tour guide. We explore a few old ruins that are hard to find. I take care of pretty much everything. They just have to show up."

"But camping is more complicated than a spa weekend," Patience said. "I think the spa weekend could work, but it needs a unique element."

"Like parasailing with shots," Felicia offered.

They all stared at her.

"What?" she asked. "Alcohol is a part of many sporting events."

"What about focusing on romance and couples instead?" Patience asked. "A romantic tour of Fool's Gold. Maybe with a gourmet picnic and champagne. Of course, it would have to be self-guided. You'd get in the way."

Aidan grinned. "I agree."

"What about the best spots to kiss in town?" Larissa waved her fork. "You know, having something like that would be fun. I'm sure a lot of couples come to camp or ski and while the wife is happy, it's more for the guy. Having a romantic tour would balance things."

Taryn nodded. "You could have packages ready, so it could be a last-minute addition. If you choose the menus for the picnic lunches or dinners in advance, Ana Raquel could keep the supplies on hand." She raised her brows. "You were planning to use her services, weren't you?"

"Uh-huh. Shelby likes her work."

He scribbled a few notes, so he didn't see the looks exchanged between the women. Shelby did, though, and knew what they were thinking. That Aidan had reached the point where he trusted her opinion.

She wanted to say it was just a friendship thing, but honestly she was getting tired of repeating herself. Not to mention the fact that they were now more than friends. A lot more.

They continued to talk about different possibilities. Aidan asked questions. When they were finally finished, he insisted on paying for lunch.

"It's the least I can do," he told her friends. "Thank you for taking the time to talk to me."

He and Shelby walked out of Jo's Bar. He smiled at her. "I appreciate you setting that up. I have a lot to think about."

"More ideas than you can use?" Shelby teased.

"Absolutely, but that's a quality problem. They're nice women. I like them."

"I like them, too," she said. That odd lurching in

her stomach returned, but she ignored it. "I like us, as well. What we've accomplished."

His expression turned predatory.

She laughed. "Not just that. Everything else."

"But *that* was good."

"It was. The best ever."

She thought he might make a joke, but his expression turned serious. He touched the side of her face with his fingers, then lightly kissed her.

"It was," he agreed.

For a second, she couldn't breathe. Before she could figure out what was wrong, the feeling passed. But questions lingered. What on earth was wrong with her? This was Aidan. Her friend and now lover. She knew him. She liked him. She was comfortable around him. They were good together and she didn't want that to change.

"I'M SO HAPPY," Amber said, brushing away tears. "Ignore the waterworks. These days I cry at everything." She took Shelby's hands. "I know selling was the right decision, but if I'd had to sell to anyone but you, I would have had regrets. As it is, I know you're going to grow the business into something amazing." Amber laughed. "And change everything. I can't wait to see where you are in a year."

Shelby swallowed. "Thank you for everything. I promise that the heart of the business will always be the same. Even if the outsides change."

They hugged.

Trisha Wynn, the attorney handling the sale,

rolled her eyes. "I have to say, this is the first time there's been hugging at a meeting like this."

Amber wiped her eyes. "Don't pretend you aren't moved."

"I'm a lawyer. I'm immune to emotion. Now let's sign our paperwork, ladies."

They all sat at the large table in Trisha's conference room. Shelby couldn't believe how quickly everything had come together. Once the business had been valued, she and Amber had settled on a price. The fact that Shelby was paying with cash rather than a loan helped speed things along. As for the money she'd borrowed from her brother—that had been accomplished with a single page note and even more hugs.

Now she signed her name where Trisha indicated. She was nervous and excited. More happy than scared, she thought, barely able to keep still in her seat. She hadn't slept in three days and should be exhausted, but she was filled with energy and possibilities.

She'd already signed the lease on the space next to the existing bakery. She had her contractor lined up, along with the building permits she would need. Bailey, Mayor Marsha's assistant, had walked her through the process and everything had gone smoothly.

She signed three more times. Trisha looked through the paperwork.

"All right, ladies, you're done. Traditionally we all shake hands, but I suppose you want more?"

Amber laughed. "Of course we do."

Everyone stood and there was plenty of hugging. Trisha grumbled but Shelby felt her hang on tight, even if it was just for a second. As she and Amber walked outside together, her former business partner handed her a set of keys.

"I won't be needing these anymore."

Shelby sighed. "Wow. We really did this. You sure you're okay with what's happening?"

"You're asking me a little late, aren't you?" her friend teased. Then Amber's chin began to tremble. "I've loved the bakery, Shelby. It's been so important to me. But having a baby is something I never thought would happen." She lowered her voice. "We got the amniocentesis results back and everything's fine. We're having a boy and he's healthy."

Shelby hugged her again. "I'm so happy for you."

"Thank you. So while I'll miss the bakery, it's nothing compared to the joy I'm feeling about my son." Amber smiled at her. "If you need anything, let me know. You're going to do great. You'll see."

SHELBY WALKED TO the bakery. Her head was spinning. There was so much to do. She had to get her temporary kitchen set up and confirm the kiosk she'd rented for the renovations. There were—

She turned the corner and saw a small crowd in front of the bakery. As she got closer, she realized that she knew everyone. In fact, all her friends were there.

Madeline stood with Destiny and Kipling. Starr chatted with one of her girlfriends. Aidan and Taryn,

Larissa, Patience, Ana Raquel. Even Sam Ridge stood on the sidewalk.

Aidan spotted her. "She's here," he called.

Everyone turned and started clapping.

"Congratulations!" Madeline yelled. "It's all yours."

There were more shouts, then plenty of hugs. Glasses of champagne were passed around. Shelby didn't know what to think, but before she could ask what was going on, Aidan stepped close to the bakery.

"Congratulations, Shelby," he said. "We're all proud of you and happy for you. You're going to do great."

He pulled a rope and a banner rolled down. On it were the stylized psychedelic daisies she'd chosen for her Flour Power logo.

Tears filled her eyes. "You did this for me," she whispered.

He raised one shoulder. "It's not every day you get to celebrate something this big."

Kipling came up and put his arm around her. "You did good, kid. Thank you for letting me be a part of this." He raised his chin toward Aidan. "He thought this up himself. I wish I had, but he's the one who arranged everything and called us all. He's a good man, Shelby. Just in case you were thinking of keeping him around."

DEMOLITION WAS LOUD and construction was louder still. Shelby supposed she'd always known that, but knowing and hearing were two different things. The construction crew had shown up bright and early every morning and worked until six.

The newly leased space was now an empty shell and on the Ambrosia side of the building everything was gone except the old kitchen. That equipment still had years left in it. They would keep it as it was.

That meant she and her team could bake from six at night until six in the morning, then sell at the kiosk a dozen yards from the bakery. But the guys working every day meant packing up everything needed to produce pastries and cupcakes and cookies, then storing it until it was needed the next day. The logistics were daunting, but worth it, she told herself.

Shelby watched the clock. It was the Friday morning of Spring Fling weekend. Tourists filled the sidewalks, taking advantage of the beautiful weather. Tomorrow was the parade. Shelby had a feeling they were going to sell out early today and with the construction going on, there was no way to bake more. They would have to adjust their schedule tonight. Which meant she needed to get home and get some sleep. But first she had a stop to make.

She walked toward Paper Moon. As she smiled at people she knew, she found herself missing Aidan. He'd only been gone overnight and he would be back on Sunday, and it wasn't like they spent every second together, but still. She didn't like knowing he was out of town.

Her emotions confused her. The odd sensations she got when she was around him. She knew some of that came from the fact that they'd had sex. But there was something else going on. Something she couldn't put her finger on. Lately she'd found herself thinking about what would happen in June. How they would go back to their regular lives. Sure, they'd still be friends, but it wouldn't be the same. Only she didn't want things to be different. So what did that mean?

She walked into the bridal salon and found Madeline straightening veils.

"Hi, you," her friend said. "What's going on? How's the construction?"

"Loud, but they're making good progress. How are things with you?"

"Okay. Work's great." Madeline wrinkled her nose. "Jonny's in Italy. I'm going to join him next week, but I miss him."

Shelby knew the feeling. Only she couldn't say that. She and Aidan were just friends, while Madeline was going to marry Jonny. Their situations were different.

Madeline put down the veil she'd been fluffing. "What's going on?"

"What do you mean?"

"I don't know. You seem like... You want a cup of coffee? I made a pot. We can go in my office. I don't have any appointments this morning and Rosalind can handle any walk-ins."

"Sure."

Shelby followed Madeline into the back. They got their coffee, then retreated to Madeline's small office. Shelby sat across from her friend.

"Is it Aidan?" Madeline asked gently. "I heard about the lunch at Jo's. He was a hit with everyone. I'm sorry I missed it."

Madeline had been unable to come because of an appointment with a bride. Shelby held her mug in both hands as she tried to figure out what to say.

"I'm confused," she admitted. "You know why I wanted to get to know Aidan."

"Of course. I have to admit, I wasn't sure about your plan, but it's working. You like him and you trust him. Right? Is there something wrong?"

"No. He's great. He's nice and funny and reasonable about stuff. I've enjoyed getting to know him. We're good together. Good friends."

"Then what's the problem?"

"I don't know. I feel strange. Uneasy."

"Have your feelings turned romantic?"

"No," Shelby said quickly. "Of course not." They couldn't have. Sex wasn't love. It was…different. "I just don't want to lose what we have."

Madeline sipped her coffee. "Okay, okay, I get it. You put a time limit on your relationship. That's what has you uneasy. Your project or experiment or whatever you want to call it was only supposed to last six months. You want to make sure that you don't lose Aidan. So don't."

"Don't what?"

"Don't stop being friends with him. There's no rule that says you have to. If it's working for the two of you, keep doing that. Hang out. Whatever."

That. Shelby held in a smile. She would like to keep doing *that* with Aidan, very much. But she knew what Madeline meant.

"We talked about staying friends. And we will… in a way. But everything will be different."

"Why does it have to be? I'm assuming he likes hanging out with you as much as you like hanging out with him."

"Yes. I think so." Now that she thought about it, she realized they never talked about their feelings. Although he'd been very clear about not wanting to screw up what they had with sex. So he must like her.

"I'm going to talk to him," she said firmly. "Man to man."

Madeline raised her eyebrows. "Excuse me?"

"I mean talk to him like a guy would talk to his friend."

"In grunts?"

"No. Being straightforward. No hints, no talking around the point. Just saying what I mean. That I want to stay friends. Real friends. Not just acquaintances who run into each other."

"Impressive. Look at you, all brave with the new business and the attitude. I like it." Madeline's humor faded. "Has this relationship with Aidan done what you wanted?"

"I hope so. I won't know for sure until I get involved with someone, but I think I'm stronger. More willing to trust. That's what I wanted. A chance to be normal."

"So it was worth it?"

"Completely."

CHAPTER EIGHTEEN

THE WOMAN—JULIE—had been crying for forty-eight hours straight. Mostly she tried to hide it, but everyone knew. Both Thursday and Friday nights, the sound of her muffled sobs had drifted through the campground, and there were still another twenty-four hours to go.

The weekend—billed as the Wild Side of the Sierras—was a camping-hiking adventure with a nature specialist as guide. The twelve campers experienced everything from bird watching to berry picking to wildflower identifying. If they were lucky, they stumbled upon a baby fawn or two. Aidan made sure they were never unlucky enough to cross the path of hungry bears.

Saturday morning the group was supposed to head to a lookout, where they could observe an eagle nest. Aidan sent them on with the naturalist but asked Julie to hang back.

She was attractive, in her midforties, with brown hair and brown eyes. Fit, if slightly high-strung. She wasn't experienced with the outdoors, but she was willing to do whatever was asked of her. Aidan knew that the reservation had been for two, but only Julie had shown up. Which probably explained the tears.

"I thought we could talk," he told her when the others had left. Charlie looked from the departing group back to Aidan, as if wanting to make sure he knew they were being left behind.

"Okay," Julie said slowly.

They sat at the picnic table by the campfire. The tents were set up in a circle, spaced a few feet apart. As Aidan used this area a lot, he'd had a Porta Potti brought in but there was no running water.

Julie rested her arms on the smooth wooden surface. "You called this meeting. What did you want to talk about?"

He patted the bench next to him. Charlie jumped up and Aidan began to rub his ears. "Whatever's going on. You're upset. Can I help?"

"Not unless you can take a hit out on someone," she said, then grimaced. "Sorry. I don't mean that."

"Bad breakup?"

"The worst." Tears filled her brown eyes. "Keith and I were together for ten years. Ten! We're both in the tech industry. He does software design and I'm in finance. We were great together. We traveled, we liked the same movies and cooking together on S-Sundays." Her voice cracked.

"But?"

She sniffed. "But we weren't going anywhere, emotionally. We kept talking about getting married, but it never seemed to happen. At first I wasn't worried, but then it became a big deal." She lowered her voice. "I'm forty-four. I'm probably never going to have kids. I accept that, but I'd always figured I'd get married."

"What happened?"

"He dumped me. There was no warning. Three weeks later, he was dating some twentysomething. A month after that, they got engaged." Tears spilled down her cheeks. "One of my friends said she heard the bitch is pregnant! I can't believe it. I wasted all that time on him and I have nothing to show for it."

She covered her face with her hands and sobbed. Aidan sat quietly, figuring she had to get it out of her system. While part of him felt uncomfortable with what was happening, he knew he wasn't responsible for what was bothering her. And telling her everything was going to fine was just plain dumb. Obviously it wasn't okay.

Eventually Julie's sobs slowed. She wiped her face and looked at him. "I'm a mess."

"Kind of."

"I miss him."

"Not really."

Her eyes widened. "How can you say that? I love Keith."

"No, you don't." He raised a shoulder. "You said yourself the relationship wasn't going anywhere emotionally. What do you miss? Be specific."

"A lot." She sniffed. "The stuff we'd do together. Hanging out. Cooking on Sunday."

"That's all what you do. What do you miss about *him*?"

Her expression was blank. "I don't understand what you're asking."

"I have a friend. She can't show up at somebody's house without bringing cookies or brownies or cake.

It's physically impossible for her to walk in empty-handed. Or if she's with this guy." He rested his hand on Charlie's back. "She'll play with him for hours. Charlie doesn't have a favorite toy so first she has to figure out which one he's in the mood for, then game on."

He looked at Julie. "It's her I'd miss. Who she is. Not the stuff we do."

Julie drew in a couple of breaths. "You're saying I miss what Keith represents. The steady guy. Being in a relationship. But that I don't miss who he is."

"It's just a guess, based on what you've said about him. For what it's worth, he's an asshole."

For the first time since showing up for the trip, Julie smiled. "I know. The new girlfriend is twenty years younger than him. What's up with that?" The smile faded. "I wanted to come on this campout just to prove something. I didn't expect to get good advice. Thank you. I'm going to think about what you said."

"He's not the only one. There are plenty of good guys out there. You have to start looking, though."

Julie nodded. "You're really easy to talk to. You know a lot about women."

Aidan grinned. "It's kind of a new thing for me, but I'm enjoying it."

SHELBY FOUND HERSELF oddly nervous as she waited for Aidan to get home from his camping trip. He'd called from the office—just to say he was back—and she'd invited him to stop by on his way back to his place. Now, as she paced the length of her living room, she fought against that weird fluttering in her stomach and a growing sense of anticipation.

She'd missed her friend, she told herself. And Charlie, of course. Because she loved that silly little dog. The way he waved his paws impatiently when she wasn't quick enough with a treat or the toy du jour. How he liked to stretch out on the back of the sofa, like a cat.

That was it, she told herself. She'd missed Charlie. And Aidan, but mostly the dog.

She heard the truck pull into her driveway and hurried out to greet her guys. Charlie had his head out the window and barked a greeting. She opened the door on his side and he jumped into her arms. He was nearly twenty pounds, so she staggered for a second, then hugged him close.

"Hey, you," she murmured, stroking his soft fur. "How was the camping trip?"

Aidan stepped out and circled the truck. "We had a good time. Charlie was a hit with everyone. They all snuck him food, so we're going to have to do extra walks for the next couple of days. The campers were great. How are you doing?"

He looked good, she thought absently. Unshaved. Tousled. Sexy. He had on an open long-sleeved shirt over a T-shirt, jeans and hiking boots. Nothing that should have gotten her heart to beating fast and yet she found herself all quivery.

"Shelby?"

"Huh?"

He smiled. "You okay?"

She nodded. "I missed you."

He put his arm around her and pulled her close. "I missed you, too. You should have come with me."

They walked toward her place. Charlie led the way, then darted inside.

"Next time," she said. "I have remodeling to monitor. I'm sure I'm making my contractor crazy, but he'll just have to deal."

"They making progress?"

"Every day."

They walked into her house. Charlie had already found the bowl of fresh water she'd put out for him. She opened the kitchen slider so he could go outside.

"Want a beer?" she asked. "You must be tired."

"I am. A beer sounds great. Then I need to get home and take a shower."

She walked to the refrigerator. "You could shower here."

She'd meant the statement innocently enough. She really was offering the shower. But something in the air changed when she said the words. She turned and found Aidan watching her from across the kitchen.

His dark eyes brightened with an intensity that stole her breath. Wanting pooled in her belly and quickly moved out to every corner of her body. She shivered and not from the cold.

"Want to join me?"

Four simple words that individually didn't mean all that much. But when strung together...well, they were a lot more significant.

She thought about what it would be like—the

small, steamy space, the hot water and a very naked, wet Aidan to do with what she would.

She smiled. "You're saying the beer can wait?"

"That I am."

AIDAN WAS UNPREPARED for the high pitched sounds that ten sixteen-year-old girls could make. His first thought was he was grateful he'd left Charlie at home. The poor pup would have been whimpering from the loud noises. To be honest, Aidan felt a little overwhelmed himself.

Starr's party was held in a section of the town's convention center. He never would have thought of that venue, but Shelby had talked to party planner Dellina Ridge, who had suggested it.

They'd taken over about a quarter of the open area near the industrial kitchen. There was plenty of room for tables and chairs and their 1950s theme.

Destiny and Kipling had provided the portable sound system and Gideon, who owned the local oldies radio station, had loaned them plenty of era-appropriate music. There were cutouts of Elvis for selfies, rented poodle skirts and a makeup station with printed instructions on how to do cat eyeliner.

Beyond the tables was a basketball court-sized concrete floor—perfect for roller skating. The menu was simple—hot dogs, mac and cheese and a salad bar. There was an ice cream sundae station and the guitar cupcake cake.

The party had started at three and dinner was still about an hour away. Aidan could see the girls were nearly finished with roller skating. He crossed to Shelby, who was setting the big table for the girls.

"We're going to need another activity," he said. "Otherwise, they'll get restless."

She smiled. "You sound nervous."

"Yeah. My female training has been with adults. Teenaged girls still frighten me."

She patted his arm. "They frighten us all. Don't worry. I have it covered." She pointed to the big double doors.

A woman walked in. She was tall and lean, with green eyes and blond hair. It took him a second to recognize her.

"She's that dance lady."

"Evie Jefferson," Shelby said, waving her over. "She owns the dance school in town. She's going to teach the girls some dances from the 1950s. That will keep them busy until dinner. Plus they'll be exhausted."

"Kipling will be thrilled."

Because after the dinner, the girls were all heading back to Starr's house for a sleepover.

"I think there's a slight chance that he and Destiny will get some sleep tonight." She laughed. "Well, except for the baby waking them up."

Evie explained the dance to the girls, then walked through it with them. Kipling moved over to stand by Shelby and Aidan.

"It's the same dance they'll see on *American Graffiti* tonight," he said.

"You know that movie takes place in the 1960s, don't you?" Aidan asked.

Kipling grinned. "I don't think they'll notice. Old is old." He pulled Aidan aside. "I heard about your gift. Thanks. Destiny and I both appreciate it. I was prepared to take it on myself, but this really helps."

Aidan had given Starr a certificate for ten driving lessons. "You have enough on your plate," he said. "Plus I think having someone other than family teach her will make it easier for everyone."

"I owe you."

Aidan started to say that was what you did for family, then stopped himself. He and Kipling weren't related. Being friends with Shelby didn't make them family. But he did think of Kipling as more than just a guy he knew.

Kipling returned to Destiny's side. They'd left the baby with a sitter and were enjoying their night out. Shelby had joined the teens and was learning the new dance. Music played and laughter filled the vast space.

This was good, he thought with contentment. How birthdays were supposed to be. When he'd been a kid, his mom had tried, but Ceallach had inevitably done something to ruin the day. It had taken Aidan a long time to figure out his father always had to be the center of attention. Even on one of his kids' birthdays.

He wondered what it had been like for Shelby—growing up terrified of her father. He doubted her birthdays had been very fun, either. At boarding school, she would have been safe, but away from family.

For the millionth time, he wondered why his

mother had stayed. He knew she would say what she felt was love, but he had his doubts. But she'd been stuck and—

Aidan watched the girls dance and Shelby laugh. The music played and the scent of the upcoming meal drifted through the space, but he was removed from it all. Thoughts formed, faded, then reformed. Then he got it.

Love didn't mean being stuck. What he'd most disliked about his parents' relationship wasn't that his mother couldn't leave. It was that she chose not to and his father had abused them all. Maybe not with his fists, but in other ways. Shelby's mother hadn't been stuck. She could have walked away at any time. And she hadn't. She'd stayed for reasons they would never understand.

It wasn't that she'd chosen her husband over her children, it was that she'd accepted what her husband had *done* to her children. Love wasn't supposed to allow pain to happen to your kids. Not when it could easily be prevented.

Whatever those women felt, it wasn't love. Because love meant giving, not taking. Love wasn't about making excuses or having to choose between the father and the child. Love wasn't being stuck— it was about being set free.

"Didn't we just do this?" Shelby asked as she followed Madeline into Jo's Bar.

"You did," her friend told her. "I was working. Now we're having a girls' lunch that I can attend."

Which all sounded great, but Shelby wasn't buying it. There was something about the way Madeline had insisted they go to lunch that made her wonder if something else was going on.

Maybe her friend wanted to talk to her about her upcoming wedding. Or there was yet another pregnancy to celebrate.

She saw Taryn and Patience were already waiting at a smaller booth along the back wall. A booth that only sat four.

"Not a big crowd today," she said as she and Madeline approached the table.

Madeline did her best to smile, but it was obviously fake. There was a hint of nervousness as she said, "Sometimes that's more fun."

Shelby sat down next to Patience, looked at the other two and asked flatly, "What's up?"

Patience sighed. "I knew we couldn't fool you for long. I was hoping for at least ten minutes."

Shelby told herself that these women loved her and she trusted them absolutely. They would never hurt her. At least not deliberately.

Jo brought over four glasses and a pitcher of iced tea, then left without saying a word. Which made Shelby think she'd been warned off.

"Now I'm scared," she said. "Is one of you sick? Am I sick? Is a meteor about to hit Fool's Gold and kill us all?"

The other three women exchanged a look. Madeline nodded.

"I'll go first," she said firmly, then reached across the table toward Shelby. "You know we all love you," she began.

Oh, God. This was going to be bad. "Yes," Shelby said slowly. "And?"

"And this is an intervention."

Which was pretty much the last thing Shelby had been expecting. "Excuse me? A what?"

"An intervention," Taryn told her. "Shelby, you're wonderful. So creative and giving. And delightfully naive."

"I have no idea what you're talking about."

"Aidan," the three of them said together.

What had been nerves quickly turned to dread. Aidan? No. What could they want to tell her? That there was another woman? That he'd been seen with someone else? What if it was true? What if he'd slept with one of his campers? It had happened before. It used to happen all the time.

No, she told herself firmly. No. They were wrong. Aidan would never do that. They were sleeping together and he wasn't the kind of man to betray that. She believed in him down to her bones.

"He's a good guy and you can't convince me otherwise," she told her friends.

"We're not trying," Patience said quickly. "It's not that at all. I've known Aidan all my life and you're right. He's great. In fact, that's the problem."

"You're not making any sense."

Taryn rolled her eyes. "I'll just say it. Shelby, you're in love with him."

She wouldn't have been more surprised if little green men had jumped onto the table and taken off with her drink.

"Wh-what?"

"You're. In. Love. With. Him." Taryn's expression turned sympathetic. "I'm sorry to be blunt, but we thought you might not have figured it out for yourself. Judging by the wide-eyed shock, you didn't."

"I'm not," she breathed, stunned by how they'd gotten it all so wrong. "We're friends."

Taryn groaned.

"We know you keep saying that," Madeline said. "All the time. That's what has us concerned. Me concerned," she amended. "Shelby, you've gone through a lot and your effort to change was so inspiring. You figured out what was wrong and how to fix it. Aidan was the perfect choice. Maybe too perfect."

"You're all crazy. It's not love. It's friendship."

Taryn shook her head. "If it walks like a duck and quacks like a duck, it's a duck. Shelby, honey, you're a down-to-the-bone, honest-to-God duck."

"I'm not. We like each other. We hang out."

"You're having sex."

Patience's voice was quiet, but firm. Shelby stared at her.

"How did you know?"

"What?" Madeline gasped. "You didn't tell me!"

"Seriously, you're going to get hung up on that?" Taryn asked. "Of course they're having sex. She's been glowing for about two, maybe three weeks. They are so doing the deed."

Speaking of glowing…Shelby felt her face heat. She kept her gaze on Patience, who gave her a rueful smile.

"I go to work really early, too," her friend admitted. "I saw you leaving his house at four in the morn-

ing. There was no other reason for you to be there."
Patience held up her hand. "I'm not judging. I'm just
worried. I think it's great you're in love with him.
We're just worried that you can't admit the truth to
yourself."

Shelby pushed aside her embarrassment and
stared down her friends. "I'm *not* in love with Aidan.
You're all sweet to be concerned, but it's fine. I'm
fine. We're—"

"We know," they said together. "Friends."

"We are."

The four of them went silent. Madeline drew in
a breath.

"Okay then. If you're sure. I'll end this the way
we started. We all love you very much and we're
concerned about you."

Shelby smiled at her. "I know, and thank you. But
there's really nothing to worry about. I'm totally and
completely fine."

"Famous last words," Taryn muttered.

"What was that?"

"Nothing. Nothing at all."

CHAPTER NINETEEN

WHEN THE FOX AND HOUND restaurant closed for its annual week of vacation, Shelby was able to use the kitchen for her baking. That allowed the contractors to pull a couple of all-nighters and finish their work one entire week early. Which was why, the week before Memorial Day, she found herself standing in front of her brand-new business, key in hand.

"You did it," Aidan said. "Are you excited?"

"Yes. And scared. The usual conflicting emotions."

He put his arm around her. "You'll do great."

He sounded exactly the same as he always did. Calm. Supportive. The man was solid. Someone she could lean on. He was nice, she trusted him and when they were intimate, he rocked her world.

Not love. Not love. She didn't know why she felt the need to chant the words, but she did. Over and over again. A ridiculous waste of time and one that also made her feel foolish. Didn't she want love in her life? Wasn't that the point of this project with Aidan? To get herself ready? So if her friends were right and she *had* fallen in love with him, wasn't that a good thing?

"You okay?" he asked.

She forced herself back to the topic at hand. "Yes. I'm great. Thanks for all your help with this."

"I didn't do anything."

"You did so much." She stared at the closed door. "Want to go inside?"

"Of course."

She turned the key over in her hand, then stepped forward. The lock turned easily. There was an alarm system and usually she would enter the bakery from the rear door, but this one time, she would start at the front and work her way back.

Directly in front of her were the cases that held the baked goods. They'd been cleaned and there was new shelving. A half-dozen bistro tables with matching chairs gave people a place to sit. There was a new coffee station on the right. She wasn't interested in competing with Brew-haha, but had needed more than the single pot she'd had before.

She knew what was behind the counter. Racks and the cold cases. Beyond that was the old kitchen. The only change had been to add two more mixers and shelving. The real magic had happened on the other side.

She turned to her left and saw open French doors. When the tea shop was open, they would be as well. When the tea shop was closed, she could lock the doors, while preserving the sense of openness.

They walked through the small restaurant. She'd had the walls painted white. Several hutches and two buffets, all in dark wood, were spaced around the edges of the room.

There were only ten tables—most seating four,

but a few could hold six. Stacks of linens sat on a side table, along with teapots still in their boxes. The tablecloths were also white, but the place mats were in a rainbow of colors. The napkins were of a similar hue, but complemented rather than matched.

She and Aidan had used an online auction site to buy several incomplete sets of china. It was amazing how much she'd been able to save by purchasing a set with six plates, but eight bowls and no side plates. Now the mismatched dishes added color and elegance to the simple decor.

Boxes of glasses, flatware and vases were ready to be put out. The serving pieces had arrived the week before and were in the kitchen. A chalkboard on the wall offered a place to list the specials of the day—whatever they might be.

She led the way into the kitchen. All the appliances gleamed. She had four ovens, an oversized professional stove and refrigerator, and a pantry fit for royalty. Everything was perfect.

For a second she couldn't believe it had all come together. That she was really that lucky.

"Tell me this isn't a dream," she whispered.

Aidan pulled her close. "You made this happen," he whispered. "I'm so proud of you, Shelby. You've done a hell of a job here."

She smiled up at him. He lowered his head and kissed her. His mouth was warm and firm. He offered as much as he took. She felt the pressure of his fingers, the strength of his body. Wanting began its insistent dance, but she ignored the beat. Instead she leaned her head against his shoulder and breathed in the scent of him.

Not love, she promised herself. Love scared her. Love meant she would be vulnerable. Maybe not physically—because she trusted him—but in every other way possible. This was so much better than love could ever be.

"Ready to get to work?" she asked.

"I am."

They went back outside and started pulling cartons, bins and bags from the back of his truck. While the bakery was closed until tomorrow and the tea shop wouldn't open until next week, tonight she was making dinner for friends and family. Sort of a thank-you for all their support.

The menu was simple. An assortment of crostini appetizers, followed by an easy salad with baby heirloom tomatoes and pears. The entrée would be her version of chicken chili verde with bacon cheddar biscuits, followed by chocolate bread pudding parfaits and custom cookies for dessert.

She'd chosen a champagne for a toast and then had gone with a simple selection of beer and wine for dinner. Which had all sounded so sensible when she'd planned it. Now she glanced at the clock and wondered if she'd overestimated her abilities.

"Two hours," Aidan told her. "Freaking out?"

"A little."

"Tell me what to do first."

She'd already made the chicken chili verde, so that was easy. She had him pour it into a giant stockpot.

"Stir that every five minutes," she told him. "We're heating it slowly."

"Yes, ma'am."

He smiled as he spoke. That easy smile that said he was happy to do what she said. That he respected her and trusted her. It was the kind of smile that made her want to step closer and be held by him, but there wasn't time.

She told him how to prep the salad. The dressing was already made. She stored that in the new, shiny, industrial refrigerator after allowing herself about ten seconds to admire all the space. The desserts were already made. She put the trays into the fridge as well, then got to work on the crostini.

While Aidan tore lettuce into bite-sized pieces and then washed them, she sliced baguettes into thin, even slices. She applied olive oil, then slid giant baking sheets into the new oven. Every five minutes, Aidan dutifully stirred the chicken.

About an hour before guests were due to arrive, she heard a voice from the front of the tea shop.

"Hey, it's me. Anyone here?" Madeline walked into the kitchen. "There you are. I came by early to see how I could help." She hugged Shelby, then walked to the sink and washed her hands. "How about if I start setting the tables?"

Only a few days ago Madeline had spearheaded the intervention that Shelby still found unsettling. She didn't blame her friends for trying to help. She just wished she could convince them there wasn't a problem. There was also the concern that her friends were upset with her for not agreeing with them.

She should have known better, she told herself happily as Madeline wiped her hands on a towel and smiled.

"So, what are your instructions?"

"We're serving everyone buffet style," she said. "We'll use the two sideboards by the door for the bar and the ones in the back for the food."

"So plates and flatware on them?"

"Yes. Bowls, too."

"I'm on it."

Time passed quickly. Madeline prepared the buffet line, Aidan stirred and made the salad and Shelby took care of everything else. Bailey and her husband, Kenny, arrived a few minutes early. Kenny immediately began opening bottles of wine and champagne while Bailey put the beer on ice. Amber and her husband arrived right after. Tom carried in a large box with a dozen or so small centerpieces.

"Our housewarming gift to you," Amber said as they hugged. "I can't tell you how beautiful everything looks."

By six thirty, the party was in full swing. Starr and a couple of her friends circulated with plates of crostini. The chicken was bubbling hot and ready to be put out on the buffet. Once she got the cheddar bacon biscuits ready to bake, Aidan had chased her out of the kitchen to go mingle with her friends.

"I'll handle this," he told her.

Shelby walked out into the tea shop and watched while the people she cared most about laughed and talked.

Two years ago, she'd been in Colorado with her

dying mother. She'd been dodging her father's fists and so alone and scared. The feeling of having nowhere to turn, no safe place to be, had only gotten worse after Kipling had been injured.

Then two men had shown up at her doorstep and changed everything. Her mother had passed in peace and Shelby had moved to Fool's Gold.

Two years ago she would never have believed she could be happy ever again. She never would have thought she would find her way to owning a business like this. She was truly blessed and so grateful.

Kipling stepped to the center of the room and held up his glass of champagne. "If I could have your attention, please," he said. "I'd like to propose a toast. To my baby sister, Shelby."

"To Shelby."

Everyone raised their glasses to her. Shelby turned in a slow circle and saw the many people who made up the fabric of her life. And Aidan, who stood by the door to the kitchen. He held his glass high. When she looked at him, he winked. And everything about her world felt exactly right.

MARGARET WAS A TALL, willowy blonde with a warm, easy smile and the physique of a professional athlete. Aidan remembered the first time he'd met her. She'd come to Fool's Gold for a hiking weekend—the most challenging trip his company offered. The rest of the group had been unable to keep up with them and by the morning of the second day, it was just him and Margaret. After long days of hiking and climbing, they'd found fun ways to fill the night.

She'd been one of the few "tourists" he'd kept in touch with. She'd married a few years back. When she'd mentioned she was going to be in the area, he'd agreed to meet her for dinner.

"I can't believe how the town's grown," she said as she sat across from him at Angelo's, where they'd scored an outdoor table. "The festivals seem to be the same, but the number of people coming to town has grown. I didn't think I would be able to book a room for the night."

The evening was warm. Under other circumstances, it might even be romantic—but not tonight. Not when he wasn't with Shelby.

The server returned with the bottle of wine Aidan had ordered. When they each had a glass, Aidan turned his attention back to Margaret.

"How are things?"

"Good. Busy. The kids are growing so fast. My oldest is nearly four. The baby's just two. It's crazy."

"But happy."

"It is. I've just gone back to work full-time." She waved to the sidewalk just beyond the restaurant patio. "There's some travel, which is hard. I want to be home with my kids. At the same time I also want to be working."

"A dilemma most working mothers face," he pointed out. "It often takes both parents working to support a family these days, but leaving every morning is difficult."

She studied him. "Yes, and why do you know that?"

"It's not a secret."

"It's not something I would expect an unmarried guy with no children to have thought about." Her gaze narrowed. "What's different?"

"Are you saying I wasn't this deep the last time we were together?"

"You were fun and charming and great in bed." She sipped her wine. "But no. Not deep."

He wasn't aware of making any changes in thinking, but he knew that they had taken place. They were inevitable and the point of the experiment with Shelby. He liked who he was now. Not the jackass he'd been, but a good man who respected others' feelings. Especially when it came to women.

"I had a bad experience a few months back," he admitted. "It caused me to look at my life and what I'd been doing in my free time."

"Aside from sleeping with tourists?" she asked, her voice teasing.

"No, pretty much just that. While the reasons were sound, the execution turned out to have some flaws." He briefly told her about the New Year's Eve debacle and Shelby's suggestion that they become friends.

"Actual friends?" Margaret asked.

"We alternate doing boy things and girl things." He laughed. "Less formally now, but it still happens. Shelby kicks butt at Texas hold 'em and I can go to lunch with a woman and simply talk." He leaned back in his chair. "Without offering advice."

"I'm not sure I believe that."

"It's true. I've learned the power of listening. Not only do some problems not have a solution, sometimes the point isn't the solution. It's sharing the feelings the problem creates. Women bond over shared emotion."

Margaret shook her head. "I honestly don't know what to say. I'm a little jealous. That would never happen at my house."

"Then you're not expecting enough of your husband. If I can learn to listen, anyone can."

"I wish that were true. How's business?"

"Excellent." He told her about the new tours he would be offering.

"I'll have to bring the whole family back here," she said with a laugh. "You're making me want to move."

"You'd be welcome." He thought about her little kids. "You'd need a babysitting service, wouldn't you? One you could trust."

"Sure, but that's hard enough to find at home. It would be impossible on vacation."

"Unless we had referrals. I'll have to talk to some of the other business owners in town. Maybe we could set up a co-op or something."

"Now you're scaring me, Aidan. What if it turns out you're perfect?"

"Nothing you need to worry about. It'll never happen."

"I don't know. You're getting pretty close."

"I'm better than I was," he told her. "I'm grateful for that." He never wanted to hurt anyone the way he'd hurt the woman he'd been unable to remember. There'd been no reason for it. No excuse.

"What happens when the six months are up?" she asked. "With you and Shelby?"

"I'm not sure."

He knew what he would like. He wanted to keep seeing Shelby. As friends and maybe something more. He liked her in a way he hadn't expected. They fit well together.

Margaret smiled at him. "Wow. I hope my husband gets that look on his face when he thinks about me."

"What are you talking about?"

"Just now, when you thought of Shelby. There was something. I can't explain it, but trust me. Every woman wants her man to look at her that way." She leaned across the table and lightly kissed him. "I hope she knows how lucky she is."

"Me, too."

Aidan started to laugh only to see movement out of the corner of his eye. He turned and saw Shelby on the sidewalk, by the restaurant. Her eyes were wide, her cheeks drained of color. When her gaze locked with his, she turned and quickly walked away.

Aidan swore and started after her.

He caught up with her before she'd gone twenty feet. After grabbing her arm, he turned her so they were facing each other.

"It wasn't a date," he told her. "I've known Margaret for years. We're friends. She's happily married with a couple of kids. You don't have anything to worry about."

Because he would never cheat on her. Not only

because he wasn't that guy, but also because of her. How he felt about her.

Shelby stared at him. "I believe you," she said slowly. "Of course I do."

Which sounded right, but she still looked upset. "Then what else is wrong?"

"I don't know."

He dropped his arm to his side. They stared at each other. Aidan felt the tension—but this one wasn't based in sexual desire. Instead it felt tight and uncomfortable. As if something was wrong. Or as if he was supposed to be doing or saying something but he didn't know what.

"I sent you a text about the dinner," he said.

"I know. You said to come by. That's why I'm here. It's not that."

"Then what?"

Her blue eyes searched his, looking for something. As if she needed something only he could give her. He knew the feeling. Sometimes when he thought about her he got confused and had no idea about the cause.

The truth crashed in on him with the subtlety of an avalanche and he suddenly knew exactly what was wrong. Or rather, what was right.

He loved her. No, he was *in* love with her. Or both. Did it matter? He loved Shelby. Why wouldn't he? She was bright and funny and caring and sweet. He loved looking at her and being with her and making love with her. He loved *her*.

Why hadn't he realized this before? Possibly because he was a guy, he told himself. Despite his recent training, he wasn't exactly intuitive. But he knew now. He loved her.

Thinking the words felt right. Now he just had to say them.

"Shelby—"

She took a step back. "I'm done."

"What?"

"I'm done. With this." She waved her hand between them. "With us. The friendship thing. I don't know what I was thinking. It was never going to work. I don't want to be friends anymore. I don't want to have anything to do with you. It was a stupid idea and I want it over."

"But I—"

"I don't want to hear it," she told him, and then she walked away.

CHAPTER TWENTY

SHELBY KNEW SHE was a big, fat failure. Or a fraud. Or both. She'd been so sure about what she wanted. So smug and determined. She'd had all the answers. Become friends with a man so she could get over being scared. Why not? It was the perfect plan.

And it had been working, too. She'd been healing. She'd felt it, had known it. And then everything had crashed in around her.

She sat in her living room, in a corner of the sofa. She'd pulled her legs up to her chest and wrapped her arms around her knees. But even that wasn't enough to hold herself together. She was unraveling, bit by bit.

Watching that woman kiss Aidan had shocked her into seeing the truth. Oh, she knew the kiss was meaningless. She trusted Aidan completely. He'd told her about the dinner and had asked her to join them if she wanted. Not the actions of the man out to cheat. Plus, she knew *him*. He had flaws, but that wasn't one of them.

No, the shock hadn't been about the kiss itself, but her instant, down-to-the-bone jealousy. The intense flash had stunned her, as had the realization that whatever emotions she had for Aidan, they were too big to be contained.

She hadn't known, she thought as she tried to steady her breathing. She hadn't realized that caring could get so large. So overpowering. She wasn't ready for that, she couldn't handle that. Loving Kipling was easy. He was her brother and she'd known him all her life. Loving her friends was also simple. They were there for her. But what if she loved Aidan?

She couldn't do it. She just couldn't risk it. Because that's what love was—a risk. She was expected to hand her heart over to some man? No way. That wasn't going to happen. She knew better. She'd seen the damage love could do. No way she was taking any chances.

She'd spent her whole life protecting herself, and with good reason. She wasn't going to stop now—no matter what. Better to be alone forever than to take the chance.

SHELBY COULDN'T REMEMBER ever visiting the offices of Score before. The PR firm had relocated about three years before—moving former Super Bowl champions Jack, Sam and Kenny to Fool's Gold. Although Jack had left Score to coach football at the local university, the other two were still working the business, along with their partner, Taryn.

Now Shelby looked at the larger-than-life-size portraits of the former football players on the reception area walls and wondered what on earth she'd been thinking. Maybe her father's fists had damaged more than her spirit, she thought sadly. Maybe they'd damaged her actual brain.

Still, there was no turning back now, she told herself as she continued along the hallway, then paused in front of the partially open door. She knocked once before entering.

Taryn was behind her desk, wearing a black-and-white floral print dress that not only fit her perfectly, but probably cost more than a used car. Shelby was sure she would recognize the name of the designer, should she bother to ask. Next to Taryn's chair was a pair of ridiculously high-heeled pumps. Taryn herself was barefoot, which made sense. Who could walk in shoes like that?

Her friend rose and walked around her desk. "Shelby, honey, what's wrong? You sounded upset on the phone."

"I'm sorry."

The response was automatic and foolish. She wasn't sorry. She was confused and angry, and confused about *being* angry, but she wasn't sorry.

Taryn crossed to her. "Let's have a seat." She motioned to the sofas at the far end of the room. "Do you want some coffee? It's early for wine, but I have a bottle in the refrigerator if that would help."

"I don't want wine or coffee. I'm fine."

They sat across from each other. Taryn's blue-violet eyes were dark with concern. Shelby couldn't blame her. She'd phoned impulsively, and had asked if they could talk. While she and Taryn often spent time together at their girlfriend lunches, their relationship was more "friend of a friend."

Taryn smiled at her. "How can I help?"

"You can't."

"Okay. That makes this more interesting."

Shelby thought maybe the other woman would insist on knowing why she'd come by or what she wanted, but Taryn sat patiently, obviously waiting for Shelby to get to whatever it was that had brought her to Score.

"I don't know why I'm here," she admitted. "I think it's because you're the—" She almost said "meanest" but knew that wasn't right. Taryn wasn't ever mean. She was actually kind and giving and she'd offered Shelby a loan. "You're the most direct of my friends."

"I'm going to take that as a compliment," Taryn told her. "What do I need to be direct about?"

"Aidan."

"Ah." Taryn relaxed. "You're thinking about the intervention."

She hadn't been, but as soon as the other woman said the words, Shelby remembered that uncomfortable conversation.

"I'm not seeing him anymore."

Taryn sighed. "I'm sorry to hear that."

"I told him it was over. Our friendship or whatever you want to call it. I'm done with him. The whole idea was stupid. A complete waste of time. I don't want to see him anymore."

She spoke defiantly, then braced herself for the scolding sure to follow. After all, Taryn believed Shelby was in love with Aidan. She would see Shelby's actions as self-destructive.

But instead of speaking, Taryn walked around the coffee table to Shelby's sofa and sat next to her. She put her arms around Shelby and held her tight.

"I'm sorry," she said quietly. "I'm sorry the fear is still winning."

Shelby struggled to get free. She scooted back a few feet. "I'm not afraid."

Taryn's expression was kind. "I don't know much about your past. Not the specifics, at least. I've heard a few things." She drew in a breath. "My father hit me, too. He was a cruel man. The details aren't important except to tell you that I had no intention of ever trusting a man enough to fall in love with him. And that when I met Angel, I nearly lost him because I wasn't willing to trust."

She tucked her dark hair behind her ears. "Learning to trust him was the hardest thing I've ever done. Because the fear's so big."

Shelby didn't know what to say. "I had no idea," she admitted. "I can't believe it. You're so confident and powerful."

"Well," Taryn murmured, "it took me a long time to get here. I put up a lot of walls. No one got in. Not even the boys."

Shelby knew "the boys" were the three men she'd worked with. Her family, before Angel. Taryn and Jack had even briefly been married.

"There's a price to be paid for everything in life," Taryn told her. "Nothing is free. If you stay safe, the price is never knowing love. Because to receive love, you have to give love. And to give love is to be vulnerable. You can build walls and be lonely or you can tear them down and hand over your heart."

"What if I don't like either solution?"

"Then you're unhappy," Taryn told her. "Like I said, there's always a price."

"I don't accept that."

"You don't have to accept gravity, either, but you're still going to fall if you step off the top of a building." Taryn leaned toward her. "You love him. We can all see it, and while it would be great for all of us to be wrong and you to be right, the odds are seriously against you. From everything I hear, he's a good guy. If you were ever going to take a chance, why not take a chance on him?"

"Because if I do, I'll die."

Shelby hadn't meant to say that, but the words came out before she could stop them.

"I didn't mean that," she said quickly.

"Yes, you did. It's not bad that you said it," Taryn told her. "At least you know your starting point. Where you go from here is up to you."

CHARLIE LED THE way back to the house, careful to sniff every plant. Aidan wasn't sure what the dog was expecting to find, but it sure seemed important. His tail wagged as he walked and every few steps he glanced over his shoulder, as if making sure Aidan was keeping up.

The last couple of days had been hard. He missed Shelby more than he would have thought possible. He was used to seeing her, talking to her, touching her. There wasn't a part of him that didn't miss her.

He dreamed about her in his sleep. There was no escape from her and his love for her.

Worse than that was not knowing what to do. His gut said to give her time. That she needed to think about whatever was bothering her. His heart wanted to go to her and hold her. Help her. Even if he was the problem, he could still help. Which sounded stupid. So he did nothing except wait.

Charlie raised his head and barked, then ran toward the house. Aidan followed and was surprised to find the front door was open. The little dog had already disappeared inside.

Aidan hurried after him. He found his living room filled with women. Lots of women.

Jo from Jo's Bar manned a blender set up in the kitchen. Taryn and Larissa were putting out platters of cookies and brownies. Patience saw him and walked over.

"We're so sorry," she said, giving him a hug. "We're here to help."

Amber waved from the kitchen. Even Destiny was there, holding her sleeping daughter in her arms.

"How are you going to help?" he asked.

Patience wrinkled her nose. "I have no idea." She turned toward the other women. "Aidan wants to know how we're going to help."

Madeline walked out of the kitchen and handed him a beer. "We generally do margaritas at times like this, but you strike me as a beer guy."

"Thanks. Don't take this wrong, but what's going on?"

Felicia Boylan walked through the front door.

"I'm sorry I'm late. Hello, Aidan. This is a Fool's Gold tradition. If a couple breaks up, the women gather together to help. Usually we're antimale, but in this case, it seems you're the wronged party. So we're bringing our traditional get-over-him party to you."

He knew they were trying to be nice, so he accepted the beer and sat on the sofa. The women gathered around him. Charlie was in doggy heaven, being petted and cuddled and fed cookies.

Taryn sat across from him. "I want to say up front that I've spoken to Shelby."

Everyone looked at her. Aidan had to fight back the need to ask how she was. Did she look okay? Was she sleeping? Was there anything he could do to—

"I'm not going to betray her confidence by telling you what she told me," she admitted. "However, I am willing to say that a lot of what she's going through has very little to do with you. I think you should give her some time. More time than you want to, I'm guessing. But she needs to figure this out."

There was a lot of information in that coded message, he thought. If Shelby was still dealing with her past, then Taryn was right—none of this was about him. Even though it still hurt.

Time. His head said that was the right thing. To give her space, to not pressure her. But his heart, his heart ached for her.

Patience sat next to him. "I'm sorry you're going through this," she said with a sigh. "Normally, when we do this, we totally trash the guys. But Shelby is our friend, so I'm not comfortable doing that." She wrinkled her nose. "Equality between the sexes can be so awkward."

Felicia sat on his other side. "When Gideon and I were still in an uncommitted dating relationship, I wasn't sure where I stood with him. He was unable to handle my declaration of love. It completely freaked him out. But he came around. I'm sure Shelby will, as well."

"You haven't asked if that's what I want," he pointed out.

"We don't have to," Madeline told him. "We can see it in your eyes. You love her." Her gaze narrowed. "You do love her, don't you?"

"Yeah. With all my heart."

Most of the women sighed.

Jo walked around, refilling margarita glasses. "We like to think only men are stupid," she said cheerfully. "But dumb is an equal-opportunity employer." She patted his shoulder. "I promise, the next time you show up for a girls' lunch, I won't say anything."

"Gee, thanks."

"I know. I'm a giver."

He managed to laugh. Conversation shifted to how everyone else was doing in their lives or how their significant others had messed up. The stories were meant to encourage him, which he appreciated, but a part of him wanted to point out that they were sharing from a place of having found their one true love. He wasn't there yet.

For a second he wondered if he should have regrets. Maybe if he'd never gotten involved with

Shelby. Only that wasn't an option. Having known her, having loved her, whatever else happened, he couldn't be sorry for what he was going through. Everything about her was amazing. He was damned lucky to have gotten as much as he had. He would shut up and be grateful. And maybe have a little faith. In her…in himself and in everything they could be.

THERE WAS SOMETHING to be said for a complete lack of conversation, Shelby thought as Angel finished dealing the cards. There was companionship, the men sitting around the table and the game itself, but no endless chatter about how everything was going to be fine.

She'd played enough times to understand the basics of the game, so close attention wasn't required. She could think or not think about what was happening in her life and let the rhythm of the cards serve as a nice distraction. They were in a back room at The Man Cave. Music played through speakers and beyond their private room they could hear noise from the bar.

She knew most of the men at the table, but a couple were a little unfamiliar. Gabriel Boylan was an ER doctor. Shelby had met Noelle, who owned The Christmas Attic, a few times and Gabriel was her husband. Also Felicia's brother-in-law. He seemed nice enough, but he'd never played cards with them before.

Angel was there, along with Justice, Patience's husband, and a few others. Shelby had been a little surprised to get the call inviting her to a game, but she'd accepted once she'd confirmed that Aidan wasn't coming. It was good to get out of the house. Mostly because everything reminded her of him.

They'd become such a part of each other's lives that separating was difficult. She missed him, missed their conversations, their time together. She missed Charlie. But she knew she'd been right to break things off. She needed to be safe, to protect her heart. The only way to do that for sure was to stay away from him.

"How's business?" Justice asked her.

The question surprised her. Usually there wasn't much talking at the games. "Um, good. The new space is working out. We're busy for lunch every day."

"You'll get tourist business for sure," Gabriel added. "Plus the ladies in town will enjoy going out to tea. Noelle gets a huge tourist trade. You should talk to her about putting flyers in her store."

"Thanks. I will."

More cards were dealt. Angel folded. Kipling studied his cards, then did the same.

"Not my night," he said easily as he picked up his beer.

"How's Destiny doing?" Sam Ridge asked.

"Good. Still trying to accomplish more than she should. Between Tonya, Starr, the upcoming tour and getting through the day, she's overwhelmed. I help when I can."

"They do love to take on too much," Justice said. "Patience acts so casual about having a baby, but it's tough on her. She's still getting up at four in the morning."

He sounded both amazed and proud.

Shelby wanted to bang her head against the table. She really didn't want to hear about how much they all loved their wives. It was depressing. Because at one time she'd thought she wanted that, too. Love. Someone in her life. But now she wasn't sure.

The price was too high. She would have to give up too much. Maybe it was better to simply be alone. At least then she was safe.

Only she missed Aidan. She wanted to see him smile at her, hear the sound of his voice. Maybe get just one quick hug. He'd changed so much in the past few months. He'd always been great, but now he was even better. While she still felt the same. *Stuck* was the word that came to mind. Talk about ironic. He would sure get that joke. She should call him and—

No! She pulled her mind back to the game. She wasn't going to give in and be weak. She would stay strong. Solitary. She'd tried becoming normal and it hadn't worked out. She didn't want to keep trying. She had her answer. Now she would move on.

"You scared when Patience went into labor?" Kipling asked Justice.

"Terrified. I've been through combat, been chased by a sniper. The only thing worse was when Lillie was taken."

Shelby frowned. "What do you mean?"

Justice sipped his beer. "Long story. My father had faked his death and was on the run from the law. He found me and wanted to hurt me, so he took Lillie. We got her back."

Shelby did her best to keep her jaw from dropping. "Seriously?"

His eyes were cold. "I would have killed him for doing it, but Ford got there first."

Shelby could tell she was going to have to have a long talk with Madeline about some Fool's Gold history. "I had no idea. I'm sorry."

"Me, too. I never would have come back if I'd known Patience and Lillie were going to be in danger."

"You don't mean that," Angel said easily. "You had to come back to find her."

Shelby was about to ask who "her" was when Justice sighed heavily.

"I know you're right, but that was the worst. Knowing that Lillie was in danger, scared. I loved her so much. Both of them. Knowing it was my fault about killed me." He held up his hand. "I know, I know. It was my father, not me. I get the distinction. But they were everything to me. Loving them, knowing they could have been hurt—" He shook his head. "I can't begin to describe what that was like."

"But it was worth it," Kipling said quietly.

"Now. I'd be lost without them."

Gabriel put down his cards. "I went through that with Noelle," he admitted. "Not being sure. She was so happy and positive all the time. I could only see the darkness."

Shelby had heard a little of his story. How he'd been a doctor in the army for several years, serving the front line. He'd been the first doctor the most seriously injured had seen. It had been his job to patch them up enough to get them to a real facility.

When he'd come to Fool's Gold to visit his brother for the holidays, he'd been exhausted. Both physically and emotionally. She supposed it was impossible to see what he'd seen, day after day, and not be affected.

"She got me through," Gabriel continued. "She was there, in my face, pulling me along."

"How much did you resist?" Kipling asked.

"As much as I could. Every step of the way. But she never gave up on me." He grimaced. "I could have lost her. Sometimes at night, I wake up in a cold sweat, thinking about that. I could have lost her."

"But you didn't," Shelby told him. "You're together now."

"We are."

They were lucky, she thought ruefully. Able to break through whatever their problems had been. They also weren't the least bit subtle.

"I know what you're doing," she said, giving in to the inevitable and putting her cards down on the table as well. "But it's not going to work."

"Why is that?" her brother asked.

"Because I don't want what you have. Any of you."

Angel smiled at her. "You're not a very good liar, Shelby."

"I'm not lying," she insisted. "I thought I did. I thought I wanted to have a husband and a family, but I don't. It's too hard. I wanted to learn to trust a man. So I did. I trust Aidan. But it doesn't matter, because in the end, love means giving over too much of myself. I'm not willing to do that."

Angel studied her. His pale gray eyes were a little unnerving. It was as if he could see into her soul.

"Sometimes you have to take a leap of faith. I know they say the best things in life are free, but every now and then the good stuff has to be earned."

"I know what you want," Kipling told her. "You want us to say that relationships don't matter. But we won't, because it's not true."

Gabriel nodded. "The people we love and who love us back are *all* that matter."

She wanted to cover her ears and not hear what they were saying. "Can't we just play cards?"

"No," Angel said easily. "Sorry, kid. This is an intervention."

"My second one in a month," she grumbled. "The last one was my girlfriends telling me I was a duck."

"What?" Kipling asked.

"Never mind." She folded her arms on the table. "Go ahead. Say what you have to say."

She would surrender to the process because it was the only way to get through the moment. Then they would move on and she would be fine.

"For what it's worth," her brother said, "you got most of it right. You can trust Aidan. He's not the problem."

"You are," Angel told her. "It was never about trusting someone else. It was always about trusting yourself."

She opened her mouth, then closed it. "You're wrong."

"He's not." Kipling's gaze was steady. "You're not freaked out because Aidan has feelings for you, but because you have feelings for him. You don't believe you can give your heart to him and survive. You don't believe you're strong." He leaned toward her. "You are, Shelby. You've been through so much already. Look where you are—with your friends, your business and with Aidan."

She didn't want to look. She wanted to cover her eyes and not see anything. She wanted to have things go back the way they'd been before she and Aidan had been friends.

Only she didn't want that. But if she couldn't go back and couldn't go forward, where did that leave her?

"You're trying to control your way to feeling safe," Angel said. "It doesn't work that way. We don't have control. All we can do is know we're strong enough to survive whatever happens. That the love makes it worthwhile."

Her eyes burned. She blinked away tears.

"You're not your mother," her brother said softly. "You'll never do what she did. But you have to believe it in your heart. You have to accept that you're going to screw up. We all do."

"Every day," Gabriel told her with a wry smile. "But we keep trying to do better."

Kipling got up and walked around the table. He pulled her to her feet and hugged her. "You think you have to be strong enough to always take care of yourself and that's a daunting task. The secret is, with love in your life, someone has your back. On the days you're not strong, he is. And you'll be there for him."

Despite her determination not to give in, the tears came. Pain and confusion and loneliness filled her until she thought she would drown from all the emotion.

"I don't know what happened," she admitted. "One second everything was fine. The next I wanted to run as far and as fast as I could."

"Sure," Angel said. "Seek cover or higher ground. It's what all wounded animals do."

She raised her head and glared at him. "Not your best analogy."

"Maybe, but it's accurate. You're wounded. More healed than you were before, but some injuries never completely go away. So you adapt. The question is do you accept where you are and make the best of it or do you spend the rest of your life feeling sorry for yourself?"

She pushed away from Kipling and walked toward Angel. "I'm not feeling sorry for myself."

"You kind of are," Justice added. "And you're stupid. You and Aidan have a great thing going. He's done everything you asked and you walked away because you're scared. Did I miss anything?"

"Nope," Angel said cheerfully. "That about sums it up. I'm hungry. Anyone want a sandwich?"

"I do," Gabriel said as he stood. "I'll go with you."

"Me, too."

All the guys left the room until it was just her and Kipling.

She put her hands on her hips. "Your friends are idiots."

"No, they're honest. And they're your friends, too."

She sniffed, then wiped her face. "If I was with my girlfriends, they'd be hugging me and telling me that Aidan was wrong."

"I thought they said you were a duck."

She stomped her foot. "You're not helping."

"Yes, I am."

She felt tears forming again. "I don't know what to do."

"Yes, you do. Suck it up, Shelby. Face down your fears. If you don't, they'll always win."

CHAPTER TWENTY-ONE

"HEY, AIDAN."

The greeting, in stereo, had him looking at the two redheads who had just walked into his office. It was early on Thursday morning. A week had gone by without Shelby. Seven entire days without her. He knew that Taryn had been right when she'd said to give Shelby time. But how long was it going to take?

In the meantime he had identical twins smiling at him. Twins who were both beautiful and bright and very comfortable in their own skin. The three of them had spent an interesting couple of nights together the previous summer.

"We were in the neighborhood and wanted to say hi," Paris said with a smile. He knew which was which because London had a small scar by the corner of her mouth. Yes, London and Paris—obviously born to parents with a strange sense of humor.

London moved close to him. "We had such a good time with you last year. We thought we could do it again."

Talk about every man's fantasy, he thought, feeling no anticipation at the thought. In fact all he felt was tired, which had nothing to do with how little he'd been sleeping and everything to do with being without Shelby.

"No, thanks."

They exchanged a look. "Why not?" Paris asked. "We were good together."

"I'm in love with someone else." It was, he realized, the second time he'd said the words out loud. Huh. It still sounded pretty damned good, so he tried it again. "I'm in love with Shelby."

Paris and London looked at each other. "Really? We would never have guessed you were the committed relationship type."

"Me, either, but it turns out I am. Very much so. I like loving Shelby. It makes me a better man."

London raised her eyebrows. "Wow, that's impressive. Most guys aren't comfortable talking about their feelings."

"You'd be amazed by what I'm comfortable with these days."

Paris sighed. "Our loss. If things don't work out, call us."

Things weren't working out, but calling them was about the last thing he wanted to do. If he couldn't have Shelby, he didn't want anyone.

He saw them out. As the twins walked away, Nick drove up. Aidan waited until his brother got out of his truck and walked toward them.

"Anything I should know about?" Nick asked, looking over his shoulder at the departing twins.

"They're in town for the weekend, if you want a going-away present."

His brother raised one shoulder. "Tempting, but

no. I think one at a time is enough for me. By the way, you look like crap."

"Thanks."

Nick's expression turned sympathetic. "Shelby?"

Aware of a few customers by the front counter and Fay close by, Aidan grabbed Charlie's leash from the hook by the door and stepped outside. The little dog trotted along with him. He and Nick headed for the trail by the office.

"I haven't talked to her in over a week," he admitted when they were out of earshot of the main building. "Taryn said to give her time, so I am, but it's tough."

"I'm sorry." Nick grimaced. "That sounds lame, but I am. You two were good together. Do you know what the problem is?"

"I can guess. She's scared. We were getting more and more involved and she couldn't handle that. Or maybe she knew that I'd fallen in love with her and it freaked her out."

Nick stumbled to a stop, then stared at him. "You're what?" He held up his hand. "Never mind. I don't want to hear you say it again." He swore. "Are you sure?"

"Yup. She's the one. I love her."

The more he said it, the better he felt. Loving Shelby was the best thing he'd ever done. It was right.

"How much time are you giving her?"

"I don't know. I don't want to rush her, but I don't want her thinking I'm not interested. Maybe a couple more days." He didn't have a plan so much as a feeling. When it was right, he would know.

"I have no idea what to say to you," Nick admitted. "You're a braver man than me."

"I can't take credit for being brave. When it comes to Shelby, I don't have a choice. Turns out she's the one."

Nick looked both intrigued and terrified. "Good luck with that."

"Thanks." Aidan saw the back of the truck was filled with boxes. "You heading out?"

"Driving to Happily Inc. tomorrow. I've shipped most of my stuff already. I'm ready to get out of here."

And then there was one. Aidan wondered what it said about his family that he was the only brother to want to stay in Fool's Gold. Del had taken off years before and the twins weren't coming back anytime soon.

"You'll need to come visit me," his brother told him. "Hell, if things work out with Shelby, come to Happily Inc. to get married. It's the country's best destination wedding spot."

Aidan grinned. "Tell you what. If Shelby and I work things out, I promise we'll come there to get married."

"Shelby might want a say in that."

"She might, but I'm pretty sure I can charm her into seeing things my way."

Or so he hoped. Because not having her as his wife was something he refused to consider.

"You take care," Nick told him. "Don't let the bastard get you down."

"He won't bother with me."

Ceallach was only interested in the talented brothers.

Aidan slapped Nick on the back. "For what it's worth, I think you're making the right decision. You need to get out of here and figure it all out. Just don't be a stranger."

"I won't. I promise. Good luck with Shelby. Let me know when she says yes."

"I will."

She would say yes, he told himself. She had to. She was the love of his life and without her, the world was a cold and dark place.

"This is completely ridiculous," Shelby complained.

"You said you wanted help," Madeline pointed out. "I'm helping."

"This isn't what I had in mind."

"Then you should have been more specific when you called."

Her friend didn't sound the least bit concerned about Shelby's reservations. In fact, she pointed to the center of the oversized dressing room and said, "Take off your clothes" in a very stern voice.

"Talk about stupid," Shelby grumbled, but she did as Madeline insisted. She pulled off her T-shirt and let her jeans fall to the floor before kicking them aside. "Happy?"

"Not yet."

They were in the largest dressing room at Paper Moon. When Shelby called Madeline and asked if they could talk, Madeline had suggested Shelby come by the store. At the time she'd thought it was because her friend couldn't get away from work.

Now she knew that Madeline had something else in mind.

"You're very petite," her friend said as she took a white lace wedding gown off a hanger. "And delicately built. The trick is to wear the dress and not the other way around. Which is harder for your figure type."

"I don't see what trying on a wedding dress has to do with anything," Shelby said. "I need to talk to you."

"And we will talk. But you have to put this dress on first. Come on, Shelby. How can it hurt?"

She wasn't sure, but the potential for pain seemed right there. She looked from the dress to her friend's very determined face, then sighed.

"Fine," she grumbled. "I'll try it on. I'm sure I'll look like an idiot, but I'll do it anyway."

"That's my cheerful friend. Always looking on the bright side. Now, with a dress like this, you don't pull it over your head. You step into it."

Shelby did as requested. The dress was lined with a cool, smooth material—maybe silk. Madeline pulled it up around her and Shelby slipped her arms into the long, lace sleeves.

The dress had a fitted bodice and was covered entirely with lace. The back formed about a three-foot train. The style was simple and elegant.

"Not yet," Madeline said, when Shelby started to turn toward the door.

Madeline pinned up her hair, then attached a short veil. "Now you can look."

Shelby walked down the short hallway to the main

salon of the bridal shop. There was a dais with a half circle of floor-to-ceiling mirrors. Madeline helped her up, then moved behind her, straightening the dress.

Shelby stared at herself. Madeline had been right. The dress didn't overwhelm her. The lace was exquisite and the fitted lines were perfect for her. Funny how until this moment she'd never once pictured herself getting married. Oh, she thought about *being* married, but not the actual wedding itself. Unlike other little girls, that hadn't been a game she'd played.

The why of it swirled in her head. She didn't want to think about it too much because then she would know what was wrong. And as soon as she knew, she would have to either fix it or accept that she was a coward.

"What do you think?" Madeline asked.

"The dress is beautiful."

"*You're* beautiful. There's a difference. The dress is simply there to reflect you. Tell me what you see."

Tears filled her eyes. "I'm a fraud," she whispered.

"Why?"

Her mouth moved, but no words came out. The truth was so elusive. Right there but when she tried to grab it… She drew in a breath.

"I'm so scared."

"Of Aidan?"

"No. Of surrendering who and what I am. I want to be in control."

"Of what?"

"Everything."

They both faced the mirror and their eyes met in the glass.

"It was all me," she continued, wiping away tears. "From the start. It was my idea to fix myself by learning to trust a man. I'm the one who picked Aidan, then convinced him. I set the rules, the boundaries. I even decided when to break them and become lovers."

"Because you needed to be in control?"

Shelby nodded. "It made me feel safe."

"Why did Aidan go along with it?"

A good question. Why did he? "Because he wanted to change, too. At first. Later, because… because he cares about me. Because he doesn't have anything to prove. Because he trusts me."

"Quack," Madeline said quietly.

Shelby laughed, then sobbed. She took a second to catch her breath. "You're saying he loves me."

"Yes. He loves you."

"You know this for sure, or you're guessing?"

"I'm pretty sure."

Shelby stared at her reflection. The bride staring back at her didn't deserve the beautiful dress or the wonderful man. She was still living in fear. Still hiding.

"What if I can't do it? What if I simply can't hand over my heart?"

"I don't know. You tell me."

What would it mean to not be with Aidan? To never see him again, never touch him or…

The pain was sharp and instant. She couldn't

breathe, couldn't think. She needed him. Wanted him. Loved him.

He'd been right, all those weeks ago. When he'd helped her see that the real pain of her childhood didn't come from her father's fists, but from the reality that her mother had stood by while it happened. Aidan wouldn't do that, and neither would she. As her brother had told her, she wasn't the type of mother who would let her children be abused. She would break the cycle.

She'd come so far. Everything she claimed to want was right there. All she had to do was take a single step of faith.

"You know, this is all going to go very badly if it turns out he's not in love with me," she said, her voice trembling as she spoke. "I'm going to feel pretty foolish."

"Won't it be better to know? You love him, Shelby. Don't you want to say it to him? At least once?"

"I do."

They looked at each other and started to laugh.

Shelby pressed her hands to her stomach. "While I love the dress…" she began.

"It's not the one. I know. But I thought trying it on would shock you and it seems to have, so yay, me."

Shelby laughed again. She turned and hugged her friend. "You're very good to me."

"And you're good to me. Now go claim your man."

"I've never claimed a man before."

"Then isn't it about time?"

It took Shelby a few minutes to change back into her street clothes. As she walked home, she thought about what she was going to say when she finally spoke to Aidan. The words were a jumble in her head. Well, she would have time. She had to go to the office and talk to Fay first. Get his schedule. Once she knew he was in town, she would call him and—

She turned the corner only to see Aidan and Charlie sitting on her front porch. The bichon saw her and raced toward her. She dropped to her knees and held out her arms. Charlie threw himself at her. She hugged him tight.

"Hey, there, my man," she whispered against his soft fur. "I've missed you so much."

He swiped her face with puppy kisses. She hung on for another second before standing and looking at Aidan.

He'd come to his feet, as well. They stared at each other.

"How are you doing?" he asked.

He didn't sound mad or disgusted or any number of negative things she deserved. He sounded like Aidan.

She thought about all they'd been through. How he was game for anything—from baby showers to pedicures to just sitting around and talking. He never said he didn't want to or complained. She remembered how he'd had this idea of the dog he wanted and had instead fallen for sweet, little Charlie. So there he was—the big, burly mountain man with a bichon frise.

She thought about how her father had hit her until she was unconscious and how her mother had never done anything to protect her. How Kipling had been the one to get her safely away. She thought of how Aidan had faced down his own parental torment.

"Shelby?"

Oh, right. He'd asked a question. "I'm okay. You?"

"Fine." He moved toward her but didn't touch her. His dark gaze settled on her face. "I had to come see you."

"I'm glad you did. I have to tell you something. A lot of things."

Fear filled her. Fear of handing the very essence of who she was to this man. And yet, there was no one else she would ever love as much. No one else she would trust or need or want to be with.

"I love you," she whispered. "I love you, Aidan. I thought I was being so strong and brave, but I was still afraid. I'm afraid right now. Maybe the fear will always be there. I don't know. What I do know for sure is that I don't want to be without you. I want us to be together. I love you so much."

One corner of his mouth turned up, then the other. "I love you, too. A lot. It kind of freaked me out when I figured it out."

Relief tasted sweet. Like the perfect cookie melting on her tongue. Only the sensation was in every part of her.

"Did you scream like a little girl?" she teased.

"Almost."

His smile faded. "Shelby, I love you and I want to be with you, but there are some things you have to know." He drew in a breath. "I get you were scared and that's okay. You're going to be scared. I probably am, too, sometimes. And we're going to screw up. We can't be together for the next seventy years and not hurt each other. That comes with being in love. But no matter what, I'm going to keep trying. I'm going to love you every day and when something bad happens, you and I are going to talk about it. Endlessly."

She started to laugh, then cry. Finally she threw herself at him. He pulled her close and hung on like he would never let go.

He was warm and solid as he held her. Everything about him was right.

"Marry me," he whispered in her ear. "Please marry me."

She looked at him. "Yes. Please. Of course."

He laughed and swung her around. Charlie barked at them, then ran in circles, as if he, too, knew something great had just happened.

Aidan kissed her, his lips lingering on hers. Then he drew back. "I hope it's okay, but I promised Nick we'd get married in Happily Inc. I guess it's some kind of destination wedding town. Is that okay?"

"It's fine, as long as I get to pick the honeymoon destination."

"What did you have in mind?"

"Somewhere sunny with a big bed."

He grinned. "Works for me."

"Now, HOW DOES this go?" Noelle asked, looking at her two cards.

Gabriel patiently pushed the cards so they faced the table. "No one is supposed to see those, honey."

"Because you'll bet against me?" she asked. "But

you love me. You can't bet against me. So I'm supposed to decide how much to put down?"

Shelby held in a grin. "Noelle, it's cards, not *Sophie's Choice*. Just go with it."

Angel sighed heavily. "Whose idea was this?"

Taryn leaned into him. "Are you saying you're not having fun?"

"I'm not sure having women join us at Texas hold 'em is a good thing."

"Later I'll take all my clothes off."

Justice raised his eyebrows. "Here or at home? Because if it's here, we might get uncomfortable. Not that it wouldn't be a good show," he added hastily.

Patience shot him a glance. "Really? You want to see Taryn naked? I never knew that."

"I don't. I was being supportive of one of your friends." He turned to Aidan. "Help."

Aidan leaned back in his chair. "See, gentlemen? Being friends with the ladies is harder than it looks. Now you're all going to apologize to me for all the insulting things you thought when you found out I was hanging out with Shelby as just a friend."

"You went to a baby shower," Kipling said. "That's kind of hard to let go."

Shelby grinned, knowing Kipling would be even more shocked by the pedicures. But that was their little secret.

She looked at Aidan and he winked back. He grabbed her left hand, stared briefly at the large diamond there, then kissed her palm.

They were officially engaged, with their wedding to follow in a few months, in Happily Inc., as per his promise to Nick. She'd chosen a beautiful resort in the Caribbean for their honeymoon. Flour Power was doing well, as was Aidan's business. Charlie was starting agility training and every single day Shelby knew that she was the luckiest person in the world.

She had family, a loving husband-to-be and a wonderful community that had allowed her to achieve all her dreams. Maybe it was a cliché, but that didn't mean it wasn't true. Love healed. She and Aidan had been healed in the best ways possible. And now they got to be in love…forever. Right here in Fool's Gold.

* * * * *

Can't get enough of Susan Mallery's hilarious and heartfelt love stories?

Then turn the page for a sneak peek of
DAUGHTERS OF THE BRIDE

CHAPTER ONE

ONE OF THE advantages of being freakishly tall was easy access to those upper kitchen cabinets. The disadvantages...well, those were probably summed up by the word *freakishly*.

Courtney Watson folded her too-long legs under her as she tried to get comfortable in a chair incredibly low to the ground. Adjusting the height wasn't possible. She was only filling in at the concierge desk while Ramona hurried off for yet another bathroom break. Apparently, the baby had shifted and was now reclining right on her bladder. From what Courtney could tell, pregnancy was a whole lot of work with an impressive dash of discomfort. The last thing she was going to do was change anything about the chair where Ramona spent a good part of her day. Courtney could pretend to be a pretzel for five minutes.

Late on a Tuesday evening, the lobby of the Los Lobos Hotel was quiet. Only a few guests milled around. Most were already up in their rooms, which was where Courtney liked the guests to spend their time at night. She wasn't a fan of those who roamed. They got into trouble.

The elevator doors opened and a small, well-dressed man stepped out. He glanced around the lobby before heading directly to her. Well, not to *her*, she would guess. The concierge desk at which she sat.

Her practiced smile faltered a bit when she recognized Milton Ford, the current president of the California Organization of Organic Soap Manufacturers, aka COOOSM. Mr. Ford had arranged for the annual meeting to be held in town, and everyone was staying at the Los Lobos Hotel. Courtney knew that for sure—she'd taken the reservation herself. But the meetings, the meals and all the income that flowed from them were taking place at the Anderson House.

"Hello." He looked at the name plate on the desk. "Uh, Ramona. I'm Milton Ford."

Courtney thought about correcting him on her name, but figured there wasn't much point. Despite his giving all that pretty catering money to one of their competitors, she would still do her job—or in this case, Ramona's—to the best of her abilities.

"Yes, Mr. Ford. How may I help you this evening?" She smiled as she spoke, determined to be pleasant.

Even if Mr. Ford had decided to hold his stupid awards luncheon at the Anderson House instead of in the hotel's very beautiful and spacious ballroom, Courtney would do her best to make sure his stay and the stays of his colleagues were perfect.

Her boss would tell her not to be bitter, so Courtney returned her smile to full wattage and promised herself that when she was done with Mr. Ford, she would head to the kitchen for a late-night snack of ice cream. It would be an excellent reward for good behavior.

"I have a problem," he told her. "Not with the rooms. They're excellent as always. It's the, ah, *other* facility we've booked."

"The Anderson House." She did her best not to spit the words.

"Yes." He cleared his throat. "I'm afraid there are…bees."

Now the problem wasn't a lack of smiling but the issue of too much of it. Joyce, her boss, would want her to be professional, she reminded herself. Glee, while definitely called for, wasn't polite. At least not to Mr. Ford's face. Bees! How glorious.

"I hadn't heard they were back," she said sympathetically.

"They've had bees before?"

"Every few years. They usually stay outside of town, but when they come into the city limits, they like the Anderson House best."

Mr. Ford dabbed his forehead with a very white handkerchief, then tucked it back into his pocket. "There are hundreds of them. Thousands. Entire hives sprung up, practically overnight. There are bees everywhere."

"They're not particularly dangerous," Courtney offered. "The Drunken Red-nosed Honeybee is known to be calm and industrious. Oh, and they're endangered. As a maker of organic soap, you must be aware of the issues we're having keeping our honeybee numbers where they should be. Having them return to Los Lobos is always good news. It means the population is healthy."

"Yes. Of course. But we can't have our awards luncheon in the same house. With the bees. I was hoping you'd have room for us here."

Here? As in the place I offered and you refused, telling me the Anderson House was so much better suited? But those thoughts were for her, not for a guest.

"Let me check," she told him. "I think I might be able to make room."

She braced herself to stand. Not physically, but mentally. Because the well-dressed Mr. Ford, for all his dapperness, was maybe five foot six. And Courtney wasn't. And when she stood...well, she knew what would happen.

She untangled her long legs and rose. Mr. Ford's gaze followed, then his mouth dropped open a second before he closed it. Courtney towered over Mr. Ford by a good six inches. Possibly more, but who was counting?

"My goodness," he murmured as he followed her. "You're very tall."

There were a thousand responses, none of them polite and all inappropriate for the work setting. So she gritted her teeth, thought briefly of England, then murmured as unironically as she could, "Really? I hadn't noticed."

COURTNEY WAITED WHILE her boss stirred two sugars into her coffee, then fed half a strip of bacon to each of her dogs. Pearl—a beautiful, blond standard poo-

dle—waited patiently for her treat, while Sarge, aka
Sargent Pepper—a bichon–miniature poodle mix—
whined at the back of his throat.

The dining room at the Los Lobos Hotel was
mostly empty at ten in the morning. The breakfast
crowd was gone and the lunch folks had yet to arrive. Courtney got the paradox of enjoying the hotel
best when guests were absent. Without the customers, there would be no hotel, no job and no paycheck.
While a crazy wedding on top of every room booked
had its own particular charm, she did enjoy the echo-
ing silence of empty spaces.

Joyce Yates looked at Courtney and smiled. "I'm
ready."

"The new linen company is working out well. The
towels are very clean and the sheets aren't scratchy at
all. Ramona thinks she's going to last until right before she gives birth, but honestly, it hurts just to look
at her. That could just be me, though. She's so tiny
and the baby is so big. What on earth was God thinking? Last night I met with Mr. Ford of the California
Organization of Organic Soap Manufacturers. Bees
have invaded the Anderson House, and he wants to
book everything here. I didn't mock him, although
he deserved it. So now we're hosting all their events,
along with meals. I talked him into crab salad."

Courtney paused for breath. "I think that's everything."

Joyce sipped her coffee. "A full night."

"Nothing out of the ordinary."

"Did you get *any* sleep?"

"Sure."

At least six hours, Courtney thought, doing the math in her head. She'd stayed in the lobby area until Ramona's shift had ended at ten, had done a quick circuit of the hotel grounds until ten thirty, studied until one and then been up at six thirty to start it all again.

Okay, make that five hours.

"I'll sleep in my forties," she said.

"I doubt that." Joyce's voice was friendly enough, but her gaze was sharp. "You do too much."

Not words most bosses bothered to utter, Courtney thought, but Joyce wasn't like other bosses.

Joyce Yates had started working at the Los Lobos Hotel in 1958. She'd been seventeen and hired as a maid. Within two weeks, the owner of the hotel, a handsome, thirtysomething confirmed bachelor, had fallen head over heels for his new employee. They'd married three weeks later and lived blissfully together for five years, until he'd unexpectedly died of a heart attack.

Joyce, then all of twenty-two and with a toddler to raise, had taken over the hotel. Everyone was certain she would fail, but under her management, the business had thrived. Decades later she still saw to every detail and knew the life story of everyone who worked for her. She was both boss and mentor for most of her staff and had always been a second mother to Courtney.

Joyce's kindness was as legendary as her white hair and classic pantsuits. She was fair, determined and just eccentric enough to be interesting.

Courtney had known her all her life. When Courtney had been a baby, her father had also died unexpectedly. Maggie, Courtney's mother, had been left with three daughters and a business. Joyce had morphed from client to friend in a matter of weeks. Probably because she'd once been a young widow with a child, herself.

"How's your marketing project coming along?" Joyce asked.

"Good. I got the notes back from my instructor, so I'm ready to move on to the final presentation." Once she finished her marketing class, she was only two semesters away from graduation with her bachelor's degree. Hallelujah.

Joyce refilled her coffee cup from the carafe left at the table. "Quinn's arriving this week."

Courtney grinned. "Really? Because you've only mentioned it every morning for the past two weeks. I wasn't completely sure when he was getting here. You're sure it's this week? Because I couldn't remember."

"I'm old. I get to be excited about my grandson's arrival if I want to."

"Yes, you do. We're all quivering."

Joyce's mouth twitched. "You have a little attitude this morning, young lady."

"I know. It's the Drunken Red-nosed Honeybees. I always get attitude when they take over the Anderson House. Gratitude attitude."

"Quinn's still single."

Courtney didn't know if she should laugh or snort. "That's subtle. I appreciate the vote of confidence, Joyce, but let's be honest. We both know I'd have a better shot at marrying Prince Harry than getting Quinn Yates to notice me." She held up a hand. "Not that I'm interested in him. Yes, he's gorgeous. But the man is way too sophisticated for the likes of me. I'm a small-town girl. Besides, I'm focused on college and my work. I have no free boy time." She wanted her degree within the next year, then a great job and then men. Or a man. Definitely just one. *The* one. But that was for later.

"You'll date when you're forty?" Joyce asked humorously.

"I'm hoping it won't take that long, but you get the idea."

"I do. It's too bad. Quinn needs to be married."

"Then you should find him someone who isn't me."

Not that Quinn wasn't impressive, but jeez. Her? Not happening.

She'd met him a handful of times when he'd come to visit his grandmother. The man was wildly successful. He was in the music business—a producer, maybe. She'd never paid attention. On his visits, he hung out with Joyce and her dogs, otherwise kept to himself, then left without making a fuss. Of course the fuss happened without his doing a single thing other than show up.

The man was good-looking. No, that wasn't right. Words like *good-looking*, or *handsome*, should be used on ordinary people with extraordinary looks. Quinn was on a whole other plane of existence. She'd seen happily married middle-aged women actually simper in his presence. And to her mind, simpering had gone out of style decades ago.

"You really think he's moving to Los Lobos?" she asked, more than a little doubtful.

"That's what he tells me. Until he finds a place of his own, I've reserved the groundskeeper's bungalow for him."

"Nice digs," Courtney murmured. "He'll never want to leave."

Although to be honest, she couldn't imagine the famous, Malibu-living music executive finding happiness in their sleepy little Central California town, but stranger things had happened.

"I'll check his arrival date and make sure I'm assigned to clean it," she told her boss.

"Thank you, dear. I appreciate the gesture."

"It's not exactly a gesture. It's kind of my job."

While she was considered a jack-of-all-trades at the hotel, her actual title was maid. The work wasn't glamorous, but it paid the bills, and right now that was what mattered to her.

"It wouldn't be if you'd—"

Courtney held up her hand. "I know. Accept a different job. Tell my family about my big secret. Marry Prince Harry. I'm sorry, Joyce. There are only so many hours in a day. I need to have priorities."

"You're picking the wrong ones. Prince Harry would love you."

Courtney smiled. "You are sweet and I love you."

"I love you, too. Now, about the wedding."

Courtney groaned. "Do we have to?"

"Yes. Your mother is getting married in a few

months. I know you're taking care of the engagement party but there's also the wedding."

"Uh-huh."

Joyce raised her eyebrows. "Is that a problem?"

"No, ma'am."

It wasn't that Courtney minded her mother remarrying. Maggie had been a widow for literally decades. It was long past time for her mom to find a great guy and settle down. Nope, it wasn't the marriage that was the problem—it was the wedding. Or rather the wedding *planning*.

"You're trying to get me into trouble," she murmured.

"Who, me?" Joyce's attempt to look innocent failed miserably.

Courtney rose. "All right, you crafty lady. I will do my best with both the party and the wedding."

"I knew you would."

Courtney bent down and kissed Joyce's cheek, then straightened, turned and ran smack into Kelly Carzo—waitress and, until this second, a friend.

Kelly, a pretty, green-eyed redhead, tried to keep hold of the tray of coffee mugs she'd been carrying, but the force was too great. Mugs went flying, hot liquid rained down and in less than three seconds, Courtney, Joyce and Kelly were drenched, and the shattered remains of six mugs lay scattered on the floor.

The restaurant had been relatively quiet before. Now it went silent as everyone turned to stare. At least there were only a couple of other customers and a handful of staff. Not that word of her latest mishap wouldn't spread.

Joyce stood and scooped Sarge out of harm's way, then ordered Pearl to move back. "What is it your sister says in times like this?"

Courtney pulled her wet shirt away from her body and smiled apologetically at Kelly. "That I'm pulling a Courtney. You okay?"

Kelly brushed at her black pants. "Never better, but you are so paying for my dry cleaning."

"I swear. Right after I help you with this mess."

"I'm going to get changed," Joyce told them. "The prerogative of being the owner."

"I'm really sorry," Courtney called after her.

"I know, dear. It's fine."

No, Courtney thought as she went to get a broom and a mop. It wasn't fine. But it sure was her life.

"I WANT TO match my dress. Just one streak. Mo-om, what could it hurt?"

Rachel Halcomb pressed her fingers against her temple as she felt the beginnings of a headache coming on. The Saturday of Los Lobos High's spring formal was always a crazy one for the salon where she worked. Teenage girls came in to be coiffed and teased into a variety of dance-appropriate styles. They traveled in packs, which she didn't mind. But the high-pitched shrieks and giggles were starting to get to her.

Her client—Lily—desperately wanted a bright purple streak to go with her floor-length dress. Her hair was long, wavy and a beautiful shade of auburn. Rachel had clients who would fork out hundreds to get that exact color while Lily had simply hit the hair lottery.

Lily's mom bit her bottom lip. "I don't know," she said, sounding doubtful. "Your father will have a fit."

"It's not his hair. And it'll look great in the pictures. Come on, Mom. Aaron asked me. You know what that means. I have to look amazing. We've only been living here three months. I have to make a good impression. Please?"

Ah, *the most amazing boy ever asked me out* combined with the powerful *I'm new in school* argument. A one-two punch. Lily knew her stuff. Rachel had never been on the receiving end of that particular tactic, but knew how persuasive kids could be. Her son was only eleven, but already an expert at pushing her buttons. She doubted she'd had the same level of skill when she'd been his age.

Lily swung toward Rachel. "You can use the kind that washes out, right? So it's temporary?"

"It will take a couple of shampoos, but yes, you can wash it out."

"See!" Lily's voice was triumphant.

"Well, you *are* going with Aaron," her mother murmured.

Lily shrieked and hugged her mother. Rachel promised herself that as soon as she could escape to the break room she would have not one but two ibuprofens. And the world's biggest iced tea chaser. She smiled to herself. That was her—dreaming big.

Lily ran off to change into a smock. Her mother

shrugged. "I probably shouldn't have given in. Sometimes it's hard to tell her no."

"Especially today." Rachel nodded at the gaggle of teenage girls at every station. They stood in various stages of dress…or undress. Some had on jeans and T-shirts. Others were in robes or smocks. And still others modeled their gowns for the dance that night. "And she *is* going to the dance with Aaron."

The other woman laughed. "When I was her age, his name was Rusty." She sighed. "He was gorgeous. I wonder what happened to him."

"In my class he was Greg."

The mom laughed. "Let me guess. The football captain?"

"Of course."

"And now?"

"He's with the Los Lobos Fire Department."

"You kept in touch?"

"I married him."

Before Lily's mom could ask any more questions, Lily returned and threw herself into the chair. "I'm ready," she said eagerly. "This is going to be so awesome." She smiled at Rachel. "You're going to do the smoky eye thing on me, right?"

"As requested. I have deep purple and violet-gray shadows just for you."

Lily raised her hand for a high five. "You're the best, Rachel. Thank you."

"That's what I'm here for."

Two hours later Lily had a dark violet streak in her hair, a sleek up-do and enough smoky eye makeup to rival a Victoria's Secret model. The fresh-faced teenager now looked like a twentysomething It Girl.

Lily's mom snapped several pictures with her phone before pressing a handful of bills into Rachel's hand. "She's beautiful. Thank you so much."

"My pleasure. Lily, bring me pictures of you with Aaron next time I see you."

"I will. I promise!"

Rachel waited until mother and daughter had left to count out the tip. It was generous, which always made her happy. She wanted her clients—and their mothers—to be pleased with her work. Now, if only one of those eccentric trillionaires would saunter in, love her work and tip her a few grand…that would be fantastic. She could get ahead on her mortgage, not sweat her lack of emergency fund. In the meantime Josh needed a new glove for his baseball league, and her car was making a weird chirping noise that sounded more than a little expensive.

If she'd mentioned either of those things to Lily's mom, she would guess the other woman would have told her to talk to Greg. That was what husbands were for.

There was only one flaw with that plan—she and Greg weren't married anymore. The most amazing boy in school slash football captain slash homecoming king had indeed married her. A few weeks before their tenth anniversary he'd cheated and she'd divorced him. Now, at thirty-three, she found herself living as one of the most pitied creatures ever—a divorced woman with a child about to hit puberty. And there wasn't enough smoky eye or hair color to make that situation look the least bit pretty.

She finished cleaning up and retreated to the break room for a few minutes before her last client—a double appointment of sixteen-year-old twins who wanted their hair to be "the same but different" for the dance. Rachel reached for the bottle of ibuprofen she kept in her locker and shook out two pills.

As she swallowed them with a gulp of water, her cell phone beeped. She glanced at the screen.

Hey you. Toby's up for keeping both boys Thursday night. Let's you and me go do something fun. A girls' night out. Say yes.

Rachel considered the invitation. The rational voice in her head said she should do as her friend requested and say yes. Break out of her rut. Put on something pretty and spend some time with Lena. She honestly couldn't remember the last time she'd done anything like that.

The rest of her, however, pointed out that not only hadn't she done laundry in days, but she was also behind on every other chore it took to keep her nonworking life running semi-smoothly. Plus, what was the point? They would go to a bar by the pier and then what? Lena was happily married. She wasn't interested in meeting men. And although Rachel was single and should be out there flashing her smile, she honest to God didn't have the energy. She was *busy* every second of every day. Her idea of a good time was to sleep late and have someone else make breakfast. But there wasn't anyone else. Her son needed her, and she made sure she was always there. Taking care of business.

She'd been nine when her father had died suddenly. Nine and the oldest of three girls. She still remembered her mother crouched in front of her, her eyes filled with tears. "Please, Rachel. I need you to be Mommy's best girl. I need you to help take care of Sienna and Courtney. Can you do that for me? Can you hold it all together?"

She'd been so scared. So unsure of what was going to happen next. What she'd wanted to say was that she was still a kid and no, holding it together wasn't an option. But she hadn't. She'd done her best to be all things to everyone. Twenty-four years later that hadn't changed.

She glanced back at her phone.

Want to come over for a glass of wine and PB&J sandwiches instead?

I'll come over for wine and cheese. And I'll bring the cheese.

Perfect. What time should I drop off Josh?

Let's say 7. Does that work?

Rachel sent the thumbs-up icon and set her phone back in her locker, then closed the door. Something to look forward to, she told herself. Plans on a Thursday night. Look at her—she was practically normal.

CHAPTER TWO

"MRS. TROWBRIDGE IS DEAD."

Sienna Watson looked up from her desk. "Are you sure?" She bit her lower lip. "What I meant is, how awful. Her family must be devastated." She drew in a breath. "Are you sure?"

Seth, the thirtysomething managing director of The Helping Store, leaned against the door frame. "I have word directly from her lawyer. She passed two weeks ago and was buried this past Saturday."

Sienna frowned. "Why didn't anyone tell us? I would have gone to the funeral."

"You're taking your job too seriously. It's not as if she would have known you were there."

Sienna supposed that was true. What with Mrs. Trowbridge being dead and all. Still... Anita Trowbridge had been a faithful donor to The Helping Store for years—contributing goods for the thrift shop and money for various causes. Upon her death, the thrift shop was to inherit all her clothes and kitchen items, along with ten thousand dollars.

Unfortunately, nearly six months before, Sienna had received word of Mrs. Trowbridge's passing. After the lawyer had given his okay, she'd sent a van and two guys to the house to collect their bequest...

only to be confronted by Mrs. Trowbridge's great-granddaughter. Erika Trowbridge had informed the men that her great-grandmother was still alive and they could take their vulture selves away until informed otherwise.

"It wasn't your fault," Seth said now as he pushed up his glasses. "The lawyer gave you the key to the house."

"Something he shouldn't have done. You know, it wouldn't have happened if they'd hired a local lawyer. But no. They had to bring one up from Los Angeles."

Sienna had apologized to Mrs. Trowbridge personally. The old lady—small and frail in her assisted living bed—had laughed and told Sienna she understood. Great-granddaughter Erika had not. Of course Erika was still bitter about the fact that Sienna had not only snagged the role of Sandy in their high school production of *Grease* but also had—perhaps more importantly—won the heart of Jimmy Dawson in twelfth grade.

"She was a nice old lady," she murmured, thinking she would have liked to have sent flowers. Instead she would donate that amount to The Helping Store in Mrs. Trowbridge's name. "I wonder if there's anything left in her kitchen."

"You think the granddaughter took things?"

"Great-granddaughter, and I wouldn't put it past her. If she had her way, Erika would clean the place out. At least we'll get the cash donation."

"I'm meeting with the lawyer in the morning."

Sienna was the donation coordinator for The

Helping Store, one of a handful of paid staff. The large and bustling thrift store was manned by volunteers. All the proceeds from the store, along with any cash raised by donations, went to a shelter for women escaping domestic violence. Getting away from the abuser was half the battle. Over the years The Helping Store had managed to buy several small duplexes on the edge of town. They were plain but clean and, most important to women on the run, far from their abusers.

Her boss nodded toward the front of the building. "Ready to tap dance?"

Sienna smiled as she rose. "It's not like that. I enjoy my work."

"You put on a good show." He held up a hand. "Believe me. I'm not complaining. You're the best. My biggest fear is that some giant nonprofit in the big city will make you an offer you can't refuse and I'll be left Sienna-less. I can't think of a sadder fate."

"I'm not going anywhere," she promised. Oh, sure, every now and then she thought about what it would be like to live in LA or San Francisco, but those feelings passed. This small coastal town was all she knew. Her family was here.

"Isn't David from somewhere back East?" Seth asked.

She pulled open her desk drawer and collected her handbag, then walked out into the hallway. "St. Louis. His whole family's there."

Seth groaned. "Tell me he's not interested in moving back."

There were a lot of implications in that sentence.

That she and David were involved enough to be having that conversation. That one day they would be married and, should he want to return to his hometown, she would go with him.

She patted her boss's arm. "Cart, meet horse. You're getting way ahead of yourself. We've only been dating a few months. Things aren't that serious. He's a nice guy and all, but…"

"No sparks." Seth's tone was sympathetic. "Bummer."

"We can't all have your one true great love."

"You're right. Gary is amazing. Okay then, let's get you to the Anderson House so you can dazzle the good people who make— Who are you talking to?"

"The California Organization of Organic Soap Manufacturers, and they're at the Los Lobos Hotel. The Anderson House has bees."

Seth's expression brightened. "The Drunken Red-nosed Honeybees? I love those guys. Did you know their raw honey has thirty percent more antioxidants than any other raw honey in California?"

"I didn't and I could have gone all day without that factoid."

"You're jealous because I'm smart."

"No, you're jealous because I'm pretty and our world is shallow so that counts more."

Seth laughed. "Fine. Go be pretty with the soap people and bring us back some money."

"Will do."

Sienna drove to the hotel. She knew the way. Not only because her hometown was on the small side—

but also because nearly every significant event was celebrated there.

The Los Lobos Hotel sat on a low bluff overlooking the Pacific. The main building was midcentury modern meets California Spanish, four stories high with blinding white walls and a red tile roof. The rear wing had been added in the 1980s, and luxury bungalows dotted the grounds.

Given the pleasant central California weather, most large-scale events were held outside on the massive lawn in front of the pool. A grand pavilion stood on the lawn between the pool and the ocean, and a petite pavilion by the paddle boat pond.

Sienna parked the car and collected her material. As she walked toward the rear entrance of the hotel, she saw that the windows sparkled and the hedges were perfectly trimmed. Joyce did an excellent job managing the hotel, she thought. She was also a generous contributor to The Helping Store. And not just with money. More than once Sienna had called to find out if there was a spare room for a displaced family or a woman on the run. A year ago Joyce had offered a small room kept on reserve for their permanent use.

Helping women in need was something Joyce had been doing forever. Nearly twenty-four years before, when Sienna and her sisters had lost their father, and Maggie, their mother, had been widowed, the family had been thrown into chaos. A lack of life insurance, Maggie's limited income and three little girls to support had left the young mother struggling. In a matter of months, she'd lost her house.

Joyce had taken them all in to live at the Los Lobos Hotel. Now Sienna smiled at the memory. She'd been only six at the time. Missing her father, of course, but also discovering the joy of reading. The day the Watson family had taken up residence in the hotel's new wing, Joyce had given Sienna a copy of *Eloise*. Sienna had immediately seen herself as the charming heroine from the book and had made herself at home in the hotel. While it wasn't the same as living at The Plaza, it was close enough to help her through her grief.

Sienna remembered how she'd called for room service and told the person answering the phone to "charge it." Most likely those bills had gone directly to Joyce rather than to Maggie. And when she'd begged her mother for a turtle, because Eloise had one, a guest had stepped in to buy her one.

While there was pain in some of the memories, she had to admit living in the hotel had been fun. At least for her. It was probably a different story for her mother.

She entered through the rear door and started down the hall toward the meeting rooms. At the far end, she saw a familiar figure wrestling with a vacuum. As she watched, Courtney tripped over the cord and nearly plowed face-first into the wall. A combination of love and frustration swelled up inside her. There was a reason the phrase was "pulling a Courtney." Because if someone was going to stumble, fall, drop, break or slip, it was her baby sister.

"Hey, you," Sienna called as she got closer.

Courtney turned and smiled.

Sienna did her best not to wince at Courtney's uniform—not that the khaki pants and polo shirt were so horrible, but on her sister, they just looked wrong. While most people considered being tall an advantage, on Courtney the height was simply awkward. Like now—her pants were too short and even though she was relatively thin, they bunched around her hips and thighs. The shirt looked two sizes too small and there was a stain on the front. She wasn't wearing makeup and her long blond hair—about her best feature—was pulled back in a ponytail. She was, to put it honestly, a mess. Something she'd been for as long as Sienna could remember.

Courtney'd had some kind of learning disability. Sienna had never been clear on the details, but it had made school difficult for her sister. Despite their mother's attempts to interest Courtney in some kind of trade school, the youngest of the three seemed happy just being a maid. Baffling.

"You here to talk to Mr. Ford's group?" Courtney asked as Sienna approached.

"Yes. I'm going to guilt that California Organization of Organic Soap Manufacturers into coughing up some serious money."

"I have no doubt. The AV equipment is all set up. I tested it earlier."

"Thanks." Sienna patted her large tote bag. "I have my material right here." She glanced toward the meeting room, then back at her sister. "How's Mom's engagement party coming? Do you need any help?"

"Everything is fine. The menu's almost finalized. I've taken care of decorations and flowers. It will be lovely."

Sienna hoped that was true. When Maggie and Neil had announced their engagement, the three sisters had wanted to throw Mom a big party. The hotel was the obvious venue, which was fine, but then Courtney had said she would handle the details. And where Courtney went, disaster was sure to follow.

"If you need anything, let me know," Sienna told her. "I'm happy to help." She would also stop and talk to Joyce on the way out. Just to make sure everything was handled.

Emotion flashed through Courtney's blue eyes but before Sienna could figure out what she was thinking, her sister smiled. "Sure. No problem. Thanks for the offer." She stepped back, bumped into the wall, then righted herself. "You should, um, get going to your meeting."

"You're right. I'll see you later."

Courtney nodded. "Good luck."

Sienna laughed. "While I appreciate the sentiment, I'm not going to need it."

She waved and headed for the Stewart Salon. The meeting room was set up with glasses of wine and plenty of hot and cold appetizers. At one end was a large screen, a podium and microphone. Sienna removed her laptop from her tote and turned it on. While it booted, she plugged it into the room's AV system. She started the video and was pleased to see the pictures on the screen and hear the music through the speakers.

"Perfection through planning," she murmured as she set the video back to the beginning.

Ten minutes later the good members of COOOSM bustled into the salon and collected glasses of wine and appetizers. Sienna circulated through the room, chatting with as many people as she could. She knew the drill—introduce herself, ask lots of friendly questions and generally be both approachable and charming so that by the time she made her pitch, she was already considered someone they knew and liked.

She made as much effort with the women as the men. While studies were divided on which gender gave more to charity, Sienna had always found that generosity came in unexpected ways, and she wasn't about to lose an opportunity based on stereotypes. Every dollar she brought in was a dollar the organization could use to help.

Milton Ford, the president of COOOSM, approached her. The little man barely came up to her shoulder. So adorable. She smiled.

"I'm ready whenever you are, Mr. Ford."

"Thank you, my dear." He shook his head. "This town does have its share of very tall women. There's a young lady who works here at the hotel. Ramona, I believe."

Sienna happened to know that Ramona was about five-two, but she didn't correct him. No doubt Courtney had done something to confuse Mr. Ford, but this wasn't the time to set him straight. Not with donations on the line.

"Shall we?" he asked, gesturing to the podium.

Sienna walked over to the microphone and turned it on, then she smiled at the crowd. "Good afternoon, everyone. Thank you so much for taking time out of your schedule to meet with me today." She winked at a bearded older man wearing overalls. "Jack, did you ever decide on that second glass of wine? Because I think it will help you make the right decision."

Everyone laughed. Jack toasted her. She smiled at him, then pushed the play button on her computer. Music flowed from the speakers. Carefully, slowly, she allowed her smile to fade. A picture of a large American flag appeared on the screen.

"Between 2001 and 2012 nearly sixty-five hundred American soldiers were killed in Iraq and Afghanistan. During that same period of time—" the screen shifted to the face of a battered woman clutching two small children "—almost twelve thousand women were murdered by their husbands, boyfriends or a former partner. Even now, three women are murdered every single day by the man who claims to love them."

She paused to let the information sink in. "Through the money we raise at The Helping Store, we provide a safe haven for women and their families in their time of need. They are referred to us from all over the state. When they arrive here, we offer everything from shelter to legal advice to medical care to relocation services. We take care of their bodies, their hearts, their spirits and their children. One woman in four will experience some kind of domestic violence in her life. We can't stop that from happening across the globe, but we can keep our corner of the world safe. I hope you'll join me in making that happen."

She paused as the voice-over on the video started. She'd planted the seed. The materials she'd brought should do the rest.

Two hours later the last of the guests left. Sienna carefully put away the pledge forms. Not only had the group been generous, they also wanted to challenge other chapters of their organization to match their donations.

"How's the most beautiful girl in the world?"

The voice came from the doorway. Sienna hesitated just a second before turning. "Hi, David."

"How did it go?" her boyfriend asked as he moved toward her. "Why am I asking? You impressed them. I know it."

He pulled her close and kissed her. Sienna allowed his lips to linger for a second before stepping back.

"I'm working," she said with a laugh.

"No one's here." He moved his hands to her butt and pulled her close again. "We could lock the door."

If the words weren't clear enough, the erection he rubbed against her belly got the message through. How romantic—going at it on a serving table, while surrounded by dirty plates and half-full glasses of wine.

Sienna chided herself for not accepting the gesture in the spirit in which David meant it. Successful and smart. He loved his family, puppies and as far as she could tell, he was an all-around nice guy.

"Remember you telling me about the time you took a girl home to meet your parents and realized you couldn't do it in their house?" she asked, her voice teasing.

He chuckled. "I do. Humiliating."

"Joyce, the owner of the hotel, is a little bit like my grandmother."

"Ouch." He drew back. "Grandma is even worse than Mom." He nibbled on her neck. "Rain check."

"Absolutely. Thanks."

He released her and pushed up his glasses. "You heading back to the office?"

She'd kind of wanted to head home after her presentation. She could deliver the pledge forms to her boss in the morning. But if she said that, David would want to make plans. Wow. She would rather go back to work than spend the evening with her boyfriend? What was up with that?

She looked at him. He was about her height, with dark brown hair and dark eyes. A nice build. He wasn't handsome, but she'd never cared much about that. Once a guy crossed the "not a troll" threshold, she was fine.

David Van Horn should have been the man of her dreams. Lord knew she'd been looking. He was the thirty-five-year-old senior vice president at the recently transplanted aerospace design firm in town. She was pushing thirty and had no idea why she hadn't been able to find "the one." Maybe there was something wrong with her.

Not a conversation she wanted to have with herself right now, she thought. Or ever.

"I don't have to go back to work," she told him.

"Great. Let's have dinner here."

"I'd love that."

A statement stretching the truth more than a little, but who was going to know?

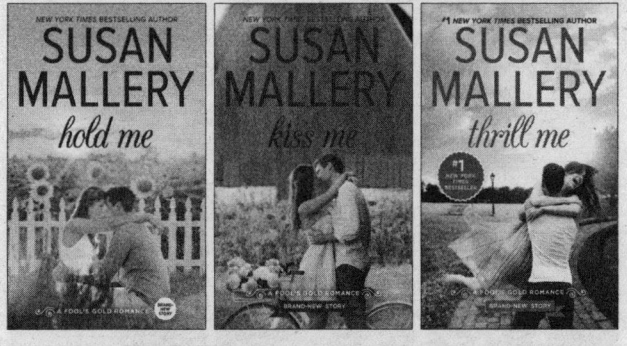

We hope you enjoyed reading

Best of My Love

by #1 *New York Times* bestselling author

Susan Mallery

If you liked this story, you will love
Harlequin® Special Edition!

Discover more heartfelt tales of family,
friendship and love from
Harlequin® Special Edition series.

Look for six new romances every month!

⊞ HARLEQUIN®

SPECIAL EDITION

Life, Love and Family

www.Harlequin.com

REQUEST YOUR
FREE BOOKS!

2 FREE NOVELS
FROM THE ROMANCE COLLECTION
PLUS 2 FREE GIFTS!

YES! Please send me 2 FREE novels from the Romance Collection and my 2 FREE gifts (gifts are worth about $10). After receiving them, if I don't wish to receive any more books, I can return the shipping statement marked "cancel." If I don't cancel, I will receive 4 brand-new novels every month and be billed just $6.49 per book in the U.S. or $6.99 per book in Canada. That's a savings of at least 19% off the cover price. It's quite a bargain! Shipping and handling is just 50¢ per book in the U.S. and 75¢ per book in Canada.* I understand that accepting the 2 free books and gifts places me under no obligation to buy anything. I can always return a shipment and cancel at any time. Even if I never buy another book, the two free books and gifts are mine to keep forever.

194/394 MDN GH4D

Name	(PLEASE PRINT)	

Address		Apt. #

City	State/Prov.	Zip/Postal Code

Signature (if under 18, a parent or guardian must sign)

Mail to the **Reader Service:**
IN U.S.A.: P.O. Box 1867, Buffalo, NY 14240-1867
IN CANADA: P.O. Box 609, Fort Erie, Ontario L2A 5X3

Want to try two free books from another line?
Call 1-800-873-8635 or visit www.ReaderService.com.

* Terms and prices subject to change without notice. Prices do not include applicable taxes. Sales tax applicable in N.Y. Canadian residents will be charged applicable taxes. Offer not valid in Quebec. This offer is limited to one order per household. Not valid for current subscribers to the Romance Collection or the Romance/Suspense Collection. All orders subject to credit approval. Credit or debit balances in a customer's account(s) may be offset by any other outstanding balance owed by or to the customer. Please allow 4 to 6 weeks for delivery. Offer available while quantities last.

Your Privacy—The Reader Service is committed to protecting your privacy. Our Privacy Policy is available online at www.ReaderService.com or upon request from the Reader Service.

We make a portion of our mailing list available to reputable third parties that offer products we believe may interest you. If you prefer that we not exchange your name with third parties, or if you wish to clarify or modify your communication preferences, please visit us at www.ReaderService.com/consumerschoice or write to us at Reader Service Preference Service, P.O. Box 9062, Buffalo, NY 14240-9062. Include your complete name and address.